Praise for the Books of
T. C. LoTempio

"Nick and Nora are a winning team!"
—Rebecca Hale, *New York Times* Bestselling author

"A fast-paced cozy mystery spiced with a dash of romance and topped with a big slice of 'cat-titude.'"
—Ali Brandon, *New York Times* Bestselling author

"Nick and Nora are the purr-fect sleuth duo!"
—Victoria Laurie, *New York Times* Bestselling author

"A page-turner with an endearing heroine."
—*Richmond Times Dispatch*

"Excellently plotted and executed—five paws and a tail up for this tale."
—*Open Book Society*

"Nick brims with street smarts and feline charisma, you'd think he was human . . . an exciting new series."
—Carole Nelson Douglas, *New York Times* notable author of the Midnight Louie mysteries

"I love this series and each new story quickly becomes my favorite. Cannot wait for the next!"
—*Escape With Dollycas Into a Good Book*

Books by T. C. LoTempio

Nick and Nora Mysteries

Meow If It's Murder
Claws for Alarm
Crime and Catnip
Hiss H for Homicide
Murder Faux Paws
A Purr Before Dying
Bell, Book and Corpses

Urban Tails Pet Shop Mysteries

The Time for Murder Is Meow
Killers of a Feather
Death Steals the Spotlight
Cats, Carats and Killers
A Side Dish of Death

Tiffany Austin Food Blogger Mysteries

Eat, Drink and Drop Dead
A Crust to Die For
A Dish Best Served Dead

Cat Rescue Mysteries

Purr M for Murder
Death by a Whisker

A Dish Best Served Dead

Tiffany Austin Food Blogger Mysteries

T. C. LoTempio

For all my Foodie Friends—especially Stephanie Lecuyer—this one's for you!

Acknowledgments

As always, I want to thank my agent, Josh Getzler, and my wonderful editor, Bill Harris, who always makes my work better. I want to thank the readers who make it possible for me to carry out my own "food fantasies" and keep me working in my old age!

One

Wednesday, 10 a.m.

"Tiffany Austin, how wonderful to see you! I'm so excited! The Foodie Fest convention right here in Branson! So, are you ready for five whole days of nothing but food, food and more food?"

I smiled at the enthusiastic woman in the registration line next to me. Ada Newman was a fairly well-known food critic who'd written a weekly column for the *Augusta Chronicle* before retiring six months ago. "I sure am," I said. "And I'm glad to see you too. I wondered if you'd be attending this event."

"Yeah, well, retiring wasn't exactly my idea," Ada said with a wave of her hand. "I had a feeling when my editor left that my days there were numbered." She let out a heartfelt sigh. "His replacement wanted me to review more trendy places. A 'hip' take, she called it. Said we needed to attract the younger set. Well, they got that in spades. Only kids thirty and under eat at the places they review now."

I'd met the editor's replacement. She wrote articles that centered around health restaurants and sushi bars, all aimed at appealing to the popular eighteen-to thirty-demographic. "Well, I'm sure all your loyal readers miss you," I said tactfully.

"That's very kind of you, Tiffany, but you know that old saying about a door closing? Well, it's true. A new opportunity practically jumped into my lap, one I just couldn't turn down."

Ada reached into her tote bag, pulled out a press pass from the *Hartwell Sun,* and dangled it before me. "I've been working there for two months now and I just love it," she gushed. "My new editor and I are very simpatico. As a matter of fact, when I heard Foodie Fest was going to be right here in Branson at the Civic Center, I suggested it for my next column, and she jumped right on it. I'm not only looking forward to the food, but all the talks and activities too." She shoved the press pass back in her bag and added, "The event I'm looking most forward to is Last Remaining Chef. I understand they're going to film it all and air it on Chef Goodwin's cable show at a later date."

I was familiar with Chef Guy Goodwin. He specialized in good ole down-home cooking with a spicy bent, and his show, *Last Remaining Chef*, had been on a national cable channel for years. All types of restaurants, from fancy-schmancy, to hotel, to burger joints all over the United States, were eligible to enter. I'd heard there had been over two thousand applicants, all hopeful of qualifying for a shot at the grand prize: ten thousand dollars' worth of advertising on the food channel and Goodwin's show for the winning restaurant, and ten thousand in cash to the winning chef. After the preliminary rounds, twenty chefs from hotels and restaurants had all qualified as finalists. A complete list of the entrants was supposed to be posted sometime later today. I'd heard that my old place of employment, the Madison, had entered, and I was curious to see if they'd qualified, and if so, who Leonardo had chosen to represent them.

"I'm looking forward to that event too," I said. "What I'd really love to get, though, is some one-on-one interviews with some of the guest chefs for my blog. I sent several email requests to the event organizer, Sophie Brinkwater, but so far I haven't heard back from her."

"That doesn't surprise me. That gal's got a lot on her plate," said Ada. "The one you should speak with is her assistant, Phoebe Fitzgerald. She's a temp, but she's really good. She set up five interviews and tastings with local and out-of-state restaurants for me, and I bet she could set some chef interviews up for you too."

"I might just do that," I said. "I'd love to score a one-on-one with Guy Goodwin, but the one I'd really like to interview is Dana Carlyle. She's always been one of my idols."

Dana Carlyle was a well-regarded chef in the food industry. She came from old Boston money—her father was Preston Carlyle, who had worked in the U.S. Department of State for years. Dana had graduated from the prestigious Cordon Bleu College of Culinary Arts in Paris, but instead of using her father's contacts to grab a plum job, she chose to start in a small restaurant in San Francisco, where she worked her way up from junior chef to executive chef within two years. She'd been executive chef at more than one Three Star Michelin restaurant in her career before starting her own restaurant chain, Dana's Delights, a few years ago. She'd written ten cookbooks, several of which I owned. To say she was one of my culinary idols was a gross understatement. She was my *primary* culinary idol.

"Dana Carlyle? Oh, dear." Ada's face fell, and she clucked her tongue. "You haven't heard?" Ada reached out and put her hand over mine. "Poor Dana was in a car accident day before yesterday. Fortunately neither driver was seriously injured, but Dana suffered a broken leg and a sprained wrist, so she's not able to attend the convention."

"Oh, no! That is a shame," I cried. "I'm glad her injuries were relatively minor, but I won't deny I'm disappointed. I think a lot of other people will be too."

"Namely the up-and-coming chefs and home cooks attending," agreed Ada. "They'll be bummed for sure. She was probably the main reason they're attending. That five-hundred-dollar registration fee isn't cheap, plus it's nonrefundable."

"They might be persuaded to make an exception considering the circumstances. After all, it's not as if Dana's accident was planned." I paused and then added, "If I'm not mistaken, wasn't Dana also supposed to receive an award at the dinner?"

Ada nodded. "Yes. The Golden Mixer Award for her contribution to the food industry." She let out a long sigh. "I understand her replacement has agreed to accept the award on her behalf."

I frowned. "Her replacement? You mean they were able to find someone to take over on such short notice? That's terrific."

"Yeah, well, that all depends on your definition of terrific," said Ada. Her brows drew together in a deep scowl. "Her replacement is Jason Barclay."

I stared at her. "Jason Barclay? Really?"

"I kid you not."

Ada dove into her tote bag again and this time pulled out a program, which she handed to me. "The substitution was so last-minute that Dana's name is still on the programs. I'm not sure if they had new ones printed up, or are just including a notice in the existing ones, you know, like they do when there's a last-minute substitution for an actor in a play. I don't think many people are aware of the switch yet. I only found out because I happened to overhear a few of the volunteers talking about it." She let out a chuckle that sounded almost sinister. "Who knows, once the news gets out about Barclay, there might be a stampede of people demanding refunds." She drew closer to me and said in a half whisper, "I heard that he approached the Foodie Fest president himself and offered to substitute once he heard about Dana."

"Are you sure? That doesn't sound like Jason." As Ada raised an eyebrow, I added, "I met him when he did a review of the Madison's restaurant. He didn't seem the type to voluntarily help out someone else."

"True, but I understand he has his reasons." She paused and then added dramatically, "I was told by someone who's very in the know that Jason volunteered to substitute for Dana in the hopes it might generate some good PR for him."

I frowned. "Are you sure about that? Jason Barclay never cared about getting good PR before."

"Well, he does now." Ada lowered her voice and added, "Apparently he wrote a proposal for a book, and word on the street is Hollywood is very hot for it."

"Wait—what?" I shook my head. "He wrote a proposal for a cookbook and now Hollywood wants to turn it into a movie?"

"Not a cookbook," replied Ada. "It's nonfiction. His auto-biography, to be precise. According to my source some of the chapters are burning hot. Apparently he rattles quite a few skeletons in the closet of people in the food industry."

"Oh, goodness. You mean he names names? Like in an exposé?"

"I don't think he used real names, but I believe the descriptions were such that it was obvious who he was talking about. Or is it whom?" She waved her hand. "You have to hand it to the guy, he knows what the public wants, what sells . . . oh, thank goodness! This line's finally moving." She reached out and gave my hand a quick squeeze. "It was nice talking to you, Tiffany. I'll probably see you around. And don't forget to get in touch with Phoebe."

Any further thoughts I might have had about Jason's book slash movie deal dissipated as my own line surged forward, and a few minutes later I found myself in front of the registration desk marked A–M. A bright-eyed blonde volunteer whose name tag read 'Joannie" handed me my welcome packet. "Tiffany Austin, welcome to the Foodie Fest convention," she said. "I just love your blog, Bon-Appetempting! I tried some of those pizza recipes you posted and they came out great!"

I'd recently hosted a pizza contest for *Southern Style* (and been instrumental in solving a murder, but that's another story), and the winning recipes had appeared on my blog. "That's great," I said. "I'm hoping to pick up some more recipes here, maybe get an interview or two with some of the chefs."

"Oh, that would be amazing," Joannie gushed. "You should hook up with Phoebe Fitzgerald. She's Ms. Brinkwater's assistant and she's tops at organizing things." Joannie gave a swift look around and then said in a low tone, "Ordinarily for something like that I'd suggest you speak with Ms. Brinkwater directly, but she's had her hands full the past few days. There have been some . . . complications with the convention program."

"I understand," I said. I didn't feel the need to mention I was aware of just what—and who—the complications might entail.

Joannie shot me a bright smile. "But Phoebe can help you with that, I'm sure. She's usually in the office area this time of day. It's in the rear of the auditorium underneath the stage." She reached into a box on the table and handed me a map. "Here's a map of the layout. Once you get to the stage, I'm sure one of the other volunteers can direct you."

"Thanks," I said. "I'll do that." I stuffed my convention materials into my tote and moved off a few paces to look at the map. The convention center consisted of two floors. The check-in and information tables were on the first floor, to the right of the entryway into the main auditorium. Behind the tables stretched a double row of vendor booths, selling everything from cookbooks to the latest in kitchenware. The vendor booths took up about a quarter of the mammoth floor space of the Civic Center. The rest of the floor had sections cordoned off and separated by curtains. These sections were reserved for the cooking classes and a few cookbook signings. Seating was limited, so early sign-up had been a must. The large first-floor stage was earmarked for guest talks, like the one Dana and now Jason was scheduled to give.

The upstairs portion of the center was devoted to the main specialty contests inspired by their cable shows of the same names, Last Remaining Chef and Market Games. For both competitions nearly half of the assigned space had been transformed into a mini-supermarket, complete with deli and liquor department. I was curious to see that! The upstairs seating area could accommodate well over three hundred people, and I had no doubt once those events started it would be a packed house, particularly Last Remaining Chef, which stretched over three days, starting Friday evening and ending Sunday afternoon. Market Games and the third major event, the food truck competition, were only one-day events. The food truck event was to be held in the center's parking lot on Friday afternoon, which reminded me that I still had some unfinished business with Dale Swenson, my editor. We'd gotten quite a bit of mail since my blog started, requesting more food photos and maybe some videos, and I'd complied with my trusty phone. While my readers seemed to like my amateur efforts, I felt an event as important as this convention deserved a more professional touch. I'd asked Dale for a photographer to accompany me, and to my surprise he'd agreed without an argument. Unfortunately, all our staff shutterbugs were currently on assignments. He'd promised to look into a freelancer but so far had had no luck. I was hopeful we could at least get one in time for the food truck competition, and also for the finale of Last Remaining Chef. Right now, though, it looked as if it would be just me and my phone for the immediate future.

I found a quiet space off to the left of the vendor tables with a few chairs, and the first thing I did after taking a seat was to pull out the program and look at it. It looked exactly like the one Ada had shown me, so I doubted there had been time to make up new ones. Sure enough, there was a piece of white paper neatly stapled to the top of one of the pages:

> We regret to inform you that Dana Carlyle will be unable to attend the conference. In her place, giving a critique on restaurant quality on Friday at 11 a.m., will be noted food critic Jason Barclay.

"Restaurant quality," I muttered. "That's a laugh. Just when did he become an expert on restaurant quality."

"I beg your pardon. As I'm sure you're well aware, I'm an expert on many things. Especially beautiful ex-chefs like yourself," said a deep voice.

I froze.

Two

"Cat got your tongue, Tiffany Austin? It is you, isn't it?"

I turned my head in the direction of the voice. The man who stood there was tall, easily over six feet. His Armani suit, tailored to show off his muscular physique, looked expensive and practically reeked money. His hair, a rich chestnut brown, was cut short, tapered down to the skin on the sides and back. Dark blue eyes bored into mine while well-shaped lips tipped slightly upward, more of a sneer than a smile.

It was indeed Jason Barclay, In the flesh, and from what I could see, he hadn't changed a bit.

I forced what I hoped was a pleasant smile to my lips. "Hello, Jason. It's been a long time."

"That it has." His gaze raked over me. "I had a feeling I might run into you here. I can't tell you how shocked I was when I learned you left your job at the Madison and relocated to Branson." When I didn't answer, he continued, "It's a pretty drastic change, don't you think? I mean, if you didn't want to work with Puccini anymore, I'm sure any restaurant within a twenty-mile radius would have hired you like that." He snapped his fingers in the air to emphasize his statement.

I cleared my throat. "I'm sure they would, but I didn't want to cook professionally any longer."

He studied me for what seemed an eternity, then shook his head. "Okay, I guess I get it. The restaurant business can be cutthroat, especially for women. But a food blogger?" His lips twisted around the last two words, as if he found the idea distasteful. I figured I shouldn't be surprised. A snob like Jason would consider food blogging the bottom of the food critique chain.

"Blogging is still very popular, Jason, weren't you aware?" I said lightly.

He waved his hand. "It's a fad, Tiffany. You're better than that. You really should reconsider your decision. You're an excellent chef, one of the best."

"Is that your professional opinion?" I asked with a curl of my lip.

His lips parted in a wide smile, revealing his perfect white teeth. "Absolutely. The Duck Devine you prepared the night I was there still registers with me as one of the best dishes I've ever eaten. Far better than anything that overrated Leonardo Puccini ever made." The corners of his eyes crinkled a bit as he added, "If you ask me, you could probably teach some of these cooking classes they're offering at this conference. Young chefs today could learn a lot from you."

"That's very . . . kind of you to say, but there are quite a few top-notch chefs on the program young chefs and home cooks can learn from," I said. "For example, Anastasia Ricci and Merlin James are scheduled to give classes, and they're both high-profile chefs with excellent reputations."

He rolled his eyes, letting me know just what he thought of the chefs I'd named. "Overrated and overbearing. I suppose it all depends on one's definition of excellent."

I stifled a laugh, remembering Ada had said pretty much the same thing about him. "It's a free country. You're entitled to your opinion."

He made an exaggerated bow. "Why, thank you. Does that motto extend to include my opinion that writing about food as opposed to making and creating it is a waste of talent?"

"Of course—even though I don't agree," I said sweetly. "And speaking about writing, I understand you've been bitten by that particular bug yourself."

His posture stiffened, and his eyes widened slightly. "Ah . . . news travels fast, I see."

"It surely does," I responded. "I heard that this book is more of an exposé. I suppose that's what got Hollywood interested?"

To my surprise, he barked out a laugh. "I wouldn't call it an exposé per se," he said. "But I have learned over the years what sells and what doesn't. When I decided to write my autobiography, I knew people wouldn't be interested in my formative years, what high school and college I went to, or how I achieved fame as a noted food critic. What would interest them are the anecdotes I have to relate about various people, both in and out of the food industry. Little, juicy nuggets about what goes on and who it goes on with." He stroked at his chin. "It would surprise you, Tiffany, what I've seen and heard in my career. Trust me, it's more than you can imagine."

I'll bet, I thought. I smiled sweetly at him. "So, Jason, just how many of these so-called juicy nuggets involve you?"

"Not as many as you might think. They aren't all about sex, if that's what you're thinking. Some of them involve other types of scandal . . . and secrets. Many types of secrets. Some could be considered quite dangerous, in fact." A faraway gleam came into his eyes. "Oh, you would be very surprised."

I gave my head an impatient shake. "Really, Jason, if these secrets are so dangerous, aren't you afraid of the consequences of revealing them, particularly on the silver screen?"

He clucked his tongue. "Now, now, Tiffany. What's the point of writing an exposé if you're not going to identify the players? Besides, I didn't use their real names."

I bit out an exasperated sigh. "You've got some ego, Jason, to think none of these people would recognize themselves and want to retaliate against you . . . particularly the ones with the so-called dangerous secrets." I made air quotes around the last two words. "Or is the word *libel* not in your vocabulary?"

He shot me an indulgent smile, much like a mother would bestow on an errant two-year-old. "I'm not afraid of any retaliation, Tiffany. You can't sue someone for telling the truth." He chuckled. "I have evidence to back up every little nugget of information I choose to reveal." He raised his hand, pointed his finger at me. "Except in your case."

I felt color rise to my cheeks. "What do you mean, my case?"

He moved a bit closer to me. "Your abrupt departure from the Madison, breaking off your relationship with young Jeff Marki, coming back to the old hometown and starting a food blog. It all seems a bit out of character for you." He tapped at his stomach. "My gut tells me there's a story there."

I met his gaze unflinchingly. "Then your gut would be wrong. I hope you're not thinking of putting that speculation in your book, or your movie."

He shrugged. "Probably not, but only because I've no concrete proof of why you left. I could, however, add in a chapter about our all-too-brief relationship."

My jaw dropped and I stared at him. "What do you mean, Jason? We never had a relationship. As I recall, you made a pass at me, and a rather clumsy one at that, which I rejected in no uncertain terms."

He clucked his tongue. "Apparently we remember what happened between us a bit differently. There were definite sparks between us. I think you would have been most amenable to my charms had not young Marki shown up like a white knight to defend your honor. Had he not burst in on us that evening, well, who knows what might have happened."

I lifted my chin. "I can answer that in one word. Nothing."

He shrugged. "If it pleases you to think that way, go right ahead. No hard feelings, as they say. And allow me to also point out that when it comes to *my* book—*my* autobiography—*my* recollection of events is the only one that matters."

"Even if it's not accurate," I began, but I never got to finish the rest of my sentence as a shrill female voice suddenly rent the air. "Jason! Jason Barclay! Thank goodness! I'm glad I found you!"

A second later a long-legged woman strode into view, and I let out an involuntary groan as I recognized Francine Weston. The features reporter for cable channel KPTX, Francine loved sensational stories, the juicier the better. The woman had no real journalistic ability I could see. The sexy outfits she wore were legendary for setting tongues wagging, and today was no exception. She was dressed in a tight red suit with an almost nonexistent skirt and a white blouse that was cut low enough to display her twin assets to their best advantage. Her trademark mane of platinum blonde hair curled around her slim shoulders in waves. One perfectly manicured hand clutched a microphone. Behind her trailed a tall man in jeans and sweatshirt, television camera perched atop one shoulder. She stepped right up to us, pointedly ignored me, and turned her full-wattage smile on Jason.

"Francine Weston, Mr. Barclay. I'm here representing KPTX's *Good Morning, Branson*, and I know our viewers would just love it if I could get an interview with you," she gushed.

Jason's eyebrows drew together, and he looked a bit flummoxed. I was pretty sure he was torn. Part of him resented the interruption and the other part didn't want to diss a member of the press, or turn down an opportunity to garner more publicity for himself or his forthcoming project. His expression cleared a bit as he remarked, "Ms. Weston, is it? Your request is a bit sudden. I was under the impression Ms. Brinkwater or her assistant handled such things."

"I know. I tried to get in touch with both of them, but so far they haven't returned my calls or emails," said Francine. "And since we're both here, and . . . free?" She shot a questioning look in my direction.

"Oh, he's free," I said. "I was just leaving." I felt a tiny sense of satisfaction in knowing that Sophie Brinkwater and her assistant had apparently blown Francine off too. I started to move away, but she stepped forward and blocked my path. "You seem familiar," she said. "Have we met?"

"No, we haven't." When she still didn't move out of my way, I added reluctantly, "I'm Tiffany Austin. I'm here representing *Southern Style* magazine."

"Austin, Austin. *Southern Style* . . . oh, right," she said. "I remember now. You're the food blogger, right? And that little blog of yours is called Appetizing something?"

Not even close, I thought, and forced my lips into a half smile. "The *little* blog has a large following, and its name is Bon-Appetempting."

"Right, right. You hosted that pizza competition a few weeks ago. I wasn't assigned to cover that." She clucked her tongue, and from her expression it was hard for me to tell if she were happy or sad about that. "It was such a shame, though, about what happened to Bart Driscoll there. That poor man—such a talent." She reached up, dabbed at her eyes. "Such a loss." Her gaze swept over to Jason. "I'm sure you agree," she said. "After all, he was a colleague of yours."

Jason frowned. "We were both food critics, but I wouldn't call him a colleague," he said with a sniff.

Francine looked a bit put off, but only for a moment. She shot Jason a catlike smile. "Of course, there are so few critics who fall into your category, Jason. May I call you Jason?" Without waiting for an answer, she turned to me. "Now, you're sure I'm not interrupting anything?"

"If you mean an interview, you can relax, Francine," I said. "I have no plans to interview Mr. Barclay. He's all yours," I added, directing a wicked smile Jason's way.

"Fantastic," gushed Francine. "I didn't want to step on anyone's toes. Well, it was nice meeting you." And with that, she turned her back on me and homed in on Jason. "I promise not to keep you long, Jason," she cooed. "I promise, I've only got a few questions for you. Now, if we could just move over here a bit? The lighting is *so* much better."

Jason started to scowl, then apparently thought better of alienating a member of the press, even if it was Francine. "Of course," he said smoothly. "But just a few questions. A very few. My schedule these days is rather tight."

"No problem." Francine looked over her shoulder and snapped the fingers of her free hand in the air. "Brent, bring that camera over here, will you? And hurry up."

Brent muttered something under his breath too low for me to hear, then moved forward. Francine, smiling all the while, took Jason's elbow and steered him into position. I seized the opportunity to take off. Before I rounded the corner I shot a quick glance over my shoulder. Francine was speaking animatedly to Jason, who, in spite of his polite words and the smile plastered across his face, seemed coiled, like a snake ready to strike, if the vein bulging in his forehead was any indication.

And Brent the cameraman? He looked more like a henpecked husband than a coworker. I found myself actually feeling sorry for him.

• • •

I glanced at my watch. According to the program, there was a half hour before the introductory luncheon for the members of the press (yours truly, yay!) and honored guests was to start. The lunch, as well as the cocktail hour and awards banquet the following evening, were to be held in the dining room of the Branson Towers, an upscale hotel situated a convenient two blocks away from the Civic Center. The hotel was fairly new, and I had no doubt they'd been ecstatic to get the Foodie Association's business. I'd heard that all of the chefs and most of the guest speakers were staying there, and I figured Jason had probably booked one of the suites. Since I had time, I decided to try and track down Phoebe Fitzgerald. Joannie had said the woman would be in her office under the stage, so after consulting my map I struck out toward that area. Two volunteers were chatting at the far end of the stage, so I made my way over to them and inquired the best way to get to Phoebe Fitzgerald's office.

"You go through there," said the taller of the two, whose name tag read *Audrey*. "There's a stairway that leads to the backstage office area. Phoebe's office is right across from the locker area, third door on the left."

I thanked them and set off for the spot Audrey had indicated, a black-curtained entry at the top of an open ramp that ran parallel to the backstage wall. I went down the short flight of steps and found myself in a dimly lighted hallway. I walked down and after a few minutes passed through a section of lockers that reminded me of the ones we'd had in high school. I found the third door on the left and knocked. I waited a few moments, then knocked again, this time calling out, "Ms. Fitzgerald? Are you there? This is Tiffany Austin from *Southern Style*. I'd like to speak with you about the possibility of setting up some chef interviews for the magazine's blog."

Still no response, so I reached out, twisted the handle. The door was locked. Apparently Phoebe wasn't there. I decided to try my luck with a written note. Fortunately the intro pack I'd gotten contained a small pad, so I tore off a sheet, dug out a pen and wrote a quick note to Phoebe. I shoved it under the door and then retraced my steps back to the main floor. I gave a cautious glance over toward where I'd last seen Francine and Jason, and let out a sigh of relief when I saw they were no longer there. I'd barely taken two steps forward when I heard an excited squeal behind me.

"Tiffany! Tiffany Austin?"

I turned. A petite middle-aged woman in a brilliant pink, purple and blue tie-dye dress was hurrying toward me so fast that the gelled spikes of her multicolored blue, green, pink and purple pixie cut bobbed up and down. "Tiffany! It's been a long time. I had no idea you'd be here. You look terrific," she cried, opening her arms to envelop me in a gigantic bear hug.

I smiled and hugged her back. "Rain! You look wonderful too! It's great to see you. I had no idea you'd be here either. This is a nice surprise."

Rain (short for Rainbow) McGill had been a food editor for a small New York paper when I'd first met her back when I worked at the Madison. She was a pert, bubbly woman in her early forties who'd since switched careers herself. She'd also given up the New York rat race and moved to Atlanta, dyed her mousy brown hair to match her name, self-published two cookbooks, one of which had spent twelve weeks on the *New York Times* bestseller list. She had her own weekly show on YouTube that garnered over a half million watches a week.

Yes, Rain had become quite the media star since she'd first reviewed my cooking.

Rain released me and took a step backward. "I guess I shouldn't be surprised you're here, Tiffany. It's just the sort of thing I'm sure your blog followers will eat up, pardon the pun."

I laughed. "You read my blog? I'm flattered. So, how is YouTube's latest sensation doing? I caught your show last week that featured *zuppa toscana.* It inspired me to make some."

"That's the main reason I do the show," said Rain with a wide smile. "It's all for the foodies. I love to inspire people to cook, although I doubt you need much encouragement. And yes, I do read your blog. I think it's . . . fab." She laid a hand on my arm. "Tell me, does an event like this get your old juices flowing? Any regrets about giving up being a chef?"

"None. Honest. I'm happy with my life right now."

"That's great. I am too. Seems like we both made the right decision to leave New York." Rain gave a quick look around the auditorium. "I heard a rumor that they got Jason Barclay of all people to replace poor Dana Carlyle."

"It's not a rumor," I said. "He's here. As a matter of fact, I saw Francine Weston from *Good Morning, Branson* interviewing him a little bit ago."

"Ah, Francine," Rainbow said with a chuckle. "She'd try to get an interview with the devil himself if she thought it might further her career. Although now that I think about it, an interview with Jason Barclay might be considered the same thing. To be honest, I'm surprised he showed up. I'd wager he's got more enemies than friends at this convention." She ducked her head and said in a half whisper, "I heard he's here to drum up some favorable publicity for a book he's writing. There's even talk of it becoming a movie."

"It's true on both counts," I said. I figured I might as well admit my encounter with Jason just in case Rain might hear it somewhere else. "I happened to run into him shortly before Francine cornered him and he mentioned it after he chastised me for quitting the Madison and taking up blogging."

"Well, to be honest, I can't fault him for that. I went back to the Madison a few times after you left, and the food was good but it just wasn't the same. In my opinion, Leonardo should at least have tried to keep you. But that's a moot point, right." She fisted a hand on her hip. "So what sort of book is he writing that's got Hollywood all agog? It has to be fiction, right? A compilation of all his most scathing reviews surely wouldn't attract a Hollywood producer."

"Actually it's his autobiography—or as he put it, more of a tell-all. He's supposed to air dirty laundry, spill some food industry secrets in it."

"No kidding!" Rain's eyes lit up. "Well, that explains the Hollywood interest. I wonder if he gives out any actual names?"

I shrugged. "It wouldn't surprise me. He mentioned having some juicy stuff on people both in an out of the food industry. He even hinted that some of the information he had might be considered dangerous."

"Dangerous? To who? Him?" Rain let out a snort. "He'd better watch out. He might have a whole slew of disgruntled husbands and boyfriends after him once that book, or movie, comes out. He's a bit of a rake, you know." She turned her hand inward, pointed at herself. "Thank goodness I have no secrets like that. My life's always been an open book."

I figured this was as good a time as any to change the subject away from Jason and his book before Rain decided to ask some more pointed questions. "I noticed the Madison registered for the Last Remaining Chef competition," I said. "I'm curious as to who Chef Leonardo chose to represent them."

"If you were still there, it would have been you," said Rain. "Any of those other chefs can't hold a candle to you. Although Marki's son is doing quite well, I understand. He was your sous chef when you were there, wasn't he?"

I nodded. "Yes. Jeff had a lot of promise. I'm glad to hear he's doing well."

"I read in the paper he just got engaged to Leonardo's daughter," Rain went on. She wrinkled her nose as she added, "Imagine having that old coot for a father-in-law. That's a fate I wouldn't wish on anyone." She raised her wrist and tapped at the face of her gold Cartier watch. "It's almost time for the luncheon to start, thank goodness. I'm starving. I skipped my usual big breakfast because I was running late. Let's head on over. I do believe seating isn't assigned, so if we're one of the first to get in, we can get a good table. I hear it's buffet-style, and several chefs have contributed dishes."

"That sounds interesting," I said. "I've always preferred buffet-style. That way you get to taste a variety."

Rain patted my hand. "I always knew you were a girl after my own heart, Tiffany. Come on, let's go."

She linked her arm through mine, and we made our way out of the Civic Center and, thanks mainly to Rain's speed walking, covered the two short blocks to the Branson Towers in record time. As we walked past the beautifully landscaped grounds, I couldn't help but admire the large garden area that overflowed with pink and purple flowers. A large fountain, square in the center, towered majestically over them. Water spurted out of a large center bowl, flanked by elegantly carved cherubs and fish that rose up out of the center of a deep, circular pool that had steps leading up to it. Beside the steps were two smaller fountains with the water spurting from the mouths of stone lions. Off to the left of the fountain, there was a small pond surrounded by some low-lying bushes. As we passed, I caught a glimpse of dozens of multicolored fish swimming around, some circling each other, others going off on their own. I would have paused for a closer look, but Rain took my elbow and propelled me forward. I made a mental note to return at some juncture and take a closer look around.

We hurried up the steps of the hotel and into the lobby, which at first glance I thought could easily rival any upscale New York hotel. I paused for a second to admire the polished marble floors and the brilliant chandeliers that twinkled overhead. There were a few people clustered around a shiny block of black marble I figured was the reception desk. I would have spent a little more time studying the lobby with all its upscale trappings but Rain once again steered me off to the left, where a large billboard had been set up. The poster on it read *Welcome Members of the Press and Honored Guests of Foodie Fest.* To the right of the board two young girls wearing name tags that identified them as Foodie Fest volunteers were just seating themselves behind a table. Just behind them were two glass doors, and as we approached they swung open, revealing an elegantly appointed dining room.

"Ooh," Rain gave my arm a squeeze. "Looks like we're the first to arrive."

We stepped up to the table and one of the volunteers glanced up and smiled. "Hello! Welcome to the luncheon. Are you guests or press?"

"We're both press," said Rain before I could answer.

"Fantastic! Then I'll be checking you in," she said. "Names and badges, please?"

We both pulled out our press passes and showed them to her. She checked off both our names and then Rain and I made our way into the room. There were six tables of eight set up for members of the press, all with pristine white tablecloths and gleaming china. A long table opposite the buffet table was set up in a similar fashion, and I figured this was earmarked for the guest speakers and judges.

Rain gave me a nudge. "I see placards at the big table," she said. "Seating's reserved there. Let's see who's attending."

No argument from me. I was curious as to just who would be attending myself. We made our way over to the table. I recognized quite a few of the names, among them Anastasia Ricci, who had been one of the pizza contest judges. Suddenly Rain let out a groan.

"Darn. Here's Jason Barclay's place, right here on the end." She pointed to the placard and pulled a face. "Thank goodness we don't have to sit with him. If we did, I'd probably lose my appetite. Oh, look! They're starting to put out the food!"

Several white-coated servers had begun to assemble the silver chafing dishes on the buffet table. "I can't wait to sample these," Rain gushed. "I heard all the chefs did something special. Kind of makes you wonder what might be in store for the awards banquet tomorrow night. I heard that's going to be buffet-style too." She chuckled. "It seems our celebrity chefs want to make a good impression, although I'll bet it's aimed more at the press—mainly the food critics—than Foodie Fest personnel."

People were starting to file in now, and Rain immediately took my hand and guided me to the table closest to the buffet. As we settled in, she glanced up and the corners of her lips immediately tipped downward. "Oh, swell. His Nibs has arrived."

I looked up. Jason had just come through the door. A slightly taller man in a tan corduroy jacket and pressed jeans was right behind him. Jason turned and said something to the taller man, who shook his head and started to move past Jason. Jason grabbed the man's arm and pulled him off to the side, shaking his finger at him all the while. The other man, apparently not to be outdone, did the same thing to Jason. Both men's cheeks were so red I feared one or both might have a stroke.

Beside me, Rain cleared her throat. "Well, well," she murmured. "What do you know? Barclay and Hudson, going at it just like old times. Some things never change."

I looked over at Rain. "Do you know that man with Barclay?" I asked.

"Sure. That's Hugh Hudson," said Rain. "He and Jason worked on the *New York Metro* back in the day when I was a food editor for the *Bronx Daily Beat*."

I looked back over at the two men. They were standing apart now and both seemed calmer, although I caught the man Rain had called

Hugh Hudson still scowling. "They were both food critics?"

"Sort of. Hugh was more of a question-and-answer guy back then." She lifted her hand, ran it through her multicolored strands. "Hugh originally had the crime beat, and he was darn good at it too. But then it got to be a bit too much for him. He wanted to do something less stressful."

I looked over thoughtfully at Hugh Hudson. "Well, food is definitely less stressful than crime. Still, that's quite a change."

Rain shrugged. "Maybe for some, but not for Hugh. His mother was a chef at L'Artusi in the Village for years. He might not be able to boil water, but he knows his food. And his palate is way better than Jason's, if you ask me." She smiled, reminiscing. "At first they got along, but then management decided to expand the food section. They gave Hugh his own column, and that was when things went off the rails. Jason didn't think Hugh was qualified to write reviews and Hugh thought Jason was ill qualified and had no business reviewing food." Rain's voice trailed off for a moment and then she continued, "One day Jason got that opportunity in Georgia and you know the rest. As for Hugh, he's happy doing food reviews for *Metro*. According to him, he should have done it sooner. Oh, look, he's coming this way. Let's invite him to sit with us." Before I could say anything, Rain jumped up in her seat and started to wave her arm back and forth. "Yoo-hoo, Hugh! Over here!" she called.

Hugh's head snapped up and he looked in our direction. He hurried toward our table and gave us both a wide smile as he sat. "Rainbow! How lovely to see you," he said. "It's been awhile."

"Yes it has," she said, reaching out to let her fingers make a trail up his arm. "Way too long," she purred.

Hugh's gaze shifted over to me. "I don't believe I've had the pleasure," he said, extending his hand. "Hugh Hudson."

"Oh, where are my manners," cried Rain. "Hugh, this is Tiffany Austin. She writes a food blog for *Southern Style* magazine." She paused and then added, "She used to be the assistant head chef at the

Madison a few years ago."

He looked at me. "From chef to food blogger, eh?" He took my hand, lifted it to his lips, and planted a quick kiss on my palm. "A pleasure, Tiffany Austin. I salute you."

"Thanks." I took a moment to study him. He was a bit older than Jason, early fifties if I had to make a guess, and an extremely good-looking man. The suit he wore wasn't nearly as expensive as Jason's, but it fit him to a tee, showing off his broad shoulders and nipped waistline.

"Yeah, you look pretty good for an old guy," said Rain. I noted the teasing note in her voice and the way she looked at Hugh, and wondered if there might be more to their relationship than she let on. Then again, the Rain I remembered had always been a terrible flirt. I remembered her making goo-goo eyes at the "old coot" Leonardo.

More people were starting to file in now, and the servers were taking their places behind the buffet table. Rain nodded in the direction of the main banquet table. "I see you had a reunion with your old chum," she said.

Hugh sighed. "You never miss a trick, do you, Rain? That man never fails to press all my wrong buttons. I haven't seen him in a few years, but he hasn't changed one iota. He still thinks the whole world revolves around him."

"So what were you disagreeing on this time? Surely not the food so soon," asked Rain.

"You'd think he'd have made some remark about that, wouldn't you? But he wanted something else." Hugh picked up his spoon, tapped it against the tablecloth. "He asked me if he could pick my brain about my crime reporting days, can you believe that?"

Rain frowned. "Your crime reporting days? Why on earth would he ask about those?"

"Who knows? I asked him why he was so interested in that and he wouldn't answer me." Hugh let out a breath. "When I first heard he was going to be here, I was hopeful he might have mellowed in all this time, but he hasn't changed a bit. His reluctant apology aside, Jason Barclay is still, and will probably always be, a first-class jerk."

Rain glanced at me, then back at Hugh. "I wonder if what he wanted to ask you could have something to do with the book he's writing," she suggested.

Hugh stared at Rain, and then barked out a laugh. "He's writing a book? You've got to be kidding. I wasn't even certain the guy knew how to read one, let alone write one."

Rain shot me a glance before she replied, "Everyone has the same reaction. Yes, his autobiography. It's rumored to be a sort of tell-all."

Hugh snorted. "A tell-all? On what? What the chefs do when dinner service is over? What really happens to all the leftover food in the kitchen?"

"It's supposed to be a bit more exciting than that," said Rain. "Supposedly he spills quite a few secrets in it."

Hugh let out a snort. "What sort of secrets could that shyster possibly reveal? What chefs are doing it with who in the pantry?"

Rain chuckled. "Well, whatever he reveals in it, it caught Hollywood's eye. Supposedly there's also some sort of movie deal in the works."

"Huh. Hollywood must be desperate." Hugh tapped his finger on the tablecloth. "I for one would not waste my money, or my valuable time, on anything he'd write," said Hugh. He cast a dark look over at where Jason sat. He was on his phone, talking animatedly into it and ignoring everyone around him.

Hugh scraped back his chair and nodded toward the buffet table, where the white-coated servers were starting to uncover the chafing dishes. "Looks like the buffet is starting, and a good thing, because I'm hungry as a bear. Are you ladies coming?"

"Absolutely," said Rain, pushing her chair back. "I can hear that Squid Ink Risotto calling my name."

I pulled my phone out of my tote and made a shooing motion with my other hand. "You two go on," I said. "I'll catch up. I want to see if

I can get hold of Phoebe Fitzgerald to set up a few interviews with some of the chefs."

Rain and Hugh didn't need any encouragement to start for the buffet. I dialed the number given for Phoebe on the program and got voicemail. I left a message, then sat for a minute, my phone pressed against my chin. I looked over once again at the main banquet table. Jason had gotten off the phone and was slouched in his chair, chin in hand, scowling. It took me a moment to realize that he was looking directly at Hugh Hudson on the buffet line, and I couldn't help but wonder, was Jason's interest in Hugh's past reporting a cover for something else? Could Hugh possibly be one of Jason's "juicy nuggets"?

Three

"Hello, kids. Mommy's home!"

I let myself in the side door of my cozy little cottage and waited. Sure enough, not ten seconds later I heard the sound of scampering feet and my "children" appeared to greet me. Cooper, my black and tan King Charles cavalier spaniel, jumped up and put both paws on my pants. Lily, my seal point Siamese, sauntered over and rubbed her furry body against my legs. Both their noses twitched as they sniffed at the large paper bag I held in my hands.

"Smells good, right? Leftovers from the lunch buffet," I said, waving it aloft. "If you're both real good, later on I'll let you have a taste of Guy Goodwin's sea bass."

Cooper let out a loud yip, and Lily meowed. They both looked at me expectantly for a moment and then, realizing that no food was immediately forthcoming, went over to their respective beds in the far corner of my kitchen and lay down.

I tossed my jacket and tote on the kitchen counter and flopped into one of the chairs at the table. I pulled my cell phone out of my pocket. In addition to copious photos, I'd also taken a short video of the buffet table to accompany my next post. I'd shut the phone down during the buffet and forgotten to turn it back on afterward, so I turned it on now, hoping that Dale might have left a message that he'd found a photographer. I did have two messages, but neither was from Dale. One was from my BFF and coworker, Hilary Hanson. The other was from my current beau, homicide detective Philip Bartell. I decided to listen to Phil's message first.

"Hey, beautiful." Phil's voice, low and sexy, came over the phone. "I'm just back from Utah and missing you. I was wondering if maybe you'd like to have dinner with me tomorrow night. Give me a call." A pause. "This is Phil Bartell, by the way."

I smiled as the message ended. Phil had been away for five days at a conference on the latest technology in homicide investigations—or as he put it, five days of utter boredom. For a minute I was tempted to accept his dinner invitation, but I knew I couldn't blow off that awards dinner. I dialed his cell and got voicemail—of course. "Hey there, Phil Bartell," I said at the beep, "I've been missing you too. Ordinarily I'd love to have dinner with you tomorrow, but it's the awards banquet at that foodie conference and I've got to attend. I'll probably be tied up all week with the various events, but the conference ends Sunday afternoon so . . . how about dinner at my place Sunday night? Let me know. Oh, and this is Tiffany Austin, by the way."

I smiled as I hung up. I'd met Philip Bartell when I'd been one of his prime suspects in a murder investigation, and although we'd tried, we couldn't deny the sparks that had flown between us. Our attempts at getting together had been thwarted when I'd gotten involved in another murder, and Phil had been more than a little annoyed at what he termed my "Nancy Drew Complex." Thankfully, it seemed we'd finally gotten past all that. We'd gone on a few dates that had gone well, and since there were no more murders on the horizon, I was hopeful that our mutual attraction might finally get off to a decent start. One thing I knew for sure: the man was an excellent kisser. Oh, yeah baby!

Next I called Hilary. She answered on the second ring. "Girlfriend! How was your first day with the foodies? Did you get to taste anything fabulous?"

I couldn't hold back a chuckle. Trust that to be the first thing on my BFF's mind. A curvy blonde, Hilary loved food in all its forms, from elegant cuisine to fast food. She herself could barely boil water, and I imagined my talent in the kitchen was part of the reason our friendship had lasted since grammar school. I remembered her coming over to my house many times to "help" me make lasagna, or Irish stew, or some other dish. Of course, in Hilary's case, the help consisted of eating whatever I prepared. Come to think of it, not much had changed in that regard.

"Lots of fabulous things," I said. "The kickoff luncheon was to die for. It was a buffet. Some of the chefs prepared entrées. For example, Guy Goodwin served up his famous sea bass with mustard sauce."

"Ooh, that's his specialty! Oh, no! How was it?"

"Heavenly. The bass was light and flaky, perfectly cooked. The mustard sauce had just the right tang to it. I think he uses a course-grain mustard. The vegetables served with it were excellent too. Steamed broccoli and baby carrots. They had just the right amount of crunch." I gave my lips a resounding smack to emphasize my point.

"Stop, you're killing me. I swear, I can taste it now," cried Hilary. I heard her take a deep breath. "Okay. What else?"

"A bacon-wrapped pork tenderloin that was succulent and divine, and a honey roast duck with fingerling potatoes. The duck was cooked perfectly, and the potatoes had a garlic seasoning that was just . . . yummy."

"You're a sadist, you know that," grumbled Hilary. "I think you enjoy torturing me this way. I wish I could have been there."

"Then do the next best thing and read my blog tomorrow. I took a video of the buffet table before the vultures descended on it. It didn't come out as well as I hoped, though. A pro would have done a better job."

"Speaking of pros, I saw Dale today. He mentioned trying to find a freelance photographer, and I suggested he contact Mac. He knows lots of freelancers." Mac was Mackenzie Huddleston, our best staff photographer and Hilary's on-again, off-again beau. "And I'm sure that no matter how bad your video is, folks will eat it up, no pun intended. I know I can't wait to see it."

I laughed. "Well, if you want to come over after work, you can not only see some of those dishes you can sample them. There was a ton of food left over, and Rain made sure we each got a giant-sized goodie bag before we left."

"Taste gourmet food? You bet I'll be there. I'll even spring for a bottle of wine, and not the bargain stuff either. A feast like this deserves the good stuff," said Hilary.

"So my sadistic streak is forgiven?"

"For the moment." A slight pause and then, "By the way, who's Rain?"

"Rainbow McGill. I've mentioned her. She used to be a food critic back when I was at the Madison."

"Oh, right, right. The chick with the multicolored hair who's got that YouTube show. Say, do you know a lot of people at work watch her?"

"That's not surprising. She's got over a half million followers."

"Wow. I wish I was talented at something so I could have a YouTube show," said Hilary.

I clucked my tongue sympathetically. "Don't tell me you regret that promotion?"

"Heck, no. I'm good with the promotion. It's just Crystal isn't exactly the easiest person to work for. She was in rare form today."

Hilary had recently been promoted to junior reporter in the Features department, a good career move save for the fact she had to now work for Crystal Worthington. The features editor was a true type A personality and a true perfectionist. Crystal seemed to still regard Hilary as a clerk and was constantly giving her menial assignments, which frustrated my BFF to no end. I had the feeling that part of her attitude toward Hilary stemmed from jealousy. Where Hilary was curvy, blonde and bubbly, Crystal was tall, rail-thin and introverted. Hilary had often compared her to the Almira Gulch character from the *Wizard of Oz*, and I had to admit, the shoe definitely fit.

"Then some of Goodwin's sea bass is just what you need. Plus the wine, of course," I said. I paused and then added, "I had an unpleasant run-in at the convention myself today. Jason Barclay was there."

I heard my friend's swift intake of breath. "Jason Barclay! Isn't he the creep who hit on you when you worked at the Madison?"

"The one and only," I responded. "Thank goodness Francine Weston interrupted our conversation. It was starting to take a very bad turn."

"Francine Weston—that barracuda? She was there?" said Hilary. "That's surprising. I wouldn't think a foodie conference would interest her."

"Me either, but I bet she found out Barclay was going to be there," I said. "She probably figured getting an interview with him would be worth her time. To be honest, I was actually glad she interrupted us. Jason claimed I'd been receptive to his advances. He intimated things between us would have escalated had not Jeff stepped in."

"Well, he's clearly in need of some medication to improve his memory," said Hilary. "What a creep—hold on. Did you say his book?"

"Yep. Rumor has it he's writing a book. His autobiography, to be precise."

"Well, that sounds like a yawn. Someone should tell him it's bad luck for food critics to write books. Look at what happened to Bart Driscoll."

"True," I agreed. "And Jason's book sounded like it could be pretty explosive. Apparently he's been privy to some scandalous information about people both in and out of the food industry that he's sprinkled in."

Hilary sniffed. "Sounds more like he's inviting trouble to me."

"Me too, but Jason doesn't seem concerned. Apparently he's got a Hollywood producer interested in it."

"You're kidding! Before it's even published?" My bestie made a sound somewhere between a sigh and a growl. "How much you want to bet he's making all this up?"

"I don't think so. He sounded so confident, almost smug, that I think he might really have dirt on people. He hinted that some of it could be dangerous. Then he hinted that he might throw in something about me . . . about our relationship."

"Your relationship? You mean when he practically assaulted you in the kitchen?"

"He doesn't think of it that way. And he made a big point of telling me that his recollection of events is the only one that matters."

Hilary made a clucking sound. "We know nothing happened, but he could twist things around to suit his version. And what if he decides to dig further into why you left the Madison? Maybe it's time to come clean with Bartell. If you're not ready to tell him about Jeff, you should at least tell what really happened with Jason." She paused. "Think about it, Tif. What if the barracuda gets wind of that? I bet she'd use it against you in a nanosecond."

"You mean Francine? Why would she do that?"

Hilary let out a huge sigh. "Apparently you never saw her interview with Bartell after Driscoll's murder. She was practically salivating all over him. It's so obvious she's got a big crush on your guy, and trust me, Francine would take any opportunity she could get to discredit you in his eyes."

I frowned. No, I hadn't seen Francine's interview with Phil, although I remembered him mentioning it to me. As I recalled, he'd been quite annoyed with the way she'd conducted it. "Francine might have a crush on Phil, but I doubt he returns her feelings," I said.

"He doesn't have to like the woman," said Hilary. "I'd be disappointed in him if he did. But once Francine plants that seed of doubt about you in his head, it could make a difference in your relationship. You know what a stickler he is for honesty. He won't like it that you kept those details from him, especially since he asked you about Jeff point-blank."

"We weren't dating when he asked me," I protested. "We were barely talking."

"Doesn't matter. Guys like him always wonder what else you might be keeping secret, and that leads to a lack of trust, which generally leads to a breakup. Please, please, promise me you'll at least consider telling him."

I knew what Hilary said made sense. "I will think about it, I promise," I said. "In the meantime, I think a nice Cabernet Sauvignon would go great with our dinner. Maybe a Caymus Special 2017?"

"A Cay—hey, hold on. Isn't that wine almost two hundred dollars?" Hilary cried.

I burst out laughing. "Very good. I see you've learned something from that wine club you joined. I think a nice pinot gris would be a fine accompaniment to our dinner. If you were serious about buying the good stuff, you can pick one up for around twenty bucks."

"That's not bad. Maybe I'll spring for two bottles. Somehow this seems like a two-bottle night for both of us," said Hilary. "By the time I get out of here I should be at your place around six. I'd like to bug out earlier, but I don't think Crystal will let me. And speaking of Crystal, I've got to get this copy over to her so she can pick it apart for the umpteenth time today."

"Good luck," I said. "Oh, and did I mention there's banana almond cream pie for dessert?" I smacked my lips. "The crust was perfect, light brown and flaky, the filling rich and robust. The slivered almonds added just the right touch. The filling was made from fresh bananas, whipped into a creamy consistency that just melted in my mouth."

Hilary let out a groan. "That did it. Before I come over I'm stopping home and changing into those elastic waist pants I always wear at Thanksgiving. So it might be more like six fifteen."

"I—and the food—will be here," I said cheerily.

No sooner had I disconnected from Hilary than my phone buzzed to signal an incoming call. I looked at the screen, saw Phoebe Fitzgerald's name, and eagerly swiped the accept button. "Tiffany Austin. Thank you for getting back to me, Ms. Fitzgerald."

The nasal voice that responded sounded annoyed. "I got the note you shoved under my office door, and your voicemail," she said. "You're quite persistent, aren't you?"

"Yes," I said. "A few people I spoke to today said that you might be able to help me in setting up some chef interviews. I thought—"

"Ms. Austin." Phoebe interrupted my spiel. "Do you know how many journalists have been nagging me for chef interviews? If I had a nickel—no, a penny—for each one, I could retire tomorrow."

"I realize that chef interviews must be a pretty popular request," I said. "And I know you must be very busy. Believe me, if I could arrange them on my own, I would."

There followed an awkward silence and then Phoebe cleared her throat and said in a more cordial tone, "I didn't mean to snap at you, Ms. Austin. It's just that it's been a rather . . . trying week. Did you have any specific chef in mind?"

"Of course, I'd love to get one with Guy Goodwin," I admitted, "but I'd be happy with any you could set up for me."

"I wish all the other journalists felt that way," Phoebe murmured, her tone a bit softer. "I assume that if you intend to video any of these interviews, you have the proper release forms."

I'd forgotten about that, but I wasn't telling her that. I'd just have Callie, Dale's admin, email me some blank forms. "Of course."

Another long pause and then, "Let me see what I can do. Like I said, it's been a trying week, and I doubt things are going to get much better. I'll get back to you."

Phoebe disconnected before I could utter a thank-you. I set my phone down and leaned my elbows on the kitchen counter. I heard a soft meow behind me and turned to see both Cooper and Lily sitting straight up in their beds, heads cocked. "Phoebe Fitzgerald might be efficient, but she sounded pretty harried just now. Three guesses who probably made her that way, and the first two don't count."

Cooper let out a sharp bark, and Lily meowed.

"Right. I bet it has to do with Jason Barclay. That man is a menace. And what do you want to bet Francine Weston is one of the nagging journalists she mentioned? Hilary thinks she might have a thing for Phil." I dragged my hand through my hair. "Aaaah. I've had better days."

My phone rang again and I glanced at the screen, wary. I relaxed when I recognized the number belonged to my favorite restaurant in Branson, Po'Boys Anonymous. I hit the accept icon, and Nita

Gillette's voice came through. "Hey, Tiff! I'm just calling to find out how the kickoff luncheon went today."

I knew that Nita and her husband, Bob, had both registered for the conference. They were scheduled to participate in the restaurant tastings, like quite a lot of other local eateries hoping to drum up more customers. "Everything was delicious," I said. "I thought I might see you there today."

"We couldn't make it," Nita said, and I could hear the disappointment in her tone. "Both our clerks called in sick, can you believe it? They've got the flu! I had to call in and register us over the phone."

"Oh, no," I said. "Does that mean you can't participate in the tastings?"

"No, that means we had to contact Bob's sister, niece and nephew and press them into service," she said with a short laugh. "Don't worry, we're going to be there every day for the tastings, but depending on everyone's schedule, Bob and I might end up taking turns, instead of working together." She sighed. "I guess all things considered it's probably a good thing we didn't qualify for the Last Remaining Chef event."

I hadn't realized that they'd entered that event. "I'm sorry you didn't make the cut," I said. "Did they finally post the list of finalists?"

"It's going up tomorrow morning. Phoebe Fitzgerald told me when I called to register. She was a bit snippy, but I guess she's under a lot of pressure."

"She was curt with me as well, when I spoke with her about getting some chef interviews. To be honest, I think Jason Barclay's being here has thrown everyone off their game."

"So it's true," Nita said with a sniff. "Barclay is the replacement for Dana Carlyle?" She let out a sigh. "Bob won't be happy to hear that."

"Not a Jason Barclay fan?"

"Neither of us are," said Nita. "A few years ago we'd entered a sandwich contest sponsored by a local magazine. Jason was one of the judges, and he flat out gave our shrimp and crab Po'Boy the lowest score in the competition. He called it 'dull' and 'unimaginative' and he panned our seasoning."

"That's absurd," I cried. "Besides being super delicious, that sandwich is your signature dish."

"Not according to Jason. Needless to say, we ended up in third place. Bob still holds a grudge. He's convinced we'd have won if not for Jason. He thinks his opinion swayed the other judges against us."

"I'm so sorry, Nita. But it does sound like vintage Jason."

"Yeah—what's that saying? A leopard never loses its spots, or something like that?"

"You're close," I said and chuckled. "Anyway, Jason's not a judge. He's just taking over Dana Carlyle's spot at the guest talks, and accepting her award at the banquet."

"Guess it's a good thing we're not on that guest list. I shudder to think what Bob might do if he got too close to Jason. Trust me, he's still itching to confront him." She was quiet for a minute and then she said, "Do you know Chef Ashley Hill?"

"I know of her," I said. "I believe she's teaching one of the cooking classes, Cajun cooking. Why?"

"Well, she's a Branson native. She and Bob went to high school together, although she was two years behind him. He tutored her in chemistry so she could graduate, and they're still pretty friendly. We went to her first restaurant opening in New Orleans two years ago. I'd be glad to have Bob give her a call to see if she could do an interview with you."

"Oh, Nita, that would be great," I said. "You're a lifesaver. At least I'll get one chef interview."

"Oh, I bet you'll get more. I know how determined you can be when you set your mind to something." A pause and then, "Sorry, I've gotta go. See you tomorrow."

I hung up and went over to my laptop, which was sitting on the other end of the kitchen island. I fired it up and sat down at the table. I called up Word, opened up a fresh document and wrote:

*National Food Association Convention—Kickoff
promises great things.*

Foodies and home cooks, rejoice! The National Food Association's local convention here in Branson promises to be informative, fun, and the best feature: food aplenty! If the kickoff luncheon is any indication, y'all are in for a real treat the next few days!

I spent the next hour writing about the luncheon, about the dishes and the chefs. I went into glowing detail about several of the dishes served at the buffet, and by the time I was finished, my mouth was watering for another helping of Goodwin's sea bass and Felipe Moreau's duck. I saved the document, then sent it to Dale Swenson along with the photos I'd taken, my video of the buffet and a brief message: *This looks like the start of something big. Thanks for this assignment. Sorry the video's so grainy. P.S. Any news on that freelance photog?*

I hit send, then glanced at the clock on the wall. I had time for a quick shower and to change into sweatpants and a sweatshirt before Hilary arrived. I went upstairs and put on the TV in my bedroom as I undressed. The news was on, and a moment later Francine Weston's face filled the screen.

"Hello, Branson," she gushed. "I'm here on the evening news with a special report on Foodie Fest, sponsored by the National Foodie Association, which is being held right here in town at our Civic Center. Today I had the good fortune to be able to get a one-on-one with everyone's favorite food critic, Jason Barclay! Hello and welcome, Jason!"

The camera panned in on Jason. He smiled affably, but I noticed the smile didn't reach his eyes. "Hello, Ms. Weston," he said politely.

"Francine, please," she gushed. "I understand that you were a last-minute substitution here at the conference, Jason. Could you tell us what prompted you to attend?"

"I was honored to have been asked to substitute for poor Dana Carlyle, who was recently in an auto accident out in LA." He looked directly into the camera and his lips parted in a wide smile. "Get well soon, Dana."

"We know you're accepting Dana's award at the Foodie Banquet. Will you be taking over Dana's place as a guest speaker as well?" asked Francine. "Participating in any of the panels, or judging any of the events?"

"I'm slated to accept that award on Dana's behalf but anything else is, unfortunately, subject to change. My schedule is very hectic."

"Would this hectic schedule have anything to do with the book you're writing? Can you tell us a bit about that?"

Jason hesitated. His brows started to draw together, and then he seemed to remember he was on TV. He gave himself a little shake and once again smiled into the camera. "All I can say at this juncture is quite a few people will be shocked by what's in my book. Quite a few."

He started to turn away, but Francine, not to be outdone, shoved the microphone in front of him. "There's also talk of your book becoming a movie. Can you give us any details?"

His expression remained impassive, but I saw his eyes flash. "Sorry," he said smoothly. "At this juncture I can neither confirm nor deny anything."

I reached out and abruptly snapped off the television. I had no desire to watch any more of the interview. I rolled my shoulders to let some of the tension out of them. From now on I was going to ignore Jason Barclay and just concentrate on the convention, all the activities and talks, and my blog. And once the conference was over, I was going to devote my full attention to the only man in my life who mattered: Philip Bartell.

After all, it's not like there would be any dead bodies around to distract us, right? Even as the thought passed through my mind, I felt a chill nicker down my spine.

I crossed my fingers and headed for the shower.

Four

Hilary arrived at my place promptly at six fifteen, wine in tow. We spent a very enjoyable evening polishing off both bottles along with the leftovers from the kickoff luncheon. We chatted about various things, from the food at the luncheon, to what was going on at the magazine, to Crystal's latest escapades. Hilary tactfully refrained from bringing up the subject of Jason Barclay or Philip Bartell, and it was after midnight when we finally said good night and I tumbled into bed.

Thanks to Lily deciding to drape herself across my new CD/Alarm/ Music System during the night, the alarm I'd set for six didn't go off, so it was nearly seven thirty when I finally opened my eyes to the bright sunlight streaming in my bedroom window. "Geez, Lily," I said as I threw off my comforter and reached for the robe at the end of the bed. "Thanks a lot. You had to pick last night to try out the new Bose as a bed?"

Lily let out a disgruntled merow, as cats are wont to do, before hopping off the Bose and onto the floor. She tossed me a look of catly disdain before she pranced out the door, tail swishing to and fro. I jammed my feet into my bedroom slippers and headed straight for the bathroom. Twenty minutes later I was showered, hair done, and dressed in burgundy slacks, a crisp white blouse and a blue-and-wine-checked vest, chugging down a fast cup of java from my Keurig. I'd put my phone on the kitchen counter and now it started to beep and twirl madly around, signaling that I had an incoming text. I picked up the phone and saw that it was from Nita:

Chef Ashley Hill can see you at nine today before her first cooking class. She said she'll be waiting for you in Booth 12-C.

I let out a loud whoop that startled both Cooper and Lily and made them look up from their bowls, then texted Nita back:

Thank you thank you thank you!!!!!! I'll let you know how it went.

I checked the rest of my messages. Nothing from Phil, but there was a text from Dale: *Great article, but I see what you mean about the photos and the video. I'm still working on that photog.*

I gulped down the remainder of my coffee and put my mug in the sink. I wanted to get to the convention center early anyway, to see if I might be able to corner Phoebe Fitzgerald or possibly approach some of the chefs on my own. Nothing ventured, nothing gained, right? I scooped up my phone and was just about to deposit it in my tote when it buzzed, this time with an incoming call. I looked at the screen, saw Phil's name, and hit the accept icon. "Well, good morning," I said.

"Good morning back." Phil's voice was rough, as if he'd just woken up, but still impossibly sexy. "I got your text yesterday and I wanted to call you, but things kinda got away from me. I made the mistake of going right into the station, and I got hit with a battery of backlogged paperwork. Plus, Brandon wanted my opinion on a robbery case he caught while I was gone."

I couldn't help but notice the frustration in his tone. Brandon was Brandon Hoffman, a young detective who'd recently been assigned as Phil's partner. According to Phil, Hoffman was like a young puppy, always trailing after him, and it didn't help things that he was the captain's nephew. I tried to keep the smile out of my voice as I answered, "No problem. Yesterday was hectic for me too."

"Yeah, I'm sorry, I forgot that you did tell me about that food convention," Phil said. "I just want to assure you that Sunday evening should be fine. I should be available that night—unless, of course, something unforeseen comes up."

I grimaced, glad he couldn't see me. In Phil's line of work, "something unforeseen" was most likely code for a murder. "Then let's hope that doesn't happen," I said, and then in a softer tone, "I'm glad you're back. I missed you."

"I missed you too," he said. "I was kind of hoping to show you how much tonight, but I guess it will have to keep till Sunday." He paused. "I didn't want to just send you another text. I wanted to hear the sound of your voice, especially since I missed your call yesterday."

"I'm glad you called," I said. "And while I'd love to stay on longer, I'm late already."

"I should get going myself. Be good, Tiffany. Try and stay out of trouble."

I laughed. "I don't think I can get into much trouble at the food convention, but I promise to be good. I'll try and pick up a special recipe for Sunday."

"Now I'm really looking forward to it," he said.

As I hung up, Hilary's words rang in my ear: *You should give Bartell your version of what happened with both Jason and Jeff. Francine would take any opportunity she could get to discredit you in his eyes.*

I dropped my phone in my tote and headed for the door.

• • •

There was a long line of people—foodies and home cooks, no doubt—waiting to enter the convention center when I arrived shortly before eight thirty. I showed my press pass to the guard at the door, and I was aware of the dirty looks and jealous glances several of the people in line threw my way. Once inside, I went directly into the main hall to locate Booth 12-C, where Chef Hill was going to conduct her Cajun cooking class. It was located not far from the stage area, and a quick peek inside assured me she hadn't yet arrived. Since I had a little time I decided to take a chance and see if Phoebe Fitzgerald was in her office. I went backstage and this time I saw a thin line of light coming from underneath Phoebe's office door. I went over and raised my hand to knock, then paused as I heard an angry voice shout.

"That man will be the death of me. I can't believe the nerve of him."

"I agree, Sophie, but you can't let him get to you."

I moved a bit closer to the door. I recognized the latter voice as Phoebe's and I figured the Sophie she was speaking with had to be

Sophie Brinkwater, the convention organizer. And there was no doubt in my mind that the man Sophie referred to was none other than Jason Barclay.

"It's hard not to," Sophie said. "In addition to being insufferable, this list of demands he left me is ridiculous. I mean, he requires a certain brand of bottled water be delivered to his hotel suite every morning? I don't think any of the markets around here even carry this brand he's specified. Not to mention all these other things he wants!" A moan and then, "He's doing this on purpose."

"Of course he is," Phoebe said in a soothing tone. "He's trying to push your buttons, and judging from your reaction, he's succeeding. After what you told me about him . . ."

Phoebe lowered her voice and I couldn't catch what else she said. From the little I'd heard Sophie say, though, it sounded as if she'd known Jason prior to the conference. Curious, I pressed closer to the door and put my ear against the wood, but all I heard was an indistinct rumble and then . . . silence. I'd just taken a few steps back into the hall when the door flew open and I found myself face-to-face with an attractive woman dressed in an expensive-looking ice-blue suit and white-and-blue-checked blouse. Her blue eyes widened at seeing me, and she fisted a hand on a slender hip. "Pardon me," she said, her tone icy. "Can I help you?"

For a second I was so startled I couldn't speak, and then I found my voice. "I-I'm so sorry. You must be Sophie Brinkwater. I-I'm Tiffany Austin. I write a food blog for *Southern Style* magazine. I've emailed you a few times . . ."

"Tiffany Austin?" Sophie raised her hand, passed it over her eyes. "I know who you are now. You wanted some chef interviews."

Phoebe came forward, an annoyed expression on her pinched face. Her brown gaze swept over me as she stepped right in between Sophie and me and put her hands on her hips. "Ms. Austin, I believe I told you that I would get back to you on that," she said, her tone none too friendly.

"Yes, I know, but I happened to get here early and I just thought I'd check in," I said.

Phoebe arched a brow. "I'm still working on it. If you'd care to check back with me later, say after lunch around one thirty, perhaps I'll have some news for you."

Sophie cleared her throat. "Just a moment, Phoebe. Maybe I can help." She turned to me and said, "I believe Dody Fenster might have some free time tomorrow. Would a pastry chef interview work for you?"

"That would be wonderful," I said. "Her banana almond cream pie at the luncheon yesterday was outstanding."

Sophie turned back to Phoebe. "Talk to Dody. Tell her I'd consider it a personal favor if she could make some time for Ms. Austin." She glanced over her shoulder at me. "How flexible are you with time?"

"Anytime she can spare will work for me," I said quickly. Taking a quick glance at Phoebe, I added, "And I have the requisite releases for a video interview." Callie had sent the form to me last night, and I'd downloaded the file and printed some out before I'd gone to bed.

"Good. Take care of that, then, Phoebe." With a curt nod, Sophie Brinkwater brushed past me and started down the long hall.

I turned back to Phoebe. "That was very nice of her," I said.

"Yes, it was," said Phoebe, her tone cold. "As I said, I'll be in touch."

And with that, Phoebe Fitzgerald cut off any chance of further conversation by closing her office door right in my face.

• • •

Contrary to my experience with Sophie Brinkwater and Phoebe Fitzgerald, my interview with Chef Ashley Hill went like clockwork. She was agreeable to being videoed, and not only did she answer my questions about her early years, she invited me to sit in on her first class while she prepared a dish she called her jambalaya with a kick. It was a little after eleven when the cooking class ended. I thanked Chef

Hill again for her time. "No problem," she said. "Any friend of Bob and Nita is a friend of mine. I'm looking forward to seeing my interview on your blog."

Chef Hill had to prepare for her next class, so I made a quick exit. I found a quiet corner, whipped out my program and consulted it. Restaurant tastings had just begun over at the far end of the auditorium, so I ambled in that direction. As I approached I noticed the tasting area was already starting to get packed with eager people. All in all there were over twenty restaurants participating, ranging from delis to upscale eateries. Most of them I was familiar with, but there were a few new places I wanted to try. Two of them, the Tender Biscuit, which specialized in breakfast food, and Down Home Taters, whose specialty was loaded potatoes of every variety, weren't yet open.

I saw a line over at the Po'Boys table and saw that Bob was there, dishing out what looked like mini po'boys, so I decided to grab one and thank him for setting up the interview with Chef Ashley. I'd just taken up my place at the rear of the exceedingly long line when I heard a shout go up from a crowd of people clustered a few feet away. I craned my neck, and a moment later saw what all the fuss was about as a tall, elegantly dressed woman clutching a book against her chest emerged from the thick of the crowd.

I recognized Damaris Alexander at once. The woman had risen to fame ten years ago when she'd won a culinary contest with an old family recipe on a national cable food show, and since had hosted several cable specials, as well as having authored eight cookbooks, five of which had ended up on the *New York Times* bestseller list. She was considered by many to be a foremost authority on Southern food, her specialty, and I myself had made several dishes from her first cookbook, *Really, Really Mouthwatering Down-Home Cookin'*. I knew she'd recently released a new cookbook, *Twenty Ways to make Real Good Fried Chicken*, and I remembered seeing on the program that she was slated for a book signing today. Without any hesitation, I gave up my place in the Po'Boys line and hurried over to join the throng of people who had clustered around her.

Damaris turned to the crowd and held up her hand. "Thank you all for this warm reception," she said in a voice rich with Southern twang. "I can't tell you what it means to me. I'll be signing copies of my new book at eleven thirty over at Booth 14-D." She waved her hand in the general direction of the booth's location, which, I noted, wasn't too far away from where Chef Hill conducted her cooking classes. "If you will all head on over there, volunteers at the table just to the left of the tent will be giving out numbers. There will be a free copy of my prior cookbook, *Southern Cooking Done Right*, for the first thirty people who sign up! Thank you and I'll see y'all in a bit."

The crowd let out a whoop and immediately started to surge toward the aforementioned booth. Damaris turned in the other direction and I didn't hesitate one iota. I went right after her. "Ms. Alexander," I called out. "Ms. Alexander, could I have a word?"

Damaris paused, then turned, the cookbook still clutched tightly against her chest. She peered at me over the rims of the gigantic tortoiseshell glasses perched on her nose. "I'm sorry," she said. "Did y'all not hear the announcement I just made? The signing will take place at Booth 14-D, which is over there." She lifted her arm and pointed.

"I'm not here for the signing," I said. I dug in my tote and pulled out the lanyard with my press pass, which I'd stuffed in my bag during Chef Hill's class and had forgotten to take back out. I slipped it around my neck and pointed to it. "I'm with the press, *Southern Style* magazine. My name is Tiffany Austin, and I write a food blog for them. I know our readers would love it if I could get an interview with you? Even better, if I could video it?" I held up my phone.

Damaris's brows drew together, cutting a deep V in the center of her high forehead. "You're asking me for an interview? I thought all that was arranged through the convention administrator, or her assistant."

"I do have a request into them," I said with a wide smile, "but since I saw you here, I just thought I'd be proactive."

"Well, I'm sorry, Ms.—Austin, was it?" I noted that all traces of a Southern accent had vanished from her voice as she continued, "I prefer to go by the rules. If Ms. Brinkwater or Ms. Fitzgerald approach me about it, I'll surely consider your request. I'm afraid, though, I don't honor ones made on the fly." She paused and then added, Southern accent back in place, "I'm sorry. I know y'all understand."

And with that, she turned on her heel and sashayed away, hips swinging. Two women who'd been standing nearby clucked their tongues. "Well, that was rude," said one.

"I've never been a fan of hers," said the other. "I bet she never grew up in the South. That accent sounded more like the Midwest to me," she added, turning to me with a wink.

I winked back, then turned and headed to the Po'Boys tasting line.

• • •

By one o'clock I'd not only tasted Bob and Nita's delicious crab and shrimp mini po'boys sandwich, I'd also tasted samples from four other eateries, among them the two new ones I'd been eager to try. Down Home Taters' loaded potato, smothered in broccoli, three different cheeses, bacon and sour cream had been delicious, and the Tender Biscuit's mini chicken and waffle had been good too—the waffle had been light and flaky, the chicken perfectly cooked and fried to a golden brown perfection. I rubbed my tummy. I'd taken pictures and videos of all of them and I felt full, but not full enough to ruin my appetite for tonight's buffet, which I had to admit I was looking forward to more than ever.

I decided to walk off my lunch, so I took the stairway to the second floor to check out the sets for the upcoming contests. Before I'd taken two steps, however, a security guard hurried over to me. "Sorry, ma'am, but this section is off-limits to the public."

I held up my press pass. "I'm not the general public. I'm the press."

He shot me an apologetic look. "That includes the press," he said. "Management doesn't want anyone other than authorized personnel poking around these sets. Sorry," he said again.

"No problem," I said, and turned to make my way back down the stairs. As I did so, I noticed someone standing off to the far left out of the corner of my eye. I turned my head slightly and saw that it was Sophie Brinkwater. She was talking into her cell phone, and judging by the look on her face, the conversation she was having wasn't a pleasant one.

"Ma'am?"

I tore my gaze away from Sophie and nodded at the security guard. "Yes, I'm going," I assured him. I saw that Sophie had vanished, so I hurried down the stairway and made my way over to a small sitting area. I found an empty bench and sat down to finish writing my notes about the tasting that would accompany my video. I'd only just started when my phone pinged with an incoming email. I looked at the screen and saw it was a generic email with the subject line Last Remaining Chef Finalists. I opened the email and ran my finger down the list. Midway down I found what I was searching for:

Madison Hotel, Starlight Restaurant,
New York City—Chef Jeffrey Marki

I sighed. While it wasn't a total shock, I had to admit part of me had hoped Leonardo might send someone other than Jeff. It was almost a certainty, now, that I'd run into him at some point. Oh, well. As I'd told Hilary more than once, it was all water under the bridge. That ship had sailed.

So why was my stomach fluttering?

"Just nerves," I muttered. After all, I hadn't seen Jeff since the night I'd ended our relationship. There were bound to be a few nerves, right? A mental image of Philip Bartell filled my head, and I heard Hilary's voice again in my head, telling me to fess all. My phone buzzed again, this time with an incoming call from a number I didn't recognize. I hesitated only briefly before hitting the accept icon. "Tiffany Austin."

"Ms. Austin?" Phoebe's voice sounded flat. "I'm glad I got you. Chef Fenster has agreed to give you some time today before she starts her prep for the banquet tonight. Can you get to her booth, 9-R, at one thirty?"

I glanced at my watch. That was fifteen minutes from now, and that booth was at the other end of the center. If I power walked I might just make it. "I'm on my way. And thank you. While I have you on the phone, do you have any other possible—"

"I'll get back to you," said Phoebe curtly, and disconnected.

"I suppose I should be grateful she managed to arrange this," I muttered. I slid my phone back into my tote and started off in the direction of Chef Fenster's booth. I soon realized that the most direct route steered me right past Damaris's booth. As I approached I saw the tent flap was open, and the crowd had dissipated. Apparently Damaris didn't encourage lingering. I started to hurry past the tent, when I heard a familiar voice from just inside. Curious, I paused and drew closer. I went over to the tent's edge and peered around the flap.

Yep, I was right. The voice belonged to none other than Jason Barclay. He stood in front of a small table, behind which Damaris sat, staring up at him. And if I were any judge, the look she shot him was none too friendly.

"You've said your piece, Jason," Damaris growled. "Don't you have someone else you can bother?"

"As a matter of fact, I do," he answered. "Lots of someones, but I get much more satisfaction out of annoying you."

"One of these days you're going to push me too far," Damaris growled. "You've got all you're going to get out of me. Now leave before I call security."

"You know you're not going to do that," said Jason. I could hear the smug tone in his voice. "If I were you, I'd think things over. It's really not so bad, you know, when you consider the alternative."

"No, thanks. I'd rather deal with a rattlesnake," spat Damaris. "Now get out!"

As Jason started to turn, I beat feet away from the tent and made straight for an empty bench a few feet away. I'd no sooner settled myself there than Jason emerged. He whipped out his phone, looked at the screen, gave a self-satisfied smile and shoved the phone in his pocket. Then he turned and started to walk right in my direction! I whipped out my program and buried my face in it. Fortunately, he seemed to be so preoccupied he didn't give me a second glance. I looked up, though, as he strode past and I gave a start. His left eye was black and blue, as if someone had given him a pretty good sucker punch.

My phone beeped with another text, and I saw it was from Dale. *Can you stop by the office before five? I have a lead on a photog for you.*

"Finally, some good news." I texted back I'd be there right after my interview with Chef Fenster, which made me realize I had about three minutes to get over to her booth. I made it there with a minute to spare, and found her deep in conversation with two men in white chef caps and aprons. She glanced up, saw me, and held up a finger. "Ms. Austin, right? I'm sorry. I just need a few moments. It's about the prep for tonight."

I stepped over to the side to wait and a few seconds later heard a voice that I recognized, Bob Gillette. I glanced up. Bob was standing a few feet away, talking to someone standing behind a pillar. His voice was raised. "If you ever try anything like that again," I heard him say, "it'll be the last time you do."

Bob turned on his heel and stalked off. A few seconds later, the person he'd been talking to emerged from behind the pillar. I sucked in a breath. Jason Barclay.

"Now, what was all that about?" I murmured. I couldn't help but think that Jason had managed to infuriate two people in the space of what? Fifteen, twenty minutes? That had to be some sort of record. As Jason stalked off, I noted someone else standing a few feet away who'd also been watching the exchange with interest. Francine Weston. Great. What was she still doing here, I wondered. Stalking Jason, hoping for some sort of sensational scoop? Somehow I wouldn't put it past her, but I couldn't worry about her now.

I had an interview to do, and then I had to stop by the office and talk to Dale before going home to get ready for the awards banquet. With any luck, tonight I'd have a freelance photographer by my side.

Five

It was a few minutes after five when I arrived at the Branson Towers. The valet service hadn't yet started, so I decided to park my car myself. Apparently a lot of other people hadn't wanted to wait for valet service either—the side lot was packed! I finally found a spot under a shady elm, right across from the garden and the fountain I'd admired the day before. I got out and made my way across the lot to the hotel entrance, thankful that I'd opted for my low kitten-heeled pumps instead of the higher heels to complement the simple black sheath I'd decided to wear.

As I stepped into the hotel lobby I gave a quick look around. Dale had said the photographer would meet me in the lobby at five, but save for a couple checking in at the reception desk, the lobby appeared deserted. I noticed a pair of closed doors off to the left of the reception area, with a large sign in front of it: *Foodie Fest Cocktail Hour. 6–7. Harmony Room.* I walked over, thinking perhaps the photographer might have gone in there to take a peek, but the doors were locked.

There was a cluster of comfortable oversized leather chairs set around a large marble fireplace just off to the left of the bar area, and I eased myself into one of the chairs to wait. I hadn't been there five minutes when I heard a familiar voice ask, "Penny for your thoughts?"

I looked up and saw Jason towering over me. I noticed he'd applied a thick layer of pancake makeup underneath his eye, but traces of his shiner were still visible. Before I could say a word, he'd settled himself in the chair next to me. "You're here early," he observed. "Meeting someone?"

"As a matter of fact, I am. He should be here any moment."

Jason gave a curt nod. "Young Marki checked in about an hour ago. I happened to be in the lobby and saw him. If he's who you're meeting, you should know he's got a very attractive woman with him."

"I'm not meeting Jeff," I said coldly. "And as for the young woman accompanying him, I'm sure it's his fiancée, Fiona Puccini."

Both of Jason's eyebrows went up. "That was Fiona? Leonardo's daughter? Well, what do you know? She's changed," he murmured.

I looked at him. "You know Fiona?"

He looked down at the floor for a few seconds before he responded. "She was one of the junior chefs at the Madison, wasn't she?" Without waiting for an answer he went on, "I remember her as a mousy little thing. She didn't seem very much at ease, either in or out of the kitchen." He chuckled. "I have to hand it to young Marki. He picked a foolproof way to ingratiate himself with Puccini—marrying his daughter."

I narrowed my gaze at Jason. "Jeff doesn't need to ingratiate himself with anyone," I said stiffly. "He's an excellent chef. And I'm sure he's marrying Fiona because he's in love with her."

Jason let out a snort. "Then he's a fool. Love is nothing more than an overrated emotion that is capable of clouding one's better judgment."

The venom in his tone startled me, and for a moment I was speechless. Then I managed to croak out, "Is that your professional opinion? It sounds more like sour grapes to me."

His lips curved upward, and he tipped two fingers to his forehead in a salute. "Touché, my dear. And since we're on the subject of love, are you ready to tell me what really drove you away from the Madison and drove Marki into Fiona's waiting arms? Because I'm not buying your 'I needed a change' story."

"I don't care if you do or not," I responded. "Get over it, Jason. It's old news."

He leaned in a bit closer. "How about if I promise not to put a thing in either the book or the movie? Then will you tell me?"

"Absolutely not."

He tapped his foot. "Your reluctance only makes me more certain that you're hiding something."

"Once again, why do you care?"

"Why? Because—"

Whatever Jason was about to say was interrupted by the sound of someone clearing his throat. Loudly. "Excuse me?"

I breathed a silent sigh of relief as I looked over at the speaker, a good-looking man with hair at least two shades redder than mine and an expensive camera slung around his neck. He ignored Jason, looked at me and smiled. "Would you be Tiffany Austin?"

"I am. You must be James Devane?"

"The one and only, but you can call me Jimmy," he said. "Mac's told me you were good-looking, but as usual, he downplayed it." He slid his gaze over to Jason and said, "I know you. You're Jason Barclay, the food critic. Wow, pal. I hope you got the number of that truck."

Jason frowned. "Truck?"

"Yeah. The one that ran into your face. That's some shiner you're trying to cover up there." He turned his head toward me and closed one eye in a wink. "Don't tell me some chef finally got fed up with your condescending reviews and let you have it."

Jason's face reddened and he reached up and touched the area around his eye gingerly. "Not that it's any of your business, but this was a total accident. I happened to trip and hit the side of my face against a door."

Jimmy didn't even bother to hide the grin that suffused his face. He held up one hand. "Yeah, okay. If you say so."

"I do. And just for the record, my reviews are not condescending. They are truthful. It is not my fault some people can't handle that." Jason stood and tugged at the lapels of his suit jacket. "If you'll excuse me, I have some things to take care of before the banquet." He gave me a curt nod. "Tiffany. Perhaps later we can continue our conversation." He ignored Jimmy completely, turned on his heel and stalked off.

Jimmy looked after Jason's retreating form and shook his head, then turned to me. "I hope you didn't mind my interrupting," he said. "You looked like you were in dire need of rescuing."

"You have no idea," I said. "That was a good comeback about the shiner," I said. "I wish I'd thought of it."

"Yeah, well, some people need to be brought back to earth every now and then, especially him," said Jimmy. "Jason Barclay has always thought he was above the rest of us poor mortals." He gave his head a shake. "Hit the side of a door, my behind. He was on the receiving end of a pretty good punch, but he'll never admit he got the raw end of the deal. Knowing him, he either got cornered by some jealous lover or husband or else he panned some poor chef's cooking once too often."

"You have him pegged pretty good. I take it you've met him before?"

He waved his hand. "Oh, yeah. Before I got into fashion photography I did lots of work for the Food Network, and local cable channel shows that he was a guest on. As a matter of fact, I was on *Hello, Atlanta* recently when he was there to give one of his scathing guest reviews. It was some Asian Mexican fusion place in Norcross. He really tore it apart. I went there a few days later, and I thought the food was pretty good." Jimmy fingered the expensive Nikon around his neck. "Some guys just invite being taken down a peg. I wonder who gave him that shiner. I'd like to shake his hand." He paused. "Or hers. I've met some women who pack a mean punch."

"I'm so glad you were able to help us out. Dale said Mac spoke very highly of you. Actually, he said we were lucky to get you."

Jimmy waved his hand. "The timing was good. I was just finishing up a shoot for *Metro* magazine when Mac gave me a shout. And since I have two weeks to kill before I leave for London, I figured hey, why not? Besides, I've always wanted to attend one of these foodie conventions anyway. I hear they're a hoot." He glanced around. "This hotel is a classy place. I see why the chefs and guest speakers are staying here."

"You aren't?"

He shook his head. "Nope. They're full up right now."

"I could make a call," I offered. "My editor, Dale Swenson, might be able to pull some strings."

Jimmy waved his hand. "It's okay. To be honest, this place is a little out of my league anyway. I got a nice room at a hotel not far from here. The Majestic. Their rates are a lot cheaper, which I'm sure will please Mr. Swenson, since *Southern Style* is footing my hotel bill," he added with a wink.

I smiled. I definitely liked Jimmy Devane. "You're probably right about that," I said. "I guess we should talk about the photos for the blog. You're the pro. What did you have in mind?"

"I thought I'd start out by taking some candid shots during the cocktail hour, you know, of you and the guests and the chefs. Mac said you wanted some professional video for your blog, so I thought I'd take some during the dinner and awards portion—concentrating on the buffet table, of course."

"That all sounds wonderful. And please, call me Tiffany." I glanced over toward the Harmony Room. There was a small cluster of people standing around now, and a second later the doors swung open. I gave Jimmy a nudge in the ribs with my elbow. "Looks like cocktail hour is starting a bit early. It's only a quarter to six."

"Don't look a gift horse in the mouth," said Jimmy. "I wouldn't mind a free drink, and I bet after your little interlude with Barclay, you could use one yourself."

We joined the crowd filing into the room. I was pretty sure I saw Phoebe Fitzgerald up near the front of the throng, dressed in a long black and red plaid skirt and red V-necked top. I was considering going after her for an interview update, but before I could do so I heard a shout. "Tiffany! I'm glad you're here. We can sit together."

I looked up and saw Rain walking purposefully toward me. She was attired in a bright neon blue pantsuit that hugged her curvaceous figure. A low-cut tank of white lace peeped out from underneath the matching jacket, and the rhinestones that were sewn into the lapels twinkled in the overhead lights. Her multicolored hair was heavily gelled so that the spikes bobbed to and fro as she bustled up to us. She smiled widely at me, and then her gaze shifted to Jimmy. She looked him up and down and then said in a throaty voice, "Well, hel-lo! Are the two of you together?"

"This is Jimmy," I said. "He's a freelance photographer who's going to be helping me out. Jimmy, this is—"

"Oh, Rainbow McGill doesn't need an introduction," Jimmy said with a smile. "I've caught quite a few of your shows on YouTube. I've even tried a few of your recipes. It's a pleasure."

Rain extended her hand. "A pleasure for me as well, to meet such a handsome fan," she cooed, batting her heavily mascaraed lashes.

Jimmy didn't appear flustered at all by Rain's obvious flirting. He shook her hand and then turned to me. "I think I'll just float around a bit, get the lay of the land. I'll catch up with you later, Tiffany. Ms. McGill."

Jimmy moved off and Rain gave me a nudge. "He's cute," she observed. "What did you say his name was?"

"James Devane, but he likes to be called Jimmy."

"Aha!" Rain snapped her fingers in the air. "I thought he looked familiar. That's Shutterbug."

I blinked. "Excuse me? Shutterbug?"

"Yes, it's his nickname. He's a very good photographer. Believe me, you're lucky to get him. He started out from humble beginnings— if I'm not mistaken, he worked on the paper with Hugh way back when he was still in school—and eventually struck out on his own as a freelancer. He's quite in demand. As a matter of fact, I think he did the cover for a few of Damaris Alexander's books. His specialty is in fashion, but he knows his way around a kitchen." She gave a quick glance around. "Speaking of Damaris, I have yet to see her. She's usually first in line for cocktail hour. Oh, well." She linked her arm through mine. "More for us, right? Let's boogie over to the bar."

I accompanied Rain to the crowded bar, where we managed to find two stools over at the far end, near the exit. I took the stool on the end and Rain slid onto the other one, next to a lantern-jawed, gray-haired man in a black jacket. He glanced over at us, frowned, then resumed drinking his mug of beer. Rain ordered a double dirty martini, and I ordered a glass of Chablis. When our drinks arrived Rain reached eagerly for hers, and as she lifted the glass she tipped it slightly, causing some of the liquid to spill over on the sleeve of the gray-haired man's jacket. "Hey," he growled, shaking his sleeve. "Watch it."

"Oh, dear. I am so sorry," said Rain. She grabbed her own napkin and started to dab at his sleeve. "Let me help clean this up."

The man jerked his arm away and rubbed his other hand across the damp sleeve. "Don't bother," he growled. "It'll dry."

"But it might leave a stain," protested Rain. She started to dig in her purse. "At least let me pay to have it dry-cleaned."

"I said don't bother. I'm leaving anyway." The man scowled, then drained his mug and slid off the stool. He grabbed a camera from underneath the bar, slapped a ten-dollar bill on the bar and shot Rain a scathing look. "Clumsy woman," he muttered, then turned on his heel and stalked off.

Rain shook her head. "Wow. He was pleasant."

"That camera he grabbed from underneath the bar looked a lot like the one Jimmy has," I said. "Maybe he's also a professional photographer."

Rain snorted. "Well, if he's hoping to get some good shots of the chefs and the food, he'd better lighten up. That guy has some attitude." Suddenly her hand shot out and she grabbed my arm, nearly causing me to spill my wine. "Speaking of guys with attitude, take a gander over at the other end of the bar," she whispered.

I did, and saw Jason seated there. There were two empty glasses off to one side, and Jason's fingers were wrapped around a glass half full of a pale liquid I took to be Scotch. He lifted the glass, downed the contents in one swallow, then held up a finger to the bartender, signaling another. Rain clucked her tongue. "Jason's never been a big drinker. He only does this when he's really irritated at something or someone."

I was about to tell Rain what Jimmy had said to Jason when we heard a loud commotion break out behind us. We turned and my breath caught in my throat as I saw who was at the center of it—Francine Weston. "Oh, no," I murmured. "What is she doing here?"

Rain chuckled. "She is the press, after all. And I see she came prepared." Francine was dressed in a tight aqua blue dress that left little to the imagination. She carried a microphone in one hand. Behind her, looking just as bored as he had the other time I'd seen him, was her trusty cameraman, Brent. "I bet she volunteered to cover this event hoping to run into Jason," Rain declared.

"You're probably right," I agreed. I glanced quickly around the crowded room, but I didn't see any sign of Jimmy. "I wonder where Jimmy is," I murmured.

"He's most likely in the kitchen by now, making nice with the chefs and snapping photos and taking videos of the food," remarked Rain.

"I sincerely hope so." I glanced over at the bar again. The bartender had just set another glass of Scotch in front of Jason, who was scowling at his phone. "Jason doesn't look happy," I murmured.

"No, he doesn't, does he?" Rain agreed. Suddenly she chuckled. "I think he's about to become even more unhappy. The barracuda's making her move."

Francine had homed in on Jason at the bar and she strode purposefully in his direction. Jason glanced up, saw her, and immediately snatched up the glass, turned and stalked off toward the rear of the room. A few seconds later he was swallowed up in the crowd, Francine in hot pursuit.

Rain looked at me. "Ten bucks says she doesn't catch him. Jason's very good at dodging people he doesn't want to bother with." She slid off her stool and picked up her glass. "Let's mingle a bit. Lots of people haven't shown up yet, like Damaris, and Sophie Brinkwater or her assistant. You'd think they'd be front and center at an event like this."

"I caught a glimpse of Phoebe earlier," I said. "But you're right, I haven't seen Damaris or Sophie. I'm sure they're here somewhere though."

Rain tapped her foot impatiently. "Hugh's not here yet either. It's not like him to be this late. He always enjoys cocktail hour."

We sauntered off toward the back of the room, near another pair of double doors that I figured opened into the dining area. Suddenly Rain stopped short and looked over her shoulder at me. "Oops. Looks as if Jason wasn't able to elude the barracuda."

I turned my head and saw Jason at the opposite end of the room. He was shaking his head at a determined-looking Francine. Francine leaned closer to him, and Jason took a step backward. His brows drew together and he shook his fist at her, then snatched up a glass from a small table. I held my breath, certain he was going to throw the contents at Francine, but instead he turned, took a sip from the glass and then pushed through the throng of people milling about and through a door marked Exit. Francine turned, a dejected look on her face, and made a cutting motion to Brent.

"Well, you win some you lose some," observed Rain. "I imagine Francine will go after someone else now. As for Jason, I hope he grabs some coffee before the dinner. I hate to think of him accepting poor Dana's award in a drunken stupor." She gave her head a shake, and the gelled spikes bobbed to and fro. "He'd better watch his step. Someone gave him that shiner he's been trying to hide—very poorly, I might add. The next time he might get more than just a black eye."

I was afraid Rain was right, but I kept silent. I glanced at my watch. It was a few minutes before six thirty. "I think I'll just take a quick run to the ladies' room before they open the doors. Want to come?"

Rain shook her head. "No, I'd rather stay here in case Hugh shows up. You go on. I'll be right here."

I asked a passing waitress where the ladies' room was and was informed that the closest one was located in the rear of the main lobby.

I headed in that direction. As I moved past the reception area, I thought I saw a familiar figure hurry past and out the front door—Bob Gillette. I shook my head. I had to have been mistaken. Why would Bob be here, unless . . . I remembered what Nita had said, that Bob was still itching to confront Jason over that sandwich contest. And then there had been the earlier incident between Jason and Bob. Had he come here tonight to finish it?

The ladies' room was just ahead, just beyond a small alcove. As I started to hurry past, I heard a slurred voice say, "It will do you no good to protest." I stopped dead in my tracks. That voice sounded like Jason's! I paused and then, overcome by curiosity, I backtracked and peered cautiously around the alcove's corner. It was indeed Jason, and he was gesturing impatiently to someone who stood in front of him. "I'm glad I ran into you," he continued. "It saves me the trouble of tracking you down. I'm doing you the courtesy of telling you, in person, that I have decided to put the incident we discussed in my book. And don't even think of getting that overprotective father of yours involved. Nothing you or he can say will change my mind."

"You're not only drunk, you're a complete cad, Jason. Ruining people's lives means nothing to you. I wish you were dead," replied his companion.

I let out an involuntary gasp. Jason's companion wasn't Bob. I knew that voice, even though it had been quite awhile since I'd heard it. It belonged to none other than Fiona Puccini, Leonardo's daughter and Jeff's fiancée.

Six

Jason let out a loud guffaw. "I think when all is said and done, it might be you who wishes you were dead, my dear," he said. "I plan on being around for quite a long time to come, I promise you."

"Promises can be broken, Jason," replied his companion. "On second thought, death is too good for you. It would be better if you suffered, like your victims."

Jason let out a laugh and moved slightly forward. I caught a flash of red as his companion moved away from him, and then the sound of a resounding slap reached my ears. I took a few steps backward and crouched behind a pillar just as a petite woman in a bright red sheath dress emerged from the alcove, rubbing at her hand. It was definitely Fiona. She'd lost weight, and her formerly dull brown hair now sported blonde highlights, but I recognized her stance, the way she carried herself. But what was she doing with Jason? From the little bit I'd overheard, it definitely sounded as if the two of them were much better acquainted with each other than Jason had let on, and I had to wonder: Just how much better? Better enough to be one of Jason's "juicy nuggets"?

Fiona started to turn in my direction and I felt a moment of panic. I had no desire to run into her right now, or Jason either, for that matter. Fortunately, Fiona stole another glance back at the alcove, then turned in the direction of the main lobby and hurried off, her heels clicking against the polished floor, still nursing her hand. I wondered idly if it might have been Fiona who'd been responsible for Jason's black eye.

I decided I'd better get out of Dodge before Jason might emerge and find me. I had a feeling he wouldn't be exactly thrilled if he thought I might have overheard his private conversation with Fiona. Fortunately, a trio of laughing women passed just then, headed in the direction of the restroom, and I joined them. I stole a quick glance over my shoulder as I did so, and saw that I'd made my exit just in time—

Jason was just emerging from the alcove. He seemed a bit unsteady on his feet, and he clutched a half-full glass of amber liquid in one hand. I also noted a large red mark on his cheek, no doubt the imprint of Fiona's hand. As I started to turn away, I caught a glimpse of another familiar figure out of the corner of my eye—the rude gray-haired man from the bar, camera slung around his neck. He waited a few moments until Jason had gotten a few feet away, and then he sauntered casually off in the same direction. Most likely he was trailing him, hoping for a photo op. A small group of women and men surged past, blocking my view for a few moments. When the group had passed, neither man was anywhere in sight.

Inside the ladies' room I freshened my makeup, ran a comb through my tumble of auburn curls, and gave myself a spritz of the Beautiful perfume I always carried in my purse. Another food critic I knew was touching up her lip gloss too and we chatted for a few minutes about the convention before I excused myself. I glanced at my watch and saw that it was almost a quarter after seven, so I quickened my steps back to the Harmony Room, where I found Rain still in the spot where I'd left her. The doors to the dining section were still closed. "And here I thought I was late," I said. "They haven't started yet?"

"They made an announcement. There'll be a slight delay. It appears the chefs are pulling out all the stops tonight to impress." Rain tapped her one perfectly manicured fingernail against her watch. "Still no sign of Hugh. I can't imagine what could be keeping him."

No sooner were the words out of her mouth than I saw the man in question enter the room, pause and glance around. I gave Rain a nudge and nodded in Hugh's direction. Rain immediately started jumping up and down and waving her arms. "Hugh! Over here!"

Hugh weaved his way over to where we stood. He bent over, gave Rain a swift kiss on the cheek, then smiled at me. "Good evening, ladies," he said. "Sorry I'm late." He touched his tie. "I had a little . . . accident. A waiter spilled wine on my tie. It left a huge stain, so I ran to my room to grab another."

Rain squeezed his hand. "Well, you're here now and that's all that matters," she said. She glanced over toward the bar, where the two bartenders were in the process of cleaning up. "Looks like you just missed out on the free liquor, though," she remarked. "I hope that means the buffet is about to start."

Hugh waved his hand. "No matter. They usually put out carafes of wine on the tables at these banquets. If I feel the need for something stronger I can always get it at the hotel bar."

"Well, you didn't miss much here," said Rain. "So far the biggest thrill of the evening was watching Jason Barclay get drunk at the bar."

Hugh pursed his lips. "So Barclay did show up, eh? I wondered if he would."

I looked at Hugh. "Why do you say that?"

Hugh shrugged. "I just know Jason, is all. This type of thing isn't his cup of tea. He'd rather pan an award than accept one. Besides, would you want to attend an affair where practically everyone attending hates your guts."

"Not everyone," said Rain. She inclined her head toward the rear of the room, where Francine Weston stood, talking to her cameraman. "She tried to corner Jason but he managed to get away from her. I bet she doesn't give up though. Francine could be the reason Jason's made himself scarce."

"Well, I can't say I blame him," remarked Hugh with a crooked smile. "If she tried to corner me, I'd hide too. That woman is scary."

"Among other things," said Rain. Suddenly she let out a squeal. "Finally! They're opening the doors. Let's go so we get a good table."

She started to move forward, but Hugh touched her arm. "No need to rush, my dear. I believe the seating at this banquet is assigned."

Rain's face fell. "Oh, that's right. Bummer."

Hugh and Rain started for the banquet room. I was just about to follow them when a voice behind me said, "Ms. Austin? I've been looking for you."

I turned and Phoebe Fitzgerald gave me a frozen smile. She pulled her oversized black cardigan tightly around her and said, "I just wanted you to know I haven't forgotten about you. There is a possibility—albeit a very slim one—that Guy Goodwin might be able to spare you a few minutes for a quick interview before the Last Remaining Chef competition begins tomorrow evening."

"Really! That would be wonderful," I cried. "When will you know for certain?"

"I'm trying to pin him down tonight, but as you can imagine, it's not easy," said Phoebe. "I promise to let you know early tomorrow, though. So if you could just stay flexible . . ."

I bobbed my head up and down. "That's not a problem. I'll be here most of tomorrow anyway, covering the food truck competition and the first installment of Last Remaining Chef."

"Good. Well, then, enjoy the banquet."

Phoebe started to turn away but I touched her arm. "Could I ask you a question?"

Phoebe hesitated, then forced a smile to her lips. "Certainly. What is it?"

"I was just wondering . . . do you know if Ms. Brinkwater and Jason Barclay have ever met prior to this convention?"

Phoebe's eyes narrowed and her lips thinned to a straight line. "That's an odd question. Why would you think that?"

There was no way in hell I was going to admit I'd overheard the conversation between her and Sophie Brinkwater, so I said the first thing that came to mind. "I happened to overhear some of the volunteers talking about Jason getting special treatment, like getting water delivered. I just wondered if perhaps Ms. Brinkwater might have a reason for giving him preferential treatment."

Phoebe pursed her lips. "Well, the fact that Jason Barclay is a nationally known food critic certainly plays into his getting special treatment," she said frostily. "That's reason enough, don't you think?"

"Of course," I murmured. "I should have thought of that. By the way, where is Ms. Brinkwater? I haven't seen her here tonight."

"She's here," said Phoebe brusquely. "She has many last-minute details to attend to, so she's not been too visible. But that will soon change. Now, if you'll excuse me." She didn't wait for me to answer, just turned and hurried off. I looked after her for a moment. Something about our little encounter didn't sit quite right with me, but I couldn't pinpoint just what. Maybe it had been her brusque manner. She hadn't really answered my question, merely sidestepped it. I also had the feeling that she was covering up for Sophie for some reason, and I wondered if the reason Sophie was making herself scarce was to avoid running into Jason. At any rate, it would be interesting to see if the convention organizer would indeed make an appearance.

I grabbed my purse and got in the line to enter the banquet room. Sure enough, the tables were all assigned. I found myself at a table near the exit with nine other reporters from small papers in the surrounding area, none of which I knew. I spotted Rain. She was seated at a table with some other prominent food critics and cookbook authors, close to the buffet, which I was sure had made her happy. Hugh was seated at a table directly behind hers with some other food critics. I sat down and watched as everyone filed in. I didn't see Damaris Alexander anywhere, and Jason hadn't shown up yet either. I noted that Jimmy was also MIA. I hoped it was because Rain was right and he was in the kitchen, busy snapping photos and shooting videos.

I slung my purse over my shoulder and made my way to Rain's table. She jumped up as soon as she saw me and gave me a big hug. "Oh, dear, I'm so sorry they seated you at that horrible table! You'll probably be one of the last up to the buffet!"

I idly wondered if Rain ever thought about anything except food. I extricated myself from her grasp and said, "I'm sure I'll get something. I see Damaris Alexander hasn't shown up yet, and I haven't seen Sophie Brinkwater either."

Rain frowned. "I'm sure I saw Sophie, out in the hall a few minutes ago. She looked somewhat out of breath, probably from rushing around, tending to last-minute details. As for Damaris, she's supposed to be at my table." She inclined her head toward an empty place setting. "Maybe if she doesn't show up you can switch seats," she said.

"I doubt that would go over big with Sophie or Phoebe," I remarked. I looked around the room. "I don't see Jason either. I hope he isn't passed out somewhere."

"Me too," said Rain. "Oh, look. Here comes Damaris now."

Damaris, elegant in a long royal blue gown, looked a bit flustered as she hurried over to the table and dropped into her chair without a glance or a word to any of the others seated. "Glad you could make it, Damaris," Rain called out. She raised her arm and tapped at her watch, which read seven twenty-five.

"Be nice, Rain," Damaris growled. "I'm in no mood. That joker Barclay sent me a text saying he wasn't able to accept Dana's award, and I'd have to do it! Can you believe the nerve of that man!"

Rain shot me an eye roll. "Ah, poor Damaris. Such are the trials and tribulations of being a bestselling cookbook author."

I looked at Damaris. "That's strange. Why did Jason send you the text? He seemed a stickler for protocol. You'd think he'd have contacted Sophie, or Phoebe?"

"How the heck should I know? Maybe he sent a text to all of us," Damaris growled.

"Regardless, it all seems very sudden," I said. "Did he mention why he couldn't accept the award?"

Damaris gave a loud sigh, then whipped her cell out of her purse. She fiddled with the screen for a few moments, then said, "This is what he sent me. Read it for yourself."

She pushed her phone at me, and I looked at the screen. Sure enough, there was a text from Jason Barclay, sent at six forty-five: *Damaris, be a peach and accept Dana's award in my absence. I've got to leave for New York immediately. Jason.* When I raised my head, Damaris snatched the phone back. She rolled her eyes as she tossed it back into her bag. "I guess I should find Sophie or Phoebe, see if he texted them about the switch. I'm sure they'll be thrilled not to have to deal with that jackass anymore."

Damaris pushed her chair back and stalked off. Rain turned to me and whispered, "New York, I bet. He probably realized he was in no condition to accept Dana's award. I've got to give him credit for that, at least."

I wasn't as generous as Rain. I couldn't help but think about the conversation I'd overheard between him and Fiona. Could that be the reason for his hasty departure?

I returned to my table and a few minutes later Jimmy appeared. He knelt beside my chair and tapped his camera. "I didn't know Chef Goodwin was here," he said. "He and I go way back, to when I did promos for the Food Network. I got some really good video of him and the dish he prepared tonight, spicy orange-glazed beef. I've had it before and it's primo." He grinned. "Your blog followers are in for a real treat, and you too."

"You're a wonder," I said. "My followers are all going to be spoiled. A few days of my efforts and they'll be clamoring for you."

"Oh, you'll get the hang of it," Jimmy said. "I looked at a few of your posts. You take the photos and video with your phone, right?" He tapped at his chin. "Phone's okay for personal use, but for something like this . . . you'd do much better with a mini camcorder. You can get a good one cheap these days, under one-fifty, name brands too. They're relatively easy to use. You just hit a button, and you can switch between video and photos."

"Sounds like something I could master," I said. "Can you give me a list of some models and prices? I'll run it past my editor."

"Sure thing." He grinned. "Tell you what, when you get the camera, I'd be glad to show you how to use it, and give you a few pointers on video taking if you're interested."

"I sure am! That would be wonderful," I said. Then I added, "Not to change the subject, but I didn't realize you were so friendly with Guy Goodwin."

"We go back a ways. Not to brag, but I know most of the chefs here," Jimmy said modestly. "Oh, and by the way, I asked him if you and I could hook up with him before the Last Remaining Chef competition starts tomorrow."

I couldn't resist letting out a squeal. "You didn't! What did he say?"

"He said sure, of course, and we should come by his tent at five, and he'd have a special dinner prepared for us. I know we're covering that food truck competition, but it's supposed to be over by four, plenty of time." Now his grin stretched from ear to ear. "I hope you like spicy. He hinted that he might make his famous ten-alarm chicken."

My mouth fell open. "Jimmy, I don't know what to say! You're a true wonder."

He chuckled. "Just a simple thank-you will suffice. Now, I'm going to go back in the kitchen, get some more candid shots of the chefs as they prep the dishes." He inclined his head toward the long table. "Get your taste buds ready. They're going to start wheeling out the food, and judging from what I saw back there, it's going to be *some* feast."

Jimmy turned and vanished just as Phoebe Fitzgerald stepped up to the podium that was set up to the left of the buffet table. She grimaced slightly as she rolled her shoulders, then rapped her knuckles against the podium, and as the conversation in the room settled into a low buzz, spoke into the microphone. "Good evening, honored guests, and welcome to the National Foodie Association Annual Awards Banquet. I'm pleased to present the woman in charge of organizing this convention, Ms. Sophie Brinkwater."

Sophie, attired in a floor-length black skirt with matching jacket buttoned up to her neck, stepped up to the stage, and in spite of her wide smile, I thought she looked a little distracted. Maybe Damaris had told her about Jason's abrupt departure. She smiled at everyone and then said, "Honored guests, members of the press. Tonight, as I'm sure you are all aware, is when the Foodie Fest honors chefs they feel have made an outstanding contribution to the food industry during the past year." She named three up-and-coming chefs, and then added, "The grand prize, the Golden Mixer Award, is being given later tonight to a chef who has made great strides in the food industry: Dana Carlyle." There was a smattering of applause, and then Sophie spoke again. "Unfortunately, Dana cannot be here tonight, but we do have someone who has agreed to accept the award on her behalf—Damaris Alexander."

Damaris rose from her chair and made a little bow. Another smattering of applause and then Sophie continued, "The awards will be given out, as is customary, during dessert. Right now, our talented chefs will be out in a few moments to join you. They're just putting the finishing touches on what we feel is quite a spread."

The double doors opened and several men in white hats and jackets began wheeling out covered silver platters. Behind them were the chefs, who smiled and waved as they took their places at their table. Sophie clapped her hands. "As you can see, our chefs have worked their magic, so please . . . feast and enjoy yourselves."

The girl next to me scraped back her chair and stood up. "You don't have to tell me twice," she said with a grin. "Let's eat."

• • •

An hour later I had to admit it: I was stuffed. The chefs had definitely outdone themselves. I'd tasted a little bit of each dish, and went back for seconds on some. I wasn't ashamed to admit that I'd had three helpings of Guy Goodwin's contribution. Jimmy was right. His spicy orange-glazed beef was seasoned perfectly, and had just the right amount of tang and spice to please the most discerning of palates. I wondered if Jimmy might be able to use his influence to get me a goodie bag to take home. I had a feeling Hilary would be forever in my debt if I brought her samples of these dishes. And dessert was still to come!

I decided that a brisk walk around the hotel grounds might help me digest enough so that I could enjoy the dessert table. I slung my purse over one shoulder and went over to Rain's table. "I'm going to take a quick walk before they serve dessert," I said. "Want to come?"

Rain shook her head. She popped another bite of spicy orange-glazed beef into her mouth, chewed, then said, "No, thanks, dear. But you have fun. Don't be too long though. You don't want to miss the awards, especially now that Damaris is accepting." She mimed stifling a yawn.

Rather than go through the lobby, I decided to go out the side door marked Exit, and a few minutes later I found myself outside. The night was clear, the moon shone brightly overhead. I walked a few steps and realized that I was on the south side of the building, just a short distance away from the gardens and fountain I'd admired. I decided I'd head over there for a closer look at the fountain. I walked briskly in that direction, but I'd only taken a few steps when I paused to listen. At first I thought I'd imagined it, but then I heard it again.

Click-clack! Yes, it was definitely the sound of heels moving swiftly, and it seemed to be coming from the direction of the fountain. The sound dissipated, and I continued on down the path. I'd almost reached the fountain when up ahead I caught a movement, a flash of red. It seemed to melt into the bushes clustered around the side of the hotel. I paused and stood still for a few moments. Everything had happened so quickly that I wasn't certain if I'd really seen something, or if it was just my imagination. I squared my shoulders and continued down the pathway, and a few seconds later the comforting sounds of rushing water reached my ears. I was a few feet away when I stopped in my tracks and blinked. I rubbed my eyes, blinked again.

Was that a shoe dangling over the edge of the fountain's circular pool?

My heart pounding, I drew closer. No, I wasn't seeing things. It was indeed a shoe, a man's shoe. I held my breath and peered over the fountain's edge. A body floated there, facedown in a growing pool of red, a body I recognized.

Jason Barclay.

For a minute I just stood there, frozen. Then I leaned over the fountain bowl for a closer look. There appeared to be a nasty gash on the side of Jason's head, which probably accounted for the growing pool of red. I hesitated, then dipped my hand beneath the water and pressed my fingers to Jason's neck. No pulse. He was dead.

I sighed, knowing what I had to do next. I took a step backward, slid my hand into my purse and fished out my cell. I punched in 911, and when the operator answered I said, "This is Tiffany Austin. I'm calling to report a body."

Seven

Fifteen minutes later an ambulance made its way across the hotel parking lot and up onto the sidewalk opposite the fountain. Two paramedics emerged wheeling a gurney. One was a bearded, dark-haired guy, thin as a rail, the other a short, stout woman with threads of silver running through her closely cropped pixie hairdo. The woman came over to me, and I saw a name tag pinned to her jacket that read *Cathy C.* "You Tiffany Austin, the one who called this in?" she asked. At my nod she remarked, "Better stay close. The police are on the way. They'll want to talk to you."

Cathy C and the other paramedic pushed the gurney next to the fountain just as a dark sedan drew up beside the ambulance. I held my breath, and sure enough, Philip Bartell emerged from the passenger side and Brandon Hoffman from the driver's. Hoffman immediately headed over to where the paramedics were bending over Jason's body. Phil made his way over to where I stood, eyes narrowed. He paused in front of me, hands on hips. "You know, when the 911 operator told me who called in the alert, I was hoping it might be another Tiffany Austin," he said bluntly.

"Nice to see you too," I said coolly. "And believe me, I'd give anything if I hadn't found Jason's body."

His eyes narrowed into mere slits. "Jason? You know the victim?"

I nodded. "Yes. It's Jason Barclay."

His eyes popped. "Jason Barclay? The food critic?" At my nod he let out a low whistle. "Swell. This just became a high-profile case." He reached into his jacket pocket, pulled out notebook and pen, and flipped to a blank page. "Okay, Tiffany. How did you discover the body?"

"I decided to take a little walk after dinner to digest. The chefs went all out with dinner. spicy orange-glazed beef, steak Diane, almond-crusted swordfish . . ."

Phil groaned and pointed his pen at me. "I only had time to grab a ham and Swiss on rye. You're getting off the subject."

"Right, sorry. I decided to check out the gardens and the fountain that I'd noticed earlier. I saw the shoe dangling over the edge of the bowl and I went and looked and . . . I found him."

Phil eyed me. "You didn't touch anything, did you?"

I shifted my weight from one foot to the other. "I did feel for a pulse. When I didn't get one I called 911." I held up both hands. "I didn't touch anything else, I swear."

He shot me a look, scribbled some more in his pad. "He was at this banquet too, I take it," he said. "Any idea what he might have been doing out here?"

"He might have taken a walk to clear his head. He was sloshing down Scotch like it was water. Or . . . he might have been meeting someone. I'm positive I heard footsteps shortly before I found his body."

Phil looked up from his scribbling. "Footsteps?"

"Yes. I heard a clicking sound going away from the fountain. It could have been high heels, or maybe men's wooden ones. They both make that type of sound." I paused and then added, "I also thought I saw a flash of something red, but it all happened so fast, I might have imagined it."

He shot me a sharp look. "With your keen powers of observation? Doubtful," said Phil. From his tone it was hard for me to tell if he was angry, just being sarcastic, dead serious, or all of the above.

"He was supposed to accept an award for Dana Carlyle tonight," I said thoughtfully, "but he sent Damaris Alexander a text asking her to do it for him."

Phil's head snapped up. "He sent a text? Do you know what time?"

My brow furrowed as I struggled to remember. "I'm not positive, but I think it was around six forty-five," I said at last.

Phil called over to Brandon, "Hoffman! Check the body and the surrounding area for a cell phone."

"I didn't notice a phone lying around," I ventured. "I'm sure if you ask Damaris she'll show you the text. It's probably still on her phone."

Phil made a grunt and continued scribbling in his notebook. I stole a quick look over at the fountain, where the paramedics were bending over Jason's body. "Blunt force trauma," I murmured.

Phil's head jerked up. "What?"

"Blunt force trauma. I'm thinking that's what he died from. I noticed the side of his head looks a little caved in, as if it was struck by something pretty heavy. I don't think it was an accident." I tore my gaze away from the body at the fountain and back to Phil. "He was writing a book, Jason was. The text he sent Damaris said he had to get to New York immediately."

Phil cocked his head. "And you think it had something to do with this book?"

I nodded. "His book was supposedly spiked with what he called 'juicy nuggets' about people he'd met during his career."

"So you think he was killed over some gossip?" Phil looked skeptical.

"His gossip was apparently good enough to interest a Hollywood producer. Jason told me some of his little tidbits were about secrets— dangerous secrets. It could be possible someone wanted to silence him to keep their secret from getting out."

"Out and possibly onto a movie screen." Phil tapped the edge of his pen against his notebook. "You certainly seem to be very well informed about all this," he remarked. He shot me a steely look. "Playing Nancy Drew again, are we?"

I was spared answering as Brandon Hoffman hurried over to us. He gestured toward the ambulance, and I saw the two paramedics transferring Jason's black-bagged body from the gurney into the ambulance. "The general consensus is he died from blunt force trauma," said Brandon. I shot Phil a smug look as Brandon added, "I gave the area a quick canvass but I didn't see any sign of a weapon. No phone either, and it wasn't on his person. The coroner will fix the accurate time, but I'd say he hasn't been dead long . . . not more than an hour tops."

Two officers had exited a squad car and were headed in our direction. "We'll need this area cordoned off," Phil said to Brandon. "I need to speak with the hotel manager and the person who's in charge of this food convention."

"Foodie," I put in. "It's a foodie convention. There's a difference."

Phil's lips puckered. "Okay, foodie convention. I don't suppose you can help me with that little detail?"

"Sophie Brinkwater is the convention organizer," I replied. I glanced at my watch. "You can most likely find her in the Harmony Room, just off the main lobby. The banquet will still be going on. They've probably just started giving out the awards."

Phil slid his notebook back into his jacket pocket as Brandon hurried off to speak to the two officers. "Looks like I'll be putting a damper on the remainder of the *foodies'* evening." He pointed his finger at me. "We can continue this tomorrow. I'll need you to come in, make a formal statement."

"Of course. I'll do anything I can to help."

Phil took a step closer to me. "I can think of one thing right off the bat: no investigating on your own," he said.

I shot him a look of mock horror. "What? But I've done so well in that area in the past, you have to admit that."

Phil reached out, placed his hands on my shoulders. "I'm serious, Tiffany," he said. "From what you've told me, you might have just missed being an eyewitness to what happened here. If you start poking around and asking questions you could make yourself a target."

I suppressed a shudder. "Fear not, I have no intention of doing that." I paused and looked him right in the eye. "So . . . I guess this is the 'something unexpected' that means our Sunday dinner date is off?"

Phil shot me a tight smile. "Could be. Of course, there's always the possibility we can get the case wrapped up by Sunday. Don't give up hope." His smile widened a bit and he motioned toward the hotel. "I'll walk you back to your banquet," he offered.

I hesitated, then shook my head. "No, I'll go in by myself. If I went in with you, it might raise questions I really don't want to answer." As Phil raised an eyebrow, I added, "Francine Weston is there. She said she was covering the banquet, but I think what she was really after was another interview with Jason. Once she hears what happened . . ." I spread my hands.

Phil made an irritated sound in the back of his throat. "She'll be all over me. Great. That woman is like an irritating fly that won't go away."

"I agree, but this is one time you might want to talk to her," I said thoughtfully. "She tried to get an interview with Jason earlier, but he cut her off. I saw her give a cutting motion to her cameraman, so she must have gotten some footage of him. There could be something on that tape that might help your investigation."

"So you're saying I should play nice with her." Phil sighed. He reached up, rubbed lightly at his forehead. "I'm starting to think I should have stayed the extra two days at my conference."

"Why didn't you?"

He leaned over and planted a hard kiss on my lips. "Why do you think?" he growled, and then he turned on his heel and was gone. I stood for a moment, savoring the touch of his lips on mine, and then I turned to walk back to the hotel. As I passed the pond, I heard something crunch underneath my shoe. I bent down to see what it was, and I picked up a small blue card. There was a tiny crack on its upper edge. I turned the card over. There was a number in the corner—738. A room key card, perhaps? I frowned. There was nothing to indicate how long the card had lain there. Anyone could have dropped it, but it was possible it could be Jason's, or even his killer's.

I was debating whether or not to ping Phil about it when I heard a familiar voice behind me. "Jeepers. What happened here?" I slid the key card into my jacket pocket and whirled around. Jeff Marki stood right behind me, his eyes wide as he took in the officers winding yellow crime scene tape around the fountain area. For a moment we just stared at each other, speechless. Jeff found his voice first. "Tiffany? Wow, you're looking well. Are you here for the food convention? I heard you write a food blog now."

I swallowed. "You look well too, Jeff. Yes, I'm covering the convention for *Southern Style*. Congratulations. I understand you're one of the finalists for the Last Remaining Chef competition."

His face split into a smile. "Yeah, can you believe that? I was stunned when Leonardo told me. I have to admit, I'm a bit nervous. I mean, there's some pretty stiff competition, and Leonardo is counting on me to finish in the top three, if not win the whole thing." He chuckled. "Leonardo's after the six months of advertising on the food channel for the Madison, and truthfully, I wouldn't mind winning that ten-thousand-dollar first prize. It would sure help." He glanced over toward the fountain area again. The officers had just finished putting up the tape. "What's going on here," he repeated. "Has something happened?"

I cleared my throat. "Yes. A body was found in the fountain."

"A body!" Jeff's face paled and his tongue darted out, licked at his lips. His voice shook as he asked, "Was it . . . was it a woman?"

I detected a note of panic in Jeff's voice. I shook my head. "No. It was Jason Barclay."

"Barclay! The food critic!" Jeff let out a breath, panic replaced by relief. "Do you know what happened? I mean, did he fall in and drown? I heard . . . I heard some people saying he got pretty drunk tonight."

"He definitely consumed a lot of alcohol." I looked Jeff in the eye and added, "You seemed a bit upset when you asked if the body was a woman's. Why?"

His gaze skittered away from mine and he was silent for a few moments. Finally he said, "Fiona's here with me. We got into a little argument, and she took off. She was pretty steamed, so . . ."

"You really thought she might have fallen in the fountain?"

He shrugged. "Anything's possible. She did have a bit to drink." There was another awkward pause, and then he said softly, "I don't know if you've heard, but . . . Fee and I got engaged recently. That's partly why I'd like to win that contest. That ten-thousand-dollar prize to the winning chef could come in very handy, and I'm sure my father and Leonardo would welcome the ten grand worth of publicity for the Madison."

"Oh, I'm sure of that," I said. "Knowing Leonardo, I bet he's already got press releases written."

Jeff barked out a shaky laugh. "I bet he does. No pressure, right?"

"Right." I reached out, touched his arm. "I did hear about your engagement, Jeff. I'm very happy for the two of you."

He let out a breath. "Thanks. I'll be honest with you, after you . . . left, I was a bit soured on relationships. But Fee kept after me, telling me not to give up. She was there for me, and we started working together pretty closely in the kitchen so . . . heck, I guess it was inevitable."

"I'm glad things worked out for you and Fiona," I said. "And . . . I'm sorry about what happened, Jeff. I'm sorry about the way things ended between us, and that I hurt you."

He swallowed, his eyes fixed on the ground. "It just happened so fast. It seemed as if one minute we were in love and the next . . . well, you weren't anyway."

We stood in silence for a long moment, and then Jeff cleared his throat. "Well, I'd better keep looking for her. It was nice to see you, Tiffany. To be honest, I'm glad we got all this awkwardness out of the way now. I mean, if you're covering the competition, we'd have probably run into each other eventually."

"True," I agreed. "I'm glad we can be civil to each other. And I'll definitely be talking to you again," I added. "After all, once you win the Last Remaining Chef competition, I'll want an exclusive interview for my blog."

"You got it." He laughed. "One thing I have to say, Tiffany. You always did believe in me—in my cooking ability," he said softly. "I'll do my best to win, believe me."

"I know you will."

With a wave, Jeff ambled off toward the parking lot. I watched him go, thinking about what he'd told me. So Fiona and he had an argument and she took off. Was that before or after I'd heard her talking with Jason, I wondered. Then another thought occurred to me. Had Fiona engineered the argument with Jeff so she could get away and talk to Jason? Phil would surely accuse me of slipping into amateur detective mode if he could hear me. I paused as another thought occurred to me. Fiona had been wearing a red dress and heels. Could she have been that flash of red I'd seen? For Jeff's sake, I hoped not.

I retraced my steps to the hotel, and the moment I stepped into the lobby I could tell that news had already spread about Jason. The doors to the Harmony Room were wide open and everyone had spilled out into the lobby, talking animatedly. Rain saw me and immediately hurried over. "You'll never believe what happened," she cried.

I held up my hand. "I know. Jason Barclay's dead. I'm the one who found his body," I said.

"Oh, my dear. How awful!" Rain dug her fingers into my forearm. "And to think we only just saw him. What do you think happened? He was drinking quite heavily. Maybe he slipped and fell into the fountain and drowned? And what was he doing out there in the first place?"

"I don't know," I said. I wasn't about to give Rain any details about Jason's death that Phil would take me to task for. "But the police are here investigating."

Rain's head bobbed furiously up and down. "Yes, a Detective Bartell and the hotel manager, Fletcher, both came in to speak to Sophie. Needless to say, it brought the banquet to an abrupt end." She lowered her voice. "He said he was from Homicide. They usually investigate murders, don't they?"

"They investigate anything considered a suspicious death," I replied. "I'm sure Jason's qualifies in that category."

"I suppose you're right." Rain sighed. "Detective Bartell interrupted the festivities just as Damaris was about to accept Dana's award. She didn't look any too pleased to have her thunder stolen, I can tell you that."

Hugh walked over to us. "Ready, Rain?" he asked. He tossed me a lopsided smile. "It's been quite an evening, eh, Tiffany?"

"It's certainly not how I anticipated this night would end," I agreed.

"Us either, and so early too." Rain shifted her bag on her shoulder and added, "Well, since the banquet ended before we could sample all the desserts, a few of us are heading over to that diner out on the highway. They're supposed to have great apple pie and peach cobbler. Not as sumptuous as what we were supposed to have, but still . . . want to come?"

I shook my head. "No, thanks. I'm still a bit full from the buffet, and I should touch base with Jimmy. Have either of you seen him?"

"No," they chorused. Rain added, "He might still be in the kitchen with the chefs—or he might have wandered outside to the crime scene, who knows."

I hadn't thought about that. Jimmy was a freelancer, after all, and photos of the crime scene would probably be in demand. Aloud I said, "I'll check it out. You two go on and I'll see you tomorrow at the convention."

Rain nodded. "Assuming there still is a convention, after all this. But I imagine since he didn't die at the Civic Center there will be."

I left Rain and Hugh and turned toward the Harmony Room. I peered in the doorway of the banquet area. No sign of either Jimmy or Phil, but Francine was there, deep in conversation with Brent.

"Make sure you get that footage edited before the eleven o'clock news," she was saying. "And go over to that sitting garden area they've cordoned off and get some good shots of that fountain before you leave. I'll meet you back at the station in an hour."

Francine turned and I saw Brent click his heels together and raise his hand in a snappy salute behind her back. "Aye, aye, Captain," he muttered. He shifted the camera on his shoulder, saw me watching him, and shot me a cheeky grin as he brushed past me. I was about to follow him when I heard, "Hey, wait up!" Francine was beside me in an instant. "Tiffany, right? I hear you're the one who discovered Jason's body."

I narrowed my gaze at her. I couldn't imagine that Phil would have told her anything, and then I remembered that 911 calls were a matter of public record. No doubt she'd made a call once she'd heard the news about Jason. I gritted my teeth. "No comment."

For a moment she looked taken aback, and then she recovered. "Oh, come on, Tiffany," she said, her voice dripping like honey. "Surely you must have something to say about it."

"Actually, I do," I said. "I think you should find Detective Bartell and show him that footage you shot of Jason earlier."

Her eyebrows rose slightly. "Footage? What footage?"

"Oh, can it, Francine. I saw you and Jason together earlier in the bar. And I know the camera was rolling because after Jason stalked off you motioned to Brent to cut."

She stiffened. "If you saw all that, then you must have figured out that Jason wasn't exactly receptive to being interviewed. Let's just say he told me, in no uncertain terms, what I could do with my microphone." She paused and then added, "He showed me too."

"I still think you should show Bartell that tape. It's your civic duty as a newspaper reporter."

She tossed me a look that a mother might bestow on an errant three-year-old. "And how do you figure that?"

"Well . . . a reporter's job is to keep the public informed, right? For all we know, you might have captured the very last footage of Jason alive."

Francine's face lit up. "You know, you're right. And won't that make a great lead-in on the eleven o'clock broadcast." She looked at her watch, then turned and spun on her heels. "Sorry, no time to chat now. I've gotta hurry if I want to get it on air."

"But what about Bartell?" I called after her. "That tape could be evidence."

"There's no guarantee it is. Bartell can catch it on the eleven o'clock news same as everyone else," she shot back.

"You don't know that, Francine," I cried. "What if there's something on that tape that might help catch whoever did this?"

She paused and I could see the wheels turning in her brain. "I won't show the entire tape," she said at last. "Only the little bit before . . . well, before Jason got a bit nasty. If Bartell plays nice with me, then I will with him." Her voice turned dreamy as she added, "I can see the lead-in now. Discord at the Foodie Fest. Prominent food critic's body found in fountain. Was it an accident? Or foul play? Detective Philip Bartell is on the case." She looked at her watch again. "I've got to get back to the station now!" She whipped out her phone, pressed a button. "Brent! Where are you? Change of plans. Meet me at the van immediately!"

Francine pushed past me out into the lobby. I pulled out my phone and sent a quick text to Phil. *Francine on her way to the studio. Going to show her footage of Jason on eleven o'clock broadcast. If you hurry you might be able to catch her.*

I slid my phone back into my pocket, and I'd just walked into the main lobby when out of the corner of my eye I saw a woman sitting on the love seat next to the fireplace jump up. My breath caught in my throat as I saw it was Fiona. I quickly slid onto a nearby club chair, slouching down low so she wouldn't see me. Fiona stood uncertainly for a moment, and then started in the direction of the reception desk— and my chair! Snagging a magazine from a nearby end table, I positioned it so that it shielded my face, but I could peer over the top. She was only a few steps away from me when the front door opened and Jeff came in. He saw Fiona and rushed over to her. "Fee," I heard him say. "I'm so glad you're okay. I was so worried."

Fiona threw her arms around Jeff and pressed her body against his. "I'm so sorry I got angry," she said. "It's just . . ."

"Just what, Fee?" Jeff's tone sounded concerned. "Something's been eating away at you these past few weeks. You've been trying to hide it, but I can tell something's wrong."

Fiona's laugh was tittering. "There's nothing wrong," she said. "I—I have a lot on my mind, is all. I mean, there's a lot to do for the wedding."

"The wedding is months away," Jeff said. "There's plenty of time. This is about more than just the wedding." A brief silence and then Jeff said softly, "Fee, I want to help you, but I can't if you don't tell me what's bugging you."

"Fine. I guess I'm still a bit . . . insecure," Fiona mumbled.

"Insecure? About what?"

She hung her head. "About us."

"Geez, Fee, we've been over this. You have no reason to feel that way."

"I'm sorry, Jeff." Fiona made a motion of brushing a tear from the corner of her eye. "I'm sorry. I know sometimes I act like such a fool."

Jeff put a finger to her lips. "It's okay, Fee. Let's go upstairs. We can talk about it."

He started to lead her toward the elevator, but she hung back. "Can we stop by the desk first? I think . . . I must have misplaced my room key," she said. "I thought I had it in my purse, but . . . I can't find it."

Jeff squeezed her arm and they both walked over to the reception desk and the bored-looking male clerk who sat there. After a brief conversation, I saw the clerk hand Fiona another key card. Then Fiona and Jeff, hand in hand, walked over to the bank of elevators. I waited until they entered and the elevator began its upward climb before I set the magazine aside and stood. I thought about the conversation I'd overheard and came to the only conclusion I could. Fiona was lying to Jeff and I had an idea that her evasiveness had to do with Jason.

My fingers slid into my pocket, and I pulled out the key card I'd found at the pond. Could this be Fiona's missing key? I turned the card over in my hand. If it were Fiona's, it had been deactivated the minute she'd accepted her new one. It was useless, save for the fact it had been found near the scene of Jason's murder.

Of course, if it wasn't Fiona's . . . but what if it were? I had two choices. I could simply turn this key in at the front desk, or I could find Phil and give it to him, explain where I'd found it. Or . . . there was a third option. I could play Nancy Drew and try and find out for myself whose room key this was. As I was debating which choice I should make, a heavy hand fell on my shoulder and spun me around.

Eight

"Boy, someone's sure jumpy."

I let out an audible sigh of relief as I saw it was Jimmy standing behind me. "You'd be jumpy too if you'd found a dead body," I snapped.

Jimmy's eyes widened. "Hey, was that you? Oh, gosh, Tiffany, I heard somebody found Barclay swimming with the fishes—literally—but I didn't realize you were the one who found him! That must have been awful!"

"It wasn't the highlight of my evening, I'll admit that," I said.

"It sure put the kibosh on the banquet," said Jimmy. "That detective, Bartell, is certainly intimidating. He did everything except utter that classic line, 'don't leave town.'" He let out a dry chuckle. "I guess he thinks that since Jason was so 'well-liked' by everyone, anyone might have done him in." He waggled his eyebrows at me. "So? Any ideas?"

I stared at him. "What do you mean?"

"Oh, I think you know," he said with a grin. "Mac told me you're quite the amateur sleuth. Are you going to try and find out who iced Barclay?"

Phil's admonition to me about playing detective rang in my ears as I answered. "The other times were different. I got involved the first time because I was considered a prime suspect. The second was because I was trying to clear Hilary's sister Arleen. I don't really have a vested interest in finding out who killed Jason."

"I would have thought finding his body would be reason enough," remarked Jimmy. "I know Barclay was a scum of a human being, but still, to die like that . . ." He let out a sigh. "I admit I'm a bit disappointed. I was kind of looking forward to seeing an amateur sleuth in action—and who knows, maybe being her sidekick."

I hesitated, thinking about the clicking heels, the flash of red, and the key card in my pocket. It certainly had seemed, from the little bit I'd overheard, that Fiona might have had a good reason for wanting Jason dead. She'd even said it out loud: *I wish you were dead.*

Had she made that wish a reality?

I frowned. The Fiona I remembered was a timid girl who was always pretty much cowed by her father. I could see Leonardo offing Jason, but Fiona? Doubtful. Still, I recalled what Phil had said: anyone can be pushed to murder, given the right circumstances. Could Jason have pushed Fiona too far? Her appearance had changed, but had her personality?

Then I thought about Jeff, about what it would do to him if his fiancée were to be arrested for murder, and I clamped my lips together. Even though I was no longer in love with Jeff, I still cared enough about him to want to spare him grief. If the only way to do that was prove Fiona hadn't killed Jason, well then . . .

I looked at Jimmy. "On second thought, maybe I do have an interest in finding out just who killed Jason."

Jimmy did a fist pump. "That's the spirit! So, what changed your mind?"

"Let's just say it occurred to me that an old . . ." I paused, hesitant to use the word *friend.* "An old . . ." I floundered for a moment for a word. "An old acquaintance of mine could be involved. And I really can't see this person as a cold-blooded killer."

"Mac said you've got really good instincts. And I meant what I said about being a sidekick. If you need any help, I'm willing and able. Whatever we find out will remain between us." He mimed locking his lips and throwing away a key.

In that instant, I made up my mind. "Let me show you something."

I led Jimmy over to the far corner of the lobby, then pulled the key card out of my pocket. "I found this by the fish pond, a few feet away from the fountain," I said. "It was in the grass." I pointed to the crack on top. "I could have done this when I stepped on it, or it might have been damaged beforehand."

Jimmy let out a low whistle. "You think maybe Barclay dropped it? Or his killer?"

"Those are two possibilities," I said. "Of course, we can't discount the idea it could have been dropped by someone who has nothing at all to do with the murder. Or it could have been there for who knows how long."

"Sure, sure," said Jimmy. "In any case, it would be interesting to find out who the key belongs to."

"That's what I was thinking, but just how do I do that? If I turn it in at the front desk, they'll just take it and not release any information on it."

"Hmm. Good point. Of course, we could always go to the room on the card and return it to the occupant."

I frowned. If this were Fiona's room key, doing that would definitely create an embarrassing moment. "I'd rather not do that," I murmured. "I have my reasons."

"O-kay." Jimmy reached up to scratch at his head. "I guess what you should do is turn it over to the cops, but like you said, you've got no idea how long that card could have been lying there. If it doesn't have anything to do with the murder, then you'd be wasting their valuable time. And Bartell strikes me as the type of guy who doesn't like to have his time wasted, am I right?" He stole a glance over at the reception area, where a young, very attractive blonde girl had replaced the male clerk. He held out his hand to me. "Tell you what. Let me have that card for ten minutes, and I bet I can get some information for you. Consider this my audition to be Robin to your Batman—or should I say Wonder Woman?"

I hesitated, then handed him the key. "Okay. You're on."

I sat down by the fireplace to wait. I saw him approach the desk, strike up a conversation with the female clerk. They spoke for a few minutes, and I saw him hand her the card. She looked at it, shook her head. I saw him reach into his pocket, pull something out and show it to her. Another brief conversation followed, and then she handed him a small square of paper, which he stuffed in his pocket. A couple sauntered up to the desk just then, so Jimmy shot the clerk another brilliant smile, then turned and made his way over to me. He held up his wrist, tapped at his watch. "A record seven minutes," he said proudly as he flopped down on the love seat next to me.

I looked at him. "So . . . what happened? Did she tell you whose room that key was for?"

He held up the key card. "Nope."

"No?" My face fell. "It surely looked as if you were having a good conversation."

"We were. She couldn't tell me anything about the card because it's not for this hotel."

My eyes popped. "It's not?"

"Nope. Branson Towers' key cards are white, this one is a light blue. Gemma—that's her name—wasn't positive, but she thinks it could be from the Cardinal Inn, which just happens to be a few doors down from where I'm staying." He paused. "I showed her my press pass, told her I was a freelance reporter. I got her to confirm that Jason Barclay was staying here in one of the suites on the tenth floor. Apparently Detective Bartell and Fletcher, the hotel manager, are up there now." He tapped the card against his palm. "So if this belongs to Jason, he had two hotel rooms."

"That would be interesting." I looked at my watch and then at Jimmy. "It's still early. What would you think about a visit over to the Cardinal Inn?"

"I'm game. Here's hoping the clerk on duty is as accommodating as Gemma." He held up the square of paper and shot me a wide grin. "She gave me her phone number."

• • •

Twenty minutes later I guided my convertible down a circular driveway and into the parking lot of the Cardinal Inn. I pulled into a spot near a large sign that read *Welcome to the Cardinal Inn*, compete with a drawing of a large red cardinal, wings spread. Jimmy pulled his silver SUV into a space across from mine, and together we walked up the concrete walkway and up a short flight of steps into the inn. I'd never been here, so I paused for a moment for a quick look around. "It's not as fancy-schmancy as the Towers," said Jimmy. "But it's kind of cozy, doncha think?"

I had to agree. Dark paneling set off the wall-to-wall thick blueberry-colored carpeting. A small sofa and love seat were positioned in front of a large bay window, and nearby was a table filled with vases of fresh-cut flowers. A chandelier hung gracefully above it. Off to the left was a stone fireplace with several comfy-looking chairs and another damask-covered love seat arranged in front of it. The mantel was a combination of walnut and oak and had designs of birds and flowers carved into it. The whole atmosphere radiated homey and cozy.

I glanced over to the right and the large mahogany reception desk. A redheaded guy who looked to be in his early twenties was seated there, his eyes glued to the computer screen in front of him. Jimmy let out a sigh. "Figures I couldn't get lucky twice in a row," he whispered. "I'm sorry to say my charm doesn't work half as well with guys."

I patted his hand. "That's okay. I got this. Sit back and relax, Robin."

I approached the desk, and the redheaded clerk glanced up. I noticed his name tag read *Jerome*. "Can I help you?" he asked in a bored tone.

"Hi, Jerome," I said with a bright smile. "Actually, it's me who might be able to help you." I pulled out the key card and held it up. "I happened to find this in the grass over at the Branson Towers. The clerk there said this might be one of your room keys."

Jerome squinted at the card. "Sure looks like it," he said. "You found it tonight, you said?" At my nod, he gave his head a shake. "This has been a banner night for missing keys," he said. He tapped at a pad on the side of the computer screen. "I've had three people report their key card missing since I came on duty at four." He pulled the keyboard in front of him. "What's the number on the card?"

"738."

Jerome tapped at the keyboard, squinted at the computer screen for a few minutes and then turned the screen so we could see. Jimmy and I leaned across the counter for a closer look as Jerome said, "Okay, that was Amanda Bridge's card." He rolled his eyes. "She's about seventy-five and a real piece of work. Here for that foodie convention. She heard that the chefs were all staying at the Branson Towers, so she went over there hoping to get some autographs and lost her card. I've already issued her a new one."

I held out the card. "Do you need this back?"

He pointed at the crack. "It wouldn't have worked anymore, but it's a moot point. It was deactivated the second I issued the new one. You can just toss it." He spun the screen back toward him.

I slid the card into my pocket. "I imagine you have quite a few people staying here for the convention?"

"Oh, yeah. Both this hotel and the Majestic got a lot of spillover, people who either couldn't get a room at the Towers or else couldn't afford to stay there."

"So I guess those other people with missing keys could also have lost them either at the Towers or the convention center," I said conversationally.

"Maybe." His eyes narrowed again. "You seem pretty interested in all this," he said, his tone rife with suspicion.

"I'm just the curious type, I guess," I said with a disarming smile. "It goes with the profession." I whipped out my press pass, held it out. "I'm a reporter, covering the convention for my magazine, *Southern Style*."

"*Southern Style*?" His eyes widened as he looked at my pass. "Oh my gosh—you're Tiffany Austin! You write the food blog!"

I smiled. "Guilty." I nodded toward Jimmy. "This is James, my photographer. He's taking photos and videos of the convention events."

Jerome ignored Jimmy and focused on me. "It's a real pleasure to meet you, Ms. Austin. I read your blog every week. I guess you could say I'm sort of an amateur chef." He leaned in a bit closer and added, "As a matter of fact, I'm attending that convention myself. Tomorrow's my day off, and I signed up for a cooking class in the morning. I'm also planning to go to the food truck competition right after." He let out a sigh. "It bums me out that I'm gonna miss Guy Goodwin's competition though. I never miss his show, but Last Remaining Chef stretches over the weekend, and I'm scheduled to work."

"That is a bummer," I agreed. "No chance you could switch with someone else?"

"I tried, but no dice. Everyone else had plans." He sighed and then his face brightened. "I did manage to get a few autographs though, even Jason Barclay's."

Jimmy let out a low moan as I dug my nails into his arm. I smiled at Jerome and said, "You got Barclay's autograph? That's quite a coup. From what I've heard, he's not the most cordial person when it comes to signing autographs."

"Yeah, I heard that too, but honest? The guy's not as bad as you might think." Jerome puffed out his chest. "Not only did he give me a twenty-dollar tip for getting him an appointment calendar, but he gave me his autograph too. If you ask me, more of our guests should be like him."

I gripped the edge of the counter so hard my knuckles were white. "Guests? Jason Barclay wa—is a guest here?" I'd caught myself in time. No need to let Jerome know his favorite guest was no longer among the living.

"Oh, yeah." He chuckled. "He's on the seventh floor too, not far from Ms. Bridge's room. He's in 715. She'd just die if she knew Barclay was just down the hall."

The phone rang just then and Jerome excused himself to answer it. I motioned to Jimmy and we moved off back into the lobby. I headed straight for the fireplace and love seat, Jimmy on my heels. Once we were seated, Jimmy gave a furtive glance around. "So Jason did have two rooms," he said. "Now the question is why?"

"Why indeed," I murmured. "It had to have something to do with his book."

Jimmy shot me a puzzled look. "You mean that appointment book?"

"No, no," I said, waving my hand impatiently. "Jason was writing a book, his autobiography."

Jimmy let out a low whistle. "Talk about boring! You mean he actually thought people would pay to read about his life?"

My lips twisted in a half smile. "Yes, and what's more, I understand he had a movie producer interested as well."

"You're kidding! They wanted to make a movie about Jason's life?" He shook his head. "Gee, I guess Hollywood will buy anything, huh?"

"I think the big attraction was the fact Jason reveals secrets in his book—dangerous ones."

Jimmy let out a snort. "How dangerous could revealing chefs' secrets be? What did he think, one of them would come after him with a cleaver?"

"I think it was more than just chef secrets," I said. "He mentioned they were about people both in and out of the food industry. He might have been using this room as a place to meet with some of those people."

"Then the guy was dumber than I thought," Jimmy said bluntly. "It sounds to me like he was practically inviting someone to murder him." He slapped his hands on his knees and rose. "Maybe there's a clue inside his room as to just what was going on," he said. "How about we take a little stroll up to the seventh floor? Who knows, maybe an opportunity will present itself." He paused. "If—and I say if—we did manage to gain entry to his room, we'd just have a quick look around. No harm in that, right?"

Once again Phil's voice warning me against investigating sounded in my ear. I resolutely pushed his voice aside. "Not as long as we don't touch anything. Let's go."

We took the elevator to the seventh floor and Jimmy read the sign directing us to the rooms. 715 was at the end of the corridor, next to the stairs. A young, pretty brunette in a chambermaid uniform was at her cart, which was positioned in front of the room across from 715. "I got this," Jimmy whispered and moved over to the chambermaid. He smiled, she smiled, and a few minutes later she pulled a key out of her pocket and opened the door of 715. "Thanks so much," I heard him say. I saw him press something into her hand, and she reached into her apron pocket, pulled out a square of paper and a pen, scribbled on it, then handed it to him with a smile. She returned to her cart and pushed it down the hall in the opposite direction. Once she was far down the hall, Jimmy motioned to me to join him.

I arched a brow at him. "Another phone number?"

"Yeah, well, this one cost me a ten spot and a promise of some drinks at the bar downstairs tomorrow night, but I figured what the heck. Violet's a pretty girl, and she was very cooperative when I told her I forgot my key in my room."

Jimmy started to reach for the door handle, but I grabbed his arm. "Wait." I felt in my pocket, pulled out a Kleenex. "Use this. We don't want to leave any prints."

One swift glance around was all it took to see that the room didn't seem as if it had been occupied. There was a full-sized bed, a desk and chair, a dresser with a large-screen TV on top, factory-produced prints on the walls and thick red-striped curtains on the window. The curtains were closed.

"I think you're right about him not sleeping here," remarked Jimmy, looking at the perfectly made-up bed. "To be honest, it doesn't seem as if anyone's been in here."

I'd moved over to the desk and, using a Kleenex, opened the middle drawer. A leather-bound appointment book lay there. I wrapped the tissue around my fingers and pulled out the book. "So much for just having a quick look," I muttered. I flipped through the pages, stopping at this week's. "There's writing here," I announced.

Jimmy came and peered over my shoulder. In the square allotted for today's date was the name Sonny, followed by the initials, DA, HH and FP. At the bottom of the page was a string of numbers. It could have been a code or possibly a phone number. "Interesting," Jimmy observed. "What do you think it means?"

"The initials might be of people he planned to meet with," I suggested. "For example, DA could stand for Damaris Alexander. I saw him with her at around one thirty. HH might be Hugh Hudson. I have no idea who Sonny might be."

Jimmy squinted at the page. "What about FP? And what do all those numbers mean?"

"No clue," I murmured. I wasn't ready to confide in Jimmy about Fiona yet. I flipped the page. Tomorrow's date had the same initials, in different squares. "Looks like he planned follow-up meetings," I remarked. "Sonny seems to be missing." I felt my breath catch in my throat as I noticed a new set of initials. BG, for ten a.m. Could it be Bob Gillette? And if so had Bob, perhaps, decided to have the meeting earlier? Like tonight, at the banquet?

"It doesn't surprise me that he had a book like this," Jimmy said. "He was one of the biggest control freaks around."

I looked at him. "How do you know that?"

"I used to date a girl who worked for him. She said that he was obsessive about everything. Names, dates, places. He'd always check and double-check all his appointments. She quit after two weeks— couldn't take his looking over her shoulder on every little detail anymore." Jimmy gestured toward the book. "So, what are you going to do? Take that?"

I shook my head. "Absolutely not. That could be construed as tampering with evidence. But I don't know of any law against taking photos of these pages." I pointed to his neck. "Since you didn't bring your camera, my phone will have to do."

I pulled my phone out of my purse, snapped photos of the pages, then closed the appointment book and slid it back in the drawer. "Nothing else to see," I said. "Let's get out of here."

We exited the room and made our way back to the elevator. Jimmy jabbed at the button. "So, what now?" he asked.

There was lots I wanted to do, but unfortunately most of it would have to wait until tomorrow. "We could go back to my place," I suggested. "I need to look over your photos and videos for the blog, anyway, so maybe something in them will pop out at us."

"In connection with the murder? I don't see how. They're mostly of the food and the chefs in the kitchen."

"But you did take some at the bar's happy hour. You might have captured Jason on film too."

My phone pinged as we entered the elevator, and I saw it was a text from Hilary. *Hey girlfriend! How was the dinner? Any excitement?*

I texted back: *You have no idea. Come over for a nightcap and I'll fill you in.*

Hilary sent back a thumbs-up emoji, and I dropped my phone back in my purse. "My friend Hilary will be joining us," I said.

"Ah, the chick Mac's been seeing. He's told me about her too. She was your sidekick on your last two capers. Hope she doesn't mind sharing the spotlight."

The elevator doors slid open and Jimmy and I exited. We walked swiftly across the parking lot to where we'd parked our cars. Jimmy held up one finger. "Just a sec," he said. He jogged over to his car, reached inside and pulled out a large brown paper bag, then hurried back over to me. He held the bag aloft. "I almost forgot. Guy gave me this huge bag of leftover food. We can heat it up during our powwow." His lips quirked slightly as he pressed the bag into my hands. "You take it, otherwise I'm sure to forget it in my car. From what Mac's told me about Hilary, I'm sure this will be very appreciated."

I chuckled. "Are you kidding? You might replace me as her best friend for this."

He walked me to my car, and as I opened the door he said, "Do you think we should tag Bartell? Clue him in about Jason's other room? We don't have to tell him we already did our own search." He patted his pocket. "I always carry a burner phone, just in case I misplace mine. I could make an anonymous call if you want."

I started to say that Phil would be able to trace a burner phone, then paused as a black sedan drew up to a halt in front of the inn and parked in the fire zone. Phil and Brandon both jumped out and hurried up the front steps and into the inn.

I tossed the bag of food onto the passenger seat and slid behind the wheel. "Not necessary," I said. "It appears they've already figured it out."

Nine

"I can't believe how murders just seem to fall into your lap!" Hilary lifted her head and sniffed at the air. "Man, does that food smell good! I'm starving."

Even though I'd only just eaten a few hours ago, I found my stomach rumbling as delicious aromas wafted out from my kitchen. Cooper and Lily had given all of us an enthusiastic greeting when we'd come in the door, no doubt due to the smells emanating from the paper bag in my hands. Now both of them squatted near the kitchen entrance, their gazes firmly fixed on Jimmy, who'd appointed himself chef for the evening, most likely because all the job entailed was warming the food up.

The man in question stuck his head out of the kitchen and grinned at Hilary and me lounging on my sofa. "Just a few more minutes," he said. He glanced down at Cooper and Lily, then at me. "I always was a sucker for pretty faces. Is it okay to give them a little taste?"

"I think they'd be insulted if you didn't," I said. "It's rich food, so not too much. Maybe just a bit of salmon for Lily, and a sliver of chicken for Cooper?"

"Gotcha." Jimmy waved his hand at my animals. "Come on, Lily and Cooper. You're in for a treat."

They immediately trotted into the kitchen, Cooper's tail wagging furiously and Lily's tail as well, although a bit more sedately. A few minutes later we heard the sounds of contented slurping and then Jimmy emerged, balancing a large tray. "It tastes even better than it smells," he said with a grin at Hilary. "Both Tiffany and I can attest to that—and Cooper and Lily too."

Hilary rubbed her hands together and sniffed at the air, then she pointed at the tray. "Is that honey-glazed salmon?"

"It is," said Jimmy. "There are also samples of steak Diane, coq au vin, chicken Kiev . . ."

"Okay, okay, I get the picture," cried Hilary. I passed out the paper plates and utensils, and for the next twenty minutes there wasn't a sound in the room other than an occasional moan from Hilary. Once everyone's plate was empty, I said, "Now that we're all well-fed, it's time to get down to business." I rubbed my hands together. "First things first. I've got to look over those photos and videos for the blog anyway, so we might as well get that out of the way first."

Jimmy set down his plate and pointed to his camera. "I can hook my camera up to your TV screen. That will make viewing much easier."

I made a sweeping bow. "I'm all for that."

Jimmy pulled a length of cable out of his camera bag, and a few minutes later we were looking at beautiful photographs of all the appetizers and main courses that had been served that evening. "Maybe this wasn't such a good idea," remarked Hilary as a photo of sea scallops and angel hair pasta in a delicate cream sauce filled the screen. "This is making me hungry all over again."

I scooped some of Guy Goodwin's beef onto a plate and handed it to her. "Here's a snack."

While Hilary munched I told Jimmy which photos I wanted to use on my blog, and he sent them over to my computer. "Great. Now let's look at the candid photos you took during the cocktail hour."

Jimmy brought up those photos and started clicking through them. Most were group shots of the reporters, milling around with drinks in their hands. Suddenly I held up my hand and motioned for Jimmy to stop at a wide shot of the bar area. Jason sat slouched at the far end, drink in hand. Hilary let out a squeal and pointed. "And look who's coming right at him in the background," she crowed. "The barracuda."

The photo did indeed show a determined-looking Francine, microphone clutched to her breast, headed right toward Jason. "You must have taken this just before Francine had her little set-to with Jason, and he left the bar," I remarked. I pointed at the screen. "There's Brent, the cameraman, just behind Francine. You can see the red light on his camera is on, which means he was filming." I tugged at a stubborn auburn curl. "Let's see, that had to be around six fifteen. It was around six thirty when I went to the restroom and saw him in that alcove."

"Whoa, whoa, back up," chorused Jimmy and Hilary. Jimmy pointed a finger at me. "You've been holding out on us. You saw Jason after he stormed out of the bar?"

I pursed my lips. "I was headed for the restroom when I heard his voice. He was in a secluded alcove, arguing with . . . someone."

"Wow, that sounds like something you should tell Bartell," remarked Hilary. "Whoever he was arguing with might be the killer." She shot me a hard stare and then wagged her finger at me. "You know who he was talking with, don't you?" she said in an accusing tone.

I hesitated, then nodded. "Yes. It was Fiona."

Hilary gasped. "Fiona? Puccini? What's she doing here?"

Jimmy frowned. "Who's Fiona?"

I turned to Jimmy. "Fiona was one of my junior chefs when I worked at the Madison." Then I looked at Hilary and added, "She's here with Jeff. He's representing the Madison in Guy Goodwin's competition. As his fiancée, it's only logical she'd want to accompany him here." I said. "Plus, I'm sure Leonardo encouraged her to."

"Maybe Daddy didn't have to. Fiona could have had a reason to come here all her own," said Hilary. She waved her arm dramatically. "Maybe she wanted to come here because she planned to kill Jason."

"I think you're giving her too much credit," I protested. "I doubt she's that devious. Besides, Jason was a last-minute addition to the program due to Dana Carlyle's accident. They didn't make the announcement until the day of registration. No one knew he'd be here."

"She might have," Hilary said stubbornly. "Who's to say he didn't contact her, told her where he'd be, demanded she come."

I shook my head. "I don't think he'd had contact with her for a while. He told me that he saw Jeff checking in with a good-looking woman. When I told him it was Fiona, he seemed genuinely surprised. He even remarked on how different she looked.”

“So maybe they hadn’t had any physical contact. It doesn’t mean he couldn’t have called her, or texted.” She grabbed a bit of her hair and gave it a tug. “Why are you making excuses for her? I think she’s a darned good suspect.”

“I can’t help thinking that the Fiona I knew could hardly be capable of cold-blooded murder. Besides, she really loves Jeff. She would never do anything to hurt him.”

“I could see where committing a murder might upset her fiancé,” put in Jimmy. “I know it would upset me.”

“You know what they say,” Hilary remarked. “Anyone can commit a murder if they’re pushed hard enough.”

“But was she? It’s hard to know the answer to that without knowing just what it was Jason had on her. Anyway, she’s not the only one with an axe to grind against Jason. I heard him and Damaris Alexander arguing earlier today too, and I’m sure Damaris is the DA in his appointment book.” I paused. “And then there’s Bob Gillette.”

Now Hilary’s eyes popped. “Bob Gillette? Po’Boy Bob? You’re kidding.”

“I wish I were, but according to Nita, Bob nurses a grudge against Jason for voting against them at a sandwich contest. I did hear Bob sort of threaten Jason, and I thought I saw him in the lobby earlier tonight right before I overheard Jason talking to Fiona. Bob would have no reason to be at the hotel tonight unless . . .”

“Unless he came here to confront Jason? You think Po’Boy Bob could have killed Jason over a sandwich contest?” Hilary said. “That’s ridiculous. Bob isn’t the type to commit murder, let alone over something that trivial.”

I shot her an innocent look. “But you just said that anyone could do murder under the right circumstances. What makes Bob different from Fiona?”

Hilary held up her hand, spread her fingers. “Should I count the ways?”

"No," I said on a sigh. I reached up to tug at an errant curl as I added, "I could even be mistaken about seeing Bob there, but I still have to tell Phil everything I saw or thought I saw, about Bob, and about Fiona."

"But not about our little excursion into Jason's second hotel room," put in Jimmy.

"Not unless he asks me directly," I responded. "Which I'm hoping he won't."

"Yeah, you're keeping enough from the poor guy," Hilary mumbled. I shot her a black look, which she ignored.

Jimmy stretched his long legs out in front of him. "Well, if you want my opinion, I'd rule out this Bob person. His motive seems a bit extreme. What we should probably concentrate on is finding out more about just who Jason had in this 'tell-all' book, and these 'dangerous secrets' he was going to expose. If you ask me, that information probably holds the key as to who would have wanted him dead. We need more to go on than just initials in an appointment book."

"Ada said that Jason sold the book on a proposal," I said. "I have no idea how much of the actual book he wrote. Even so, getting a copy of either the outline or the manuscript would be a good starting point," I said. "But I have no idea how we'd ever do that. After he first mentioned his book to me, I checked his social media and his webpage. He makes absolutely no mention whatever of his book. No mention of having a literary agent, or what house is publishing his memoirs. He was serious about wanting to keep it under wraps until he was ready."

"Like I said, control freak," put in Jimmy with a sly smile.

"Or he didn't want to do anything to jeopardize his pending movie deal," I said.

"*Or* he could have been afraid of just what did happen—that someone might come after him," suggested Hilary. "So the million-dollar question becomes, who's on that list and who had the biggest motive to want Jason dead?" Hilary sighed. "My money's still on

Fiona. I bet whatever secret she has is a real doozy."

"I'm not discounting her as a suspect," I said. "I'm just saying there are lots of others to consider as well. Damaris Alexander, for instance. I overheard them arguing earlier. Jason mentioned some sort of deal, and she said she'd rather do business with a rattlesnake."

Jimmy whistled. "Damaris is quite a character. I did one of her book covers. She can be very demanding—and secretive. I've heard stories that make me think she was quite wild in her youth. It wouldn't surprise me if Barclay did manage to unearth a skeleton or two of hers."

"I think her motive probably depends on the skeleton," I said. "She's built up quite an image as a successful down-home Southern cook. Having her past as a wild child come out certainly wouldn't enhance her career, but I doubt it would end it either. It would have to be something really, really serious."

I whipped out my phone, called up the photos I'd taken of the appointment calendar. Jimmy and Hilary crowded around me. "Wow, that's a lot of initials," remarked Hilary. "We probably should be making up a murder board."

Jimmy looked at her. "A what? It sounds . . . gruesome."

"It's basically a list of suspects, with how they relate to the deceased," I answered. "I don't have an easel handy, so we'll have to wing it with this photo." I pointed at one of the date squares. "I'm sure HH stands for Hugh Hudson. He's a former crime-reporter-turned-food-critic, and Rain said that Hugh and Jason worked together for a time. Apparently it didn't go well. I remember Hugh mentioning at the luncheon that Jason wanted to pick his brain about his crime career, and Hugh refused. I also saw Jason give Hugh a couple of 'you should be six feet under' looks."

"Interesting. Do you think that maybe this Hudson fellow did something back when he was a crime reporter that Jason found out about? That he wanted to expose in his book?"

"It's a definite possibility." I tapped at the screen. "Hugh came in late to the banquet. So did Damaris. It was around six thirty when Jason stalked off after talking with Fiona. Hugh arrived around seven fifteen and Damaris close to seven thirty. If the time of death was in that time frame, then either one of them had plenty of time to murder Jason."

"So would Fiona," pointed out Hilary. "Or it could be someone else entirely. It all depends on whether or not what he had on them was serious enough to kill over." She glanced at her watch and said, "Say, it's time for the eleven o'clock news. Shall we see if Francine made the broadcast in time with her tape?"

Jimmy fiddled with the remote and a few seconds later the face of Hal Inwood, the news anchor, filled the screen. "And now, Francine Weston gives us her special report on the tragedy at the National Foodie Convention banquet tonight. Francine."

Francine's face, looking somber and dejected, filled the screen. "I'm reporting on the Foodie Fest convention here in Branson, where just a few hours ago noted food critic Jason Barclay was found brutally murdered."

The screen cut over to Jason, walking back to Francine, drink in hand. Francine's voice blared out, "This could possibly be the last footage taken of Jason Barclay alive. It was taken shortly before his body was discovered by a hotel guest."

Jason turned around to face the screen. "I told you," he said, his words slightly slurred, "that you'll learn about my book when everything is in place, and not a second before. But mark my words, it will be well worth the wait. And that is my final comment on the subject." He started to hold up his hand, no doubt with the uncomplimentary gesture Francine had referred to, but the video cut out abruptly and the next instant Francine's face once again filled the screen. "A sad bit of irony from Jason Barclay, with what might well indeed have been his final comment. Detective Philip Bartell is on the case, so I'm sure his murderer will soon be brought to justice. This is Francine Weston, KPTX News."

"You can be sure she'll be sniffing out this story," said Hilary. "I'm surprised she didn't mention your name, Tif, as the person who discovered the body."

"I probably have Phil to thank for that," I said. I frowned at Inwood's face on the TV screen. "Damn," I murmured. "I wish I could see those last few seconds again."

Hilary practically jumped out of her seat. "You saw something," she cried. "What did you see?"

I pushed the heel of my hand through my hair. "It was only there for a second, but . . ." I grabbed the remote, muted Inwood's voice. "There was a gray-haired man in the background. He was only on-screen for a split second but I recognized him. It's the same man who was at the bar. Rain sat next to him, and she accidentally spilled her drink on him." I looked at Jimmy. "Can I see your photo of the bar again?"

Jimmy called up the photo and handed me his camera. "Ah, there he is." I pointed to a slouchy figure at the other end of the bar from Jason. "You can only see his profile, but that lantern jaw is hard to miss. He had a camera like this one. I thought he was probably a photographer." I handed Jimmy back the camera. "He was lurking around that alcove too, and he was right behind Jason when he left that alcove. I figured he must be following him hoping for a photo op, but . . . it could have been more."

"You think he's the killer?" Hilary squealed. "Maybe he's Sonny!"

"If he really is a photographer, he might have seen something if he was following Jason," put in Jimmy. "He might even have seen the killer." He turned to me. "I could make some inquiries among the girls who were checking everyone in, see if they can tell us something about him."

I shot him a look. "Let me guess. They gave you their phone numbers too?"

"Let's just say I've got a definite rapport with them." He looked at the photo again. "I can blow this up, maybe call a few contacts, see if anyone might know him. "It's a long shot, but I'll give it a try." He shot me an admiring glance. "Mac was right. You've got a definite knack for putting pieces together."

"That only works when you've got enough pieces," I said with a sigh. I rose and stretched. "I think it's time to call it a night. I've still got to write up my blog on the banquet—with a short mention of Jason's passing—for tomorrow's blog and attach those photos and that video you took of the buffet. Dale should love it."

Jimmy rose. "It's not that late. When I get back to my hotel, there are a few people I can contact who might be able to give me a line on our mystery photog."

I shot Hilary a swift glance. "It would be helpful to establish a definite time of death. It's a sure bet Phil isn't going to share that info with me."

"Oh, no." Hilary took a step backward. "I'm not doing it."

"Oh, come on, Hil," I said in a coaxing tone. "You know he's like putty in your hands."

My friend glared at me and crossed her arms over her chest. "I know what you want, and I'm not doing it. There's only so many times I can go to the well on this."

Jimmy shot both of us a puzzled glance. "What are you two talking about?"

Hilary pointed at me. "Tif wants me to use my past relationship with Howard Sample, the assistant district coroner, to wheedle information out of him. I'm not doing it. The last time he pestered me with calls and candy afterward for two weeks before I finally had to let him down gently. And I'm especially not doing it now that Mac and I are officially dating."

"I'm sure Mac would want you to do everything you could to aid in Tiffany's investigation," Jimmy said. "After all, he's helped out a time or two himself, right?"

Hilary sighed and slid me a glance. "I'll think about it. But if you ask me, what we should concentrate on is finding a way to get our hands on a copy of Jason's manuscript. I don't suppose you've got any ideas on that front?"

"Not at the moment," I said, my lips curving into a sly smile. "But I might know someone who does."

Ten

I arrived at *Southern Style*'s offices a few minutes after seven Friday morning. Donna, the receptionist, was just settling in behind the desk when I pushed through the plate glass doors. "Tiffany," she cried, setting down her go cup. Her eyes slid to the clock on the wall. "Wow, you're here really early."

"Yeah, I have a few things I have to take care of before I go over to the conference and I wanted to get an early jump," I said. I'd seen Dale's BMW in the parking lot, so I knew my editor was in. "I'll just go on up," I said, waving my own go cup. "I texted Dale last night and told him I'd be here bright and early."

"Well, you certainly weren't kidding," she said with a chuckle. Cocking her head to one side she added, "Speaking of that foodie convention, I imagine what happened to Jason Barclay must have put a damper on last night's festivities. I saw him on TV a few times. He was a pretty good food critic, but some of those reviews could be really brutal. The guy really enjoyed tearing restaurants apart." When I didn't respond she added, "I saw Francine Weston's report on the news last night. So Jason was writing a book, huh? He sure sounded mysterious about it. It piques your curiosity, you know. Makes you wonder what it could have been about. I don't suppose you have any ideas?"

Thankfully the phone rang just then, forestalling any further conversation. Donna went to answer it and I gave her a cheeky wave and bolted for the bank of elevators. Fortunately one was right there, and I took it straight up to the floor where the administrative offices were located. I alighted and hurried down the empty corridor to Dale's office. His door was slightly ajar and I could see the lights were on. I rapped lightly and gave the door a push. It swung back, revealing Dale seated behind his desk, hunched over his computer. His hair was mussed and his jacket was thrown across the back of a nearby chair, a sure sign he was deep in editor mode. He glanced up and regarded me over the rims of his glasses. "Well, when you said in your text you'd be by early you weren't kidding," he grumbled. "I suppose if I weren't here you'd have shown up at my apartment and dragged me out of bed."

"Be careful what you wish for," I said cheerily, sliding into one of the overstuffed chairs in front of his desk. I set my cup carefully on the edge. "If you read my text, you know I've got a lot to do today before I cover the food truck competition at eleven."

Dale leaned back in his chair and whipped off his glasses. He rubbed at his eyes, put the glasses back on, and looked at me. "I just finished reading your post," he said. "It's great. And that guy— Devane? You were right about the professional touch. Those are top-notch photos and video."

"Thanks. I thought it was pretty good myself. Jimmy had a few ideas on how I might be able to take better photos and video, too. He said something about a camcorder that was inexpensive and easy to operate."

"A camcorder, huh? Well, we can discuss that when I'm more awake." He linked his fingers together. "I liked the understated way you mentioned Barclay. Not much detail, just a brief mention about him and what a loss his death is—although I bet not many people in the food industry would agree with that sentiment."

"I'm sure they wouldn't, but the blog isn't written for them," I said. "Discretion is the better part of valor, right?"

His eyes narrowed. "I know I'm going to regret asking this, but you're not the hotel guest who discovered the body, are you?"

I leaned back in my chair and crossed my legs at the ankles. "Well . . . Technically I was a guest of the Foodie Convention."

"I knew it," he muttered. Then he lifted his hand to stifle a yawn. "Sorry. Didn't get too much sleep. I got here at the crack of dawn today."

I eyed him. "Why so early? My blog post couldn't have needed that much editing."

He shrugged. "I just thought it would be advisable to be present and available today with as few distractions as possible." He paused and then added, "Manchetti called a board meeting for this morning."

I raised an eyebrow. Enzo Manchetti, the owner and chairman of the board of *Southern Style*, rarely came to the office, let alone call board meetings. "He did? That's odd. Is something up?" I asked.

"Dunno, since I'm not a board member, but don't worry. I'm sure the gossip chain will be in full force afterward. When I know, you'll know."

"I take it your desire to come here early means you've already spoken to Marcia?" Marcia Allen, Manchetti's see-all-and-know-all admin, was usually the last employee to leave and the first to arrive, usually getting in the office just as the sun was rising.

"I managed to accidentally run into her as she was getting off the elevator. If she knows anything, she's not saying. The woman's definitely close-mouthed. I don't think even a crack hypnotist could get anything out of her."

"Typical Marcia." I leaned forward, pushed my go cup toward Dale. "I notice that you are severely lacking in the caffeine department. Did you forget to stop for coffee this morning?"

"Actually I did stop but they weren't open yet. That's how early I got here." He inclined his head toward the empty Keurig coffee maker on the table near the window. "And Carrie's been locking up the coffee. Can you believe it, some people have been helping themselves to my stash! And she never gave me the key to the closet, so . . ."

I gave my cup another push. "You can have mine," I offered. "I had a quick cup before I left home anyway. And I haven't touched this one yet."

"Thanks." He reached out, grabbed the cup, lifted the tab and took a long sip. "Aah—that hit the spot," he said, putting the cup down. "I owe you for that."

I scooted forward on my chair so that I was almost sitting on the edge. "I was hoping you'd say that."

Dale's eyes narrowed. "Uh-oh. So the coffee was a bribe? I should have known." He leaned back in the chair and crossed his arms over his chest. "Okay, out with it. What do you want? A raise? An assigned parking spot?"

"Both of those would be nice, but not what I'm after right now. Did you happen to catch Francine Weston's interview with Jason on the news last night?"

"I'm pretty sure most of Branson did." Dale leaned back, steepled his fingers beneath his chin. "I can't imagine Barclay actually writing a book, let alone one possibly under consideration as a movie."

"Oh, he was definitely writing one. A tell-all masterpiece. Apparently he named names and revealed people's deepest, darkest secrets in it."

Dale raised an eyebrow. "And who told you all that? Him? And you believed him?"

"He did and yes, I do believe it." I cleared my throat. "There was a little incident between us back when I was the assistant head chef at the Madison. Long story short, he tried to come onto me, and I turned him down flat. One of my sous chefs had to escort him from the kitchen."

"I see. And he told you he was going to put that in his book?"

"He never said one way or the other, but I'd rather err on the side of caution, if you get my drift."

Dale picked up a pencil, tapped it against the blotter. "I get it. You think Jason might have exaggerated what went on between the two of you, and you don't want to be mentioned. I'm not clear, though, on how I can help with that."

"I've checked social media and his webpage, and Barclay makes absolutely no mention of anything connected to this upcoming book. No editor, publishing house, or even an agent. I think he kept everything under wraps deliberately because . . . because he also knew that some of these secrets he planned to reveal were a bit . . . dangerous."

"Dangerous?" Dale stopped tapping and set the pencil down. He took off his glasses and set them on the desk, another thing he did when something really interested him. "How so?"

"I don't know. I was kind of hoping that maybe you could get in touch with a few of your literary friends and pick their brains, get some details."

Dale rubbed at his eyes. "I doubt any of my friends would know any details about that. And if Jason's book is that explosive, it's very likely the publisher's legal department had everyone concerned sign a non-disclosure agreement."

"I didn't think of that," I admitted. "But maybe they might know who Barclay's agent or publisher was. Surely that information wouldn't be included in an NDA."

"Possibly, but if you're thinking about contacting either the agent or publisher, I doubt either would be in a position to share information about what might or might not be in that book, especially with an outsider."

"One never knows unless one asks," I said primly.

Dale sighed and put his glasses back on. "Okay, Tif. I wouldn't want anything bad to be printed about my star blogger. I'll see if I can find out anything."

"I appreciate it," I said, rising. "If you find out anything, text me. I've got the food truck competition at eleven, and after that, the first round of Last Remaining Chef. Oh, and lest I forget, I've also got an exclusive interview and dinner with Guy Goodwin in between."

His head snapped up. "Guy Goodwin! For real? How on earth did you manage that?"

"Actually, I didn't. We can thank Jimmy Devane. Apparently he and Guy are like this." I held up two fingers pressed close together.

I headed for the door. As I laid my hand on the knob, Dale called after me, "You know, you might want to have a word with Twyla Fay."

I paused. "Twyla Fay? Why?"

"Well, if I'm not mistaken, her niece works for a literary agency in

New York. I understand Darlene is just like her aunt—she loves a good gossip. I'll bet she could find out what you want to know, and more." He made a shooing motion with his hand and turned back to his computer again. "Off with you, now. Some people have work to do."

• • •

Twyla Fay's office at *Southern Style* was a lot like the woman herself—big, bold and full of color. She'd been known to change the color of her office walls nearly as much as she changed those brightly colored caftans she was so fond of wearing. I raised my hand and knocked on her office door. "Twyla? It's Tiffany. Can I speak to you for a few minutes? I need to ask you something."

I heard the sound of scuffling footsteps, a drawer closing. Then, "Come on in."

I opened the office door and fought the urge to shield my eyes. The last time I'd been in Twyla's office, the walls had been a soft periwinkle blue. Now they were a deep violet, almost neon. I averted my gaze and focused on the woman seated behind the massive oak desk. Twyla's bulky frame was encased today in a low-necked caftan of different shades of purple, the most predominant one matching the office walls. I also noted that her chair had been reupholstered to match said walls. I also noted, with some amusement, that she'd added a purple streak to her Lucille Ball red hair. Her thick lips parted in a wide smile and she waved her hand impatiently.

"Well, don't just stand there," she said. "Come on in and have a seat."

She nodded toward two chairs in front of her desk. They had also been reupholstered, but to a slightly lighter shade of purple than the walls and Twyla's captain chair. "Like my new color scheme?" she asked as I sat down. "I heard that purple is going to be the next up-and-coming fashion color and I wanted to be the first around here to set the tone."

I placed my purse on the other chair and scooted to the edge of mine. "That you have," I remarked. "It's . . . very nice."

Twyla threw her head back and laughed. "Oh, you can tell me if you think it's too much. So far everyone who's been in here has had something to say about it." She waggled her heavily penciled eyebrows. "But ask me if I care."

I knew Twyla's late husband had left her extremely well off. She didn't need to work, but she stayed at *Southern Style* because she loved what she did—and also because she enjoyed her role as head gossip maven. Twyla pretty much did what she wanted, and knowing her penchant for change, I had no doubt the walls would revert to some other color within the next few weeks. I smiled at her. "I'm sure you don't."

"Good. Now that's out of the way . . . you said you want to ask me something?"

"Yes." I hesitated, not quite sure how to broach what I wanted to know. "I suppose you've heard about Jason Barclay."

Twyla clucked her tongue. "Who hasn't? What a horrible way to end a banquet. I was never a fan, but to die like that . . ." She cocked her head at me. "They said he was found by a hotel guest. It was you, wasn't it?"

I sighed. "Unfortunately, yes."

More tongue clucking. "Pardon my saying so, but you do seem to be making a habit out of finding dead bodies. That's not a particularly attractive aspect in a young single woman—although Philip Bartell might disagree." She shot me a sly look. "He might find that quality irresistible."

I ignored her and asked, "Did you happen to catch Francine's interview with Jason on the eleven o'clock news last night?"

She let out a grunt. "I try not to catch anything of Francine's, but I did see that interview. All three seconds of it."

"He certainly was defensive about that book he's writing," I ventured.

Twyla lifted her hand and waved it in the air, causing the stack of bangle bracelets on her wrist to jangle. "That book of his is old news, at least to me. My niece, Darlene, works for a literary agency in New York. She's a junior agent there, and she told me about it months ago."

"No kidding!" I tried to keep my voice calm as I continued, "Does her agency represent him?"

"No, her agency deals primarily in fiction, mostly children's. But she knows another junior agent at the agency who does." Twyla leaned forward in her chair, her expression one similar to the cat who ate the canary. "The agent told Darlene that book was shrouded in secrecy. Apparently Jason sold it on the strength of an outline and the first three chapters. The agent showed it to some guy who produces movies for one of the big cable channels, and he was pretty hot to acquire the rights. Anyway, the editor at the publishing house who bought it has been pestering Barclay's agent for months. He had a deadline for delivering the finished product and he didn't meet it. He'd asked for an extension, which is almost up. The editor was getting nervous, wondering if there was ever going to be a finished version."

My face fell. "So neither the editor or his agent had access to the entire manuscript?"

Twyla shook her head. "Not that I know of. However . . ." She twirled her hand in the air. "There was a light at the end of the tunnel. Jason contacted his agent yesterday and said he'd deliver the finished product this coming Monday. Of course, now that won't be possible but . . . who knows?"

"What if the manuscript is found? Would they still publish the book?"

Twyla held up a hand to inspect her perfectly manicured nails, also painted a vivid purple. "Oh, they'd publish it all right. All the royalties would just revert to his estate. I think he's got a sister in Duluth somewhere who'd be thrilled to get her hands on that money, if Barclay left it to her. They weren't close, so who knows? Maybe he left it to a charity, although that's pretty hard to believe too. Jason wasn't exactly the charitable type."

"What would happen to the movie deal, I wonder?"

"I'm sure the agent would push that through somehow." Twyla shrugged. "It's a moot point, though, unless the manuscript is found. Personally, my best guess would be it's on his computer, which I'm sure Bartell has impounded by now."

"I'm sure he has," I murmured. I crossed my legs at the ankles and leaned forward, putting my elbows on the edge of Twyla's desk. "I don't suppose your niece happens to know who Barclay's agent and editor are?"

"Aha!" She pointed a finger at me. "You are playing detective again!"

"Maybe," I responded. "Jason told me a bit about his book. He said he was revealing people's secrets, and some of them might be considered dangerous. I can't help but think that could be the reason he was murdered."

Twyla let out a snort. "Dangerous, huh? Are we talking jealous husband or lover dangerous?"

"Possibly, but I got the sense it was more than just that."

"Hmm." Twyla reached up to fiddle with her necklace, a gold chain with—yes, you guessed it—a purple stone dangling from it. "From what I know about Jason, he was the type who'd dig deep for dirt. And depending on how deep the dirt is, well, there could be a pretty long list of people who might have wanted him dead."

I could just tell Twyla was chomping at the bit to share whatever it was she knew, so I leaned forward and said conspiratorially, "Anyone in particular come to mind?"

Her lips curved in a feline smile and she leaned across the desk. "Well, since you asked . . . there were rumors that he and that Southern cookbook author, Dimity something, once had a torrid affair, and during one of their pillow talk sessions she confessed to committing some sort of crime back in her misspent youth."

I gasped. "Are you sure the name was Dimity? Could it have been Damaris?"

Twyla snapped her fingers. "Damaris, yes, that's the name. I knew it was something weird. And then there was a young girl in New York. Supposedly he had some revealing, ah, shall we say, photographs. The kind your parents would disown you over. He was threatening to sell them to some men's magazine."

"New York, you say?" My mind flew immediately to Fiona. She'd accused Jason of ruining people's lives. Could those photos be of her?

"There are so many rumors about Jason I couldn't even begin to list them all. The darned book would be bigger than *War and Peace*," Twyla said with a sigh. She held up her hand and started to tick off on her fingers. "Supposedly he had an affair with a Mafia princess that ended badly, a top executive's wife he had a long affair with, a soap opera star that he broke up with so callously it supposedly drove her to an overdose . . . that's just the tip of the iceberg. There were lots of men, too."

I felt my jaw drop. "Are you saying Jason was bi?"

"Oh, Lord, no, no, no." Twyla shook her head and waved her hands back and forth. "He was definitely heterosexual but he was a master at ferreting out secrets about the men he knew as well as the women he romanced. There were so many. I recall hearing something about a reporter he worked with who'd been dabbling in insider trading, a prominent New York lawyer who took several bribes, not to mention all the chefs and restaurateurs he'd pissed off over the years . . . and that list would include your old boss, Leonardo Puccini, by the way. He's gotten lots of chefs and restaurants blacklisted. You'd need a giant scorecard to list them all." She paused. "And I bet none of them would be happy about seeing their secrets revealed in one of those streaming movies, either."

"But not all of them made his cut, I'm sure," I said. "Or were at the Branson Towers yesterday."

"That's a fact. It might not even be anyone he mentioned in this book of his. Trust me, he had plenty of enemies. I guess it all depends on what one would consider a dangerous secret. And I don't know as

I'd put too much stock in what he told you. Jason liked to exaggerate." She paused. "Except about that movie deal. That was on the level."

I didn't say it out loud, but I had the feeling that in this instance, Jason hadn't stretched the truth. I removed my elbows from Twyla's desk and rose. "Thanks for the info, Twyla. And if you could text me those names, I'd appreciate it. Right now I've got to get down to the police station and finish giving my statement from last night."

"I'll give Darlene a call." She reached out suddenly and touched my arm. "Can I give you a bit of advice? If I were you I'd watch out for Francine Weston. It looks to me like she's on this story, and she's going to be like a Rottweiler with a bone, more so than usual. She might try to get in your way."

I chuckled. "I didn't think it was possible for Francine to be more annoying than she already is."

"Well—she's got a reason." Twyla withdrew her hand, drummed her fingers on the desktop and hesitated for a few seconds before she added, "I've heard from several dependable sources that old Joe Bateman is thinking of putting KPTX up for sale. Apparently he purchased some beachfront property in Hawaii, and he's chomping at the bit to retire there and live the good life. It's common knowledge Francine has only kept her job because Joe has a thing for those postage-stamp-sized skirts she wears. If the station gets sold, well . . . she could be out on that shapely derriere of hers."

"I see. So you're thinking she feels the need to prove her worth?"

"Exactly. She's looking for a big scoop to make her mark. And if she thinks you're on to something she might attach herself to you, and mark my words, that woman is trouble with a capital T."

"Thanks, Twyla, but I can handle Francine," I said. I walked over to the door, paused with my hand on the doorknob as a thought occurred to me. "If that sale rumor is true, I don't suppose you have any insights into who might be interested in buying the TV station?"

That catlike smile again. "There is a board meeting today, but you knew that, didn't you? Manchetti's been toying with the idea of expanding for months now. When you stop to think about it, it makes perfect sense." Her hand flapped in a shooing motion. "Ta for now, dear. You run along to the police station and your hunky Detective Bartell. No worries. I'll be in touch about the rest."

Eleven

As I drove to the police station, I mentally reviewed my conversation with Twyla, particularly the last part. I'd also heard from several people at the magazine over the past few months that Manchetti was toying with a possible expansion. He'd originally put his son in charge of it, but plans had come to a standstill once Roberto had gone to prison. Was it possible Manchetti had revived his expansion plan and was seriously considering buying the TV station? I thought about the board meeting today and decided it could be a distinct possibility. If that happened, what would it mean for my blog? Would they still keep it on?

"Maybe they'd reassign me to do something else," I mused. "Maybe I'd end up with Hilary on Features. Or maybe . . . Good Lord," I muttered as I shut off the engine. "Maybe they'd stick me working with Francine—unless they terminate her." I sighed. "I probably wouldn't be that lucky."

I pushed that thought from my mind, exited my car, hurried up the short flight of stone steps and pushed through the double plate-glass doors and into the main lobby of the police station. I took a quick look around. It certainly seemed as if the station were hopping, and it was only a few minutes after nine thirty on a Friday morning. A policeman stood in one corner, taking down a report from a young girl in jeans and a too-tight sweater. Off to my left another officer was speaking to an elderly woman who kept dabbing at her eyes with a Kleenex. As I passed them I heard the officer say, "So he's got a white spot underneath his chin? And two white forepaws?"

I didn't wait to hear if they were talking about a cat or a dog but made my way straight to the wide reception desk. A bored-looking woman wearing a starched denim shirt, her long hair done in a braid slung over one shoulder, was frowning at the computer screen in front of her. She glanced up, eyed me warily as I approached.

I noticed a name tag pinned to her shoulder that read *Officer K. Olsen.* "Good morning, Officer Olsen," I said, flashing her a bright smile. "I'm here to see Detective Philip Bartell."

Her eyes narrowed. Apparently she wasn't buying my attempt at being buddy-buddy. "Do you have an appointment?"

"No, but he asked me to come by this morning to give my statement about what took place last night at the Branson Towers."

Her eyebrows rose. "Just one moment."

She picked up the phone, pressed a few buttons, then turned her face away and spoke softly into the phone. After a few moments she replaced the receiver and turned back to me. "It'll be just a few minutes," she said.

I nodded and moved over toward the bank of chairs opposite the desk. I'd no sooner seated myself than a door off to the left opened, and Brandon Hoffman came out. He looked around, and Officer Olsen pointed to where I was sitting. Brandon nodded and walked over to me. His lips tipped up in a smile. "Good morning, Tiffany," he said.

"Good morning, Brandon," I said. "I'm waiting for Detective Bartell. He wanted me to come in to give a formal statement about last night."

"I know. Unfortunately he's occupied at the moment, so I'm going to take your statement." He made a sweeping gesture with his arm. "If you'll come with me?"

I rose and fell into step beside Brandon. "So Phil's busy, huh?" I said. Briefly I wondered if he was still a little bit annoyed with me. "What is he, hiding from me? Or is he interrogating a suspect?" I remarked with a chuckle.

Brandon shot me a serious look. "I can't comment on that," he said.

I stopped walking so Brandon stopped as well. I stared at him. "He's interrogating a suspect? In Barclay's murder? So quickly?"

Brandon made another motion with his arm. "As I said, I can't comment on that. Now, if you'll just step this way . . ."

I fell into step beside him once again, but my thoughts were in a whirl. Phil had homed in on someone pretty fast. Was it Fiona? Or possibly Damaris? Or was it someone else entirely? And if so . . . who?

• • •

Twenty minutes later I finished giving my formal statement to Brandon. I'd reiterated what I'd told Phil last night, about seeing the flash of red and hearing the footsteps, but I'd left out some of the more salient details that I'd been going to share . . . mainly, the conversation between Jason and Fiona, and seeing (or thought I saw) Bob Gillette lurking around, and my finding of the hotel room key. I probably could have told Brandon, but I wanted to tell Phil all this directly so I could watch him clench his teeth and see his face turn beet-red.

Call me crazy, but I had to take my fun where I could get it.

Brandon escorted me back out to the waiting area. "I'll have this typed up for your signature right away," he said. "It shouldn't take more than fifteen or twenty minutes."

I looked at my watch. It was just ten a.m., so I would still have plenty of time to get to the convention center and meet Jimmy before the food truck competition began. As if he were reading my mind, Brandon said, "I know you've got to get to the convention center. No worries, you'll be out of here in plenty of time."

Brandon disappeared into the back room and I settled in one of the chairs to wait. I pulled out my phone and texted Jimmy. *At police station. Should be at center before eleven.*

Less than a minute later Jimmy texted back. *OK. I'm at the center now. BTW Bartell texted me early this morning, said he wanted me to forward him any photos I might have taken.*

Next I texted Hilary. *Hey. Given any more thought to what we discussed last night?*

Five minutes later I got a response: *Don't push it.*

I chuckled. A response like that undoubtedly meant my chum was leaning toward giving in and making a call to Sample. At least I hoped that was what it meant.

Another text from Hilary: *Things are hopping around here. Board had a big meeting today. U know anything about it?*

I texted back: *Manchetti called meeting. We'll talk later after you have a chat with Sample.*

Hilary: *U know, sometimes I really hate U.* Followed by several images of grumpy emojis and a few unladylike hand gestures.

I grinned. From that response, I was fairly certain Hilary was pretty darn close to contacting Sample. I started to text back when a shadow fell across my chair. I looked up and saw Brandon holding a sheet of paper. "All set," he said with a smile. "You just need to sign this, and you can be on your way."

He pulled a pen out of his jacket pocket and I signed the statement. Brandon folded it in half and tucked it into his pocket. "Thanks for coming in, Tiffany," he said. "I'm sure Detective Bartell will be in touch if he needs anything else."

"I'd still like to speak with him," I said. "Please tell him I'll try and get in touch with him later."

Brandon frowned. "Is it something else connected with the case? If so, maybe I could be of assistance?"

"Thanks, but what I need to speak to Detective Bartell about is rather . . . personal," I said. Technically I wasn't lying. Phil took my amateur detective status as deeply personal, and confessing what I'd done in that area so far was going to qualify as a doozy.

Brandon, who was well aware that Phil and I had dated a few times, probably figured what I wanted to talk to him about was relationship-related, and I saw his cheeks flush a delicate shade of pink. "Sure. I'll tell him." He mumbled and then moved off. I gathered up my purse. As I turned to leave, I saw Brandon open the door that led to the inner offices. Phil stood just inside the door talking to a man. I sucked in a breath. I knew that man.

It was Bob Gillette.

•••

My thoughts whirled as I drove to the convention center. What was Bob doing there? Was he the person Phil had been interrogating? The thought occurred to me that could have been the reason he'd asked to see Jimmy's photos. He wanted to see if Bob was in any of them, which thankfully he was not.

But how had he known to interrogate Bob?

I pulled into the convention center parking lot and saw the KPTX truck parked off to one side. "Don't tell me Francine is here," I muttered as I slid into a spot under a shady elm. Apparently Twyla had been right about her smelling a story. And then a lightbulb went off in my head.

The argument I'd overheard between Bob and Jason the other day. Francine had been there, watching it. If Phil had approached her about the Jason video, and I was pretty sure he had, did she say something about that to Phil? I set my lips. Of course she had. How better to sniff out a good story than to ingratiate herself with the investigating officer by giving him a lead on a potential suspect? Phil had surely found Jason's appointment book when he and Brandon went through the room at the Cardinal Inn. He'd have seen the initials BG in it, and if Francine had told him about the argument she'd witnessed between Bob and Jason, he'd have wanted to bring Bob in for questioning. Which made sense, because once the altercation was brought to his attention, he'd have been bound to check it out. But was he seriously considering Bob as a suspect?

There was one person, other than Phil and Bob, who would know the answer to that.

I pulled out my phone and sent Nita a quick text. *Hey! Was just down at police station. Thought I saw Bob there?*

I waited a few minutes but no answering text appeared. I hadn't gotten a message that there had been a problem sending, so I just had to assume Nita was probably busy right now getting ready for the lunch crowd and couldn't answer immediately. I slid my phone back into my jacket pocket, locked my car, and headed for the back parking lot, where the food truck competition was scheduled to start. I'd been told that a record number of trucks had entered the competition, and as I approached I could see that had been no exaggeration. There had to be at least twenty trucks lined up in their respective numbered spaces. There was a table set up opposite slot number one with two bright-eyed volunteers, a blue-eyed blonde and an olive-skinned brunette, sitting behind it. I went over and they handed me a sheet of paper that listed all the trucks, where they were from and their specialties. "They should be starting to give out samples soon," said the brunette. "Enjoy."

I walked down the line, taking in all the contestants. There were a few local food trucks I recognized: Min-Hah's Noodles and Burgers on Wheels, both owned by local Bransonites. I'd eaten at both trucks and their food was excellent. Some of the other trucks were from other towns in Georgia, and there were about ten others from out of state. The trucks offered a wide variety of food, from burgers and hot dogs to pizza to different kinds of ethnic foods. I remembered our invitation to join Guy Goodwin before Last Remaining Chef began and figured that I'd better watch my food intake. After all, how often did one get to eat a Guy Goodwin meal!

I looked around but didn't see any sign of Jimmy. I pulled out my phone and checked, but I hadn't received any texts from him or Nita. I sent Jimmy a quick one: *I'm here. Where R U?* and slid my phone back into my pocket. I decided that while I was waiting for him I'd check out slot number one, which was occupied by a truck called Everything but the Kitchen Sink. The name turned out to be appropriate—the truck, owned by the Pappas brothers, served everything from hot dogs and burgers, to steak sandwiches, to falafel, gyros, moussaka, Greek salads and more. The smells were irresistible, and my stomach let out a loud growl. Well, after all, I was here to report on the food, right? I'd just pace myself.

I'd just taken a bite out of the lamb gyro I'd ordered—the pita was fresh, the lamb beautifully seared, and there was just the right amount of tzatziki (some places smothered the gyro in sauce, so you could barely taste the lamb)—when I saw a familiar figure a few trucks ahead of me. Two, in fact. Fiona and Jeff.

I paused, mid-bite, and sauntered over to the side of the Kitchen Sink truck. They were standing beside a truck entitled Holy Smoke BBQ but it didn't look as if they were about to sample their goods. Judging from their body language, it looked to me as if they hadn't patched up their argument of last night. Jeff's shoulders were slouched, and the expression on his face appeared strained. Fiona kept dabbing at her eyes as if she were fending off tears, and for all I knew she might have been. I shoveled another bite of gyro into my mouth and moved cautiously forward, keeping my face averted. The two of them were so intent on their conversation that, thankfully, I didn't think they noticed me as I moved over to Noodle Heaven, a Chinese food truck that was parked two down from the BBQ truck. I stood beside the truck, keeping in the shadows. From this spot I could hear every word they said, because they weren't exactly whispering.

"I don't understand why you can't tell me," Jeff was saying. "We're engaged to be married, Fee. We shouldn't have any secrets from each other."

Fiona averted her face. "I have no secrets from you, Jeff. I told you that," she said.

"I want to believe you, Fee," said Jeff. "Darling, if there's something I should know, now would be the time to tell me!"

"I told you," she practically shouted at him. "If you don't trust me—well, I don't know what else I can say!"

And then Fiona turned on her heel and stalked off—thankfully, in the other direction from where I was standing. Jeff stood looking after her retreating form, a confused look on his face. I was pretty sure the secret Fiona was keeping from Jeff was her relationship with Barclay. Was that because she was the girl Twyla had mentioned, the one who was in some embarrassing photographs? As I pondered this I felt my phone vibrate with an incoming call. I whipped the phone out and looked at the screen.

Darlene Rogers. That had to be Twyla's niece! Heart thudding in my chest, I hit the accept icon.

Twelve

"Ms. Austin? This is Darlene Rogers, Twyla Thorpe's niece," said a pleasant, well-modulated voice. "She said that you wanted to speak with me?"

"Yes, and thank you so much for calling me so quickly," I said.

"Well, when Aunt Twyla asks for a favor, I've always found it best to comply quickly," Darlene said with a laugh. "I'm afraid she wasn't too specific with me about just what it is you want. She just said you needed to pick my brain about a book. I'm unclear as to whether you're writing one and need guidelines, or if there's a particular book that we've represented that you need info on."

Apparently Twyla had left out some salient details when she'd spoken with her niece. "It's a particular book," I said. "But it's not represented by your agency."

I could hear the puzzlement in her tone. "I'm sorry—I don't follow."

"I understand that you are acquainted with someone at the agency who does—or rather, did—represent Jason Barclay."

"Oh." The voice that had sounded so friendly moments ago now took on a guarded tone. There were a few moments of silence, and then Darlene said, "I'm not sure I can be of much help to you. My friend didn't tell me a lot of details. To be honest, she doesn't know all that much. No one talks much about that book."

"I don't need to know details," I said quickly. "I just wanted some basic information."

Another few seconds of silence and then, "How basic?"

"The name of Jason's agent, and the name of the publisher and editor who bought his book."

Darlene let out a nervous laugh. "That's pretty basic, all right," she said. Another pause and then, "Aunt Twyla said you were a very discreet person. I can tell you that everyone connected with that book is very sensitive about it. I think the guy swore them all to secrecy.

You would think state secrets were revealed in it or something."

"I spoke with Jason Barclay about his book before he . . . died," I said. "He told me that he intended to reveal people's secrets in it, and he hinted that some of those secrets might be dangerous. I believe that's why he was killed."

"I saw something about his death on the news," Darlene said. "What you just told me, well, that probably explains why everyone at Trilby's agency is so paranoid about the book. Can I ask why you want this information?"

"I'm the one who discovered Jason's body," I said. "And I think that an old . . . that someone I know could be a suspect in his murder. I tried getting this information on my own but you're correct, Jason was secretive about it. I couldn't find a thing online about his having a literary agent or a publisher."

"It's like I said . . . this project is guarded, like it was going to cause Armageddon or something. Barclay was fanatical about it."

"I thought that might possibly be because he was also in negotiations for a movie deal," I ventured.

"Yeah, that's true." I heard tapping sounds. "Those secrets must really be something. But I don't know how much those people would be able to help you. As far as I know, they don't have the manuscript, they just have the outline and first three chapters. Jason was supposed to deliver the completed manuscript next week but . . ."

"That ended with his death," I finished. "To be honest, I don't know how much help they might be either, but it's possible that something Jason may have said to one of them could provide a clue to his killer—or possibly to what he might have done with the manuscript."

"Well, from what I've heard they'd kill the fatted calf for anyone who could hand over that book. And Aunt Twyla did mention that you were some sort of amateur detective," said Darlene. "I know she'd want me to help any way I could. It's just . . . well, it's just that if anyone should find out who gave you this information . . . well, not only me, but the girl who confided in me would get in a heap of trouble. I don't think I'd lose my job, but I bet they'd fire her in a nanosecond, and she's a good friend. I don't want that on my conscience."

"Don't worry," I said. "I would never reveal the name of my source. Wild horses, ancient Egyptian water torture, getting burned at the stake . . . they'd never get your name out of me. And if by some miracle I did find that manuscript—well, who knows. Your friend might end up with a promotion—you too."

A low chuckle and then: "I have to say you're pretty convincing. Okay then. His agent was Monica Freers at the Pen and Ink Agency on Eighteenth Street here in New York. The book was sold to a relatively small press that specializes in biographies, Shady Elm Press out of Chicago. The editor there is Allison Dugan." A pause. "And you didn't hear any of this from me."

"Any of what?" I said. "Thank you, Darlene. Rest assured, no one will ever know how I found out."

"Thanks, I appreciate that. And good luck. I hope you do find that manuscript."

Darlene hung up, and I did a quick search on the Pen and Ink Agency and Shady Elm Press. I'd just finished entering the phone numbers into my contact list when I heard a familiar voice behind me. "There you are! I've been looking all over for you. What are you doing, hiding behind this food truck?"

I smiled at Jimmy as I slid my phone back into my pocket. "I had a pretty productive morning. I found out who Jason's agent and publisher are."

He let out a low whistle. "Boy, you work fast! How did you do that?"

I put a finger to my lips, made a motion of locking them and throwing away the key. "Sorry. A good reporter never reveals their source."

He grinned. "I can respect that. So, can you tell me who the agent and publisher are? Maybe I know them."

"His agent is Monica Freers at the Pen and Ink Agency. She sold the book to a small press out of Chicago, Shady Elm Press."

"Never heard of Monica Freers, but I have heard of Shady Elm. They're a very reputable publisher. They specialize in biographies, but they do other types of nonfiction books as well. They publish lots of cookbooks. As a matter of fact, I do believe one of our suspects has had several of her cookbooks published there."

I stared at him. "Damaris Alexander?" At his nod, I let out a low whistle. "Talk about a coincidence—or is it?"

"You think Damaris could have had something to do with Shady Elm publishing Barclay's book?"

I struggled to recall the conversation I'd overheard between them. "Damaris mentioned making some sort of deal. Maybe she was talking about his publishing contract. She's sold a kajillion cookbooks, so she must be a big moneymaker for that publishing house. Maybe she's got influence there, and she used it to help Jason get published."

"Why would she do that? They're not exactly best buds."

"It might have been in exchange for something," I ventured. "She gets Jason's book accepted, and he doesn't reveal any secrets she might have revealed to him. But maybe—"

"Barclay changed his mind," Jimmy finished my sentence. "He tells her he's going to put it in the book anyway, because it will help it become a bestseller!"

"Then he tells her he won't do it unless she does something else for him, and she tells him she's done making deals."

"Because she's decided to do away with him!" Jimmy said in a stage whisper, waggling his eyebrows dramatically. "Wow, well, if that's what went down, all I can say is . . . that must be one heckuva secret."

I slanted him a glance. "I don't suppose you had any luck finding out any info on our mysterious gray-haired man from the volunteers."

"Nope. I spoke to a half dozen girls, showed them that photo, but it didn't ring any bells. Kind of makes you wonder just how the guy got in here."

Further conversation on the subject was halted as people started teeming over to the food truck area to sample their goodies, and Jimmy and I spent the next hour and a half doing the same, and taking photos and videos. Neither of us wanted to stuff ourselves before our dinner meeting with Guy Goodwin, so we ended up splitting the food samples between us. I was enthusiastic about everything I'd tasted at Everything But the Kitchen Sink, and we spent a good bit of time chatting up the chefs and taking photos and videos. We also spent time at the Holy Smoke BBQ truck, where I deemed their pulled pork BBQ sandwich the best I'd had in a long time. Ditto the drunken noodles and eggplant at Thai-licious, one of the Thai food trucks in the competition.

The judges showed up at one o'clock, and we dogged their steps for the last hour. I spotted an old acquaintance. Giovanni "call me John" Ferrante was one of the judges, and he tossed me a cheery wave as he ambled from truck to truck with the other two judges, both noted food critics from Las Vegas. At this competition the public was also allowed to vote for their favorites, and their votes would be combined with the judges' scores to determine the winner. I would definitely have voted for both the Kitchen Sink and Thai-licious, but as members of the press, neither Jimmy nor I was allowed to vote. Tons of people were filling out the ballots and stuffing them in the ballot boxes placed throughout the lot, and from snatches of conversation I'd overheard, it sounded as if most people shared my sentiments about the top two. I had the feeling it was going to be a close race.

At two o'clock, when the competition ended, I left Jimmy to do some follow-up video and moved over to a quiet corner to call the Pen and Ink Agency. I asked to speak to Monica Freers and was told that she was away on vacation and not due back for two weeks. I left a message on her voicemail and then hung up. I couldn't help but wonder, though, if Jason's untimely death had anything to do with this "vacation." It seemed odd, considering that Jason had been supposed to deliver the manuscript on Monday. I had an idea this so-called vacation was her way of avoiding the press, and the inevitable questions surrounding Jason's book.

Next I called Shady Elm Press and asked to speak to Allison Dugan. I fully expected to get another voicemail, so when the Muzak cut off and I heard a soft voice with a trace of what I thought might be a British accent say, "Allison Dugan," I was so startled that for a moment I didn't know what to say. "This is Allison Dugan," she said again, and this time there was no mistaking the impatience in her tone. "Is anyone there?"

"Yes, hello, I'm sorry. It seems we've got a bit of a bad connection," I lied.

Allison seemed a bit less annoyed. "A bad connection, you say? Perhaps you should try this call again."

"No, no," I said quickly. "It seems to have cleared up. I can hear you fine now."

"Good. Well, then, I've a pretty busy day, so if you'll just tell me who you are and what you want, we can get right to it."

I said the first name that popped into my head. "My name is Crystal Worthington. I'm a reporter for *Southern Style* magazine here in Georgia. I'm writing an article on selling nonfiction and I was referred to you by several people in the literary industry as an expert in the field. I was hoping you could give me a few moments of your time, answer a few questions?"

"That's very flattering." I heard the tone in Allison's voice change from guarded to almost preening. "Just what is it you wanted to know?"

I decided to dive right in. "Can one get a contract on a book that's not yet completed?"

She laughed. "Of course. That's very common, actually, particularly with the biographies we deal with. Nonfiction in general is easier to sell than fiction in that regard. Usually fiction requires the full manuscript, unless you are an established author, say, like a Stephen King. Nonfiction usually requires no more than a basic outline, perhaps a chapter or two, and a marketing plan."

"A marketing plan?"

"Oh, yes. It's all about the platform."

"Platform? I'm sorry, but I'm not familiar with that term."

There followed a long, drawn-out sigh and then Allison said in a tone I expected she reserved for mentally challenged persons, "It's all about the author, and his or her credentials. Their fame, their savvy with social media. Do they Facebook? Tweet? Insta? What's their topic? How hot is it? How likely is it to sell, garner attention?" She gave a throaty chuckle. "I don't mind telling you the juicier the topic, the better."

"That's very interesting," I said. "I don't know if you've heard, but we've had an incident here in Branson recently concerning a media figure who was supposed to be writing his autobiography. Jason Barclay."

The sharp intake of breath was impossible to miss. "Yes," she said, and just like that her tone changed from amenable to detached and crisp. "I've heard."

"I actually spoke with Mr. Barclay shortly before he died," I rushed on. "He alluded to the fact that this book of his was going to be one of those hot, hot items you were just speaking about. In fact, he hinted that it was going to be more of a tell-all type of book than an autobiography."

"Did he now?" Her tone sharpened even more. "Just what exactly did Jason tell you about his book? I can't imagine it was too much, since he swore practically everyone connected with it to secrecy."

"That's very true. He didn't say much at all, but he did hint that a lot of people would be very surprised by its contents. He was very circumspect about who his agent and publisher were. It was sheer luck I found you. I did a search on publishing houses that specialized in biographies, and Shady Elm popped up." I crossed my fingers, hoping she'd buy that explanation.

"O-kay," she said after a long pause. "But if Jason didn't give you my name, how did you know that I'm his editor—or rather, that I was."

That was my opening, and I grabbed it. "Call it Lady Luck again," I said. "I know Damaris Alexander has had several of her cookbooks published at Shady Elm, and I saw your name on one of the dedication pages. So, I thought perhaps she might have steered Jason your way." I crossed my fingers. I had no idea if Damaris had mentioned Allison in her dedications or not, but I guessed I'd soon find out.

"Ah, good old Damaris. Yes, I used to be her editor. As if thanking me in glowing terms could make up for all the drama that would ensue with each book. It was a godsend when they moved me over to doing biographies exclusively, and now someone else has the dubious honor of working with her. That woman is a piece of work." A sharp intake of breath and then she continued, "Damaris recommended he have his agent contact me, and she gave him a good reference. For the first time in years, I actually felt like sending her a thank-you card. That book— well, let's just say it would have made my career. And now I have no idea what's going to happen."

"So you're not going to publish the book now he's deceased?"

"Oh, we'd love to publish it. We don't have it, and we have no idea where it might be. Jason was extremely secretive about its location. I'd ask him for more chapters and he'd put me off, telling me that it would be best to read the manuscript in its entirety. The closer we got to the anticipated publication date, the more I worried, and I left him a voicemail every day asking for something . . . anything, no exaggeration, which of course he summarily ignored. Then, magically, he called me late Wednesday night and informed me that he'd made a decision about the chapter that was holding him up, and he'd deliver the finished product Monday. A few hours later, I heard on the news that he was dead." She sighed. "I have no idea what's going to happen now. I put a call in to the law enforcement in Branson, asking if they should find the manuscript if it could possibly be emailed to me. The detective I spoke with said that they had Jason's laptop but the manuscript wasn't on it. He also said that if and when it was found, the manuscript would be construed as evidence. I wouldn't be permitted to have it until Jason's murderer is caught and the case closed." Another sigh. "So basically, I'm screwed."

"And the movie deal that was in the works? What would happen to that?"

"Damien Kazmir—the interested producer—wants to buy the outline, worst-case scenario. His writers could take that and make a script from it. I believe his agent is still negotiating, though." Her tone sharpened. "How did you hear about that movie deal?"

"A local reporter got wind of it, and asked Jason about it on an interview," I said quickly. "He refused to comment. You know, there could be something in that outline that could help the police investigation, help them solve Jason's murder more quickly."

"I doubt it would be of any help. It wasn't written in great detail, although he did list some specific people. I'm sure those names were altered though. I mean—Thor? Sonny? Hansel? They can't possibly be real names." Another short pause and then, "We've gotten way off track. What did you say your name was again? Kristie something?"

Oops, time to go. "I'm sorry, Ms. Dugan, but I just remembered an important meeting I have to get to. Thanks so much for your time."

"Hey, wait a—"

I hung up midway through Allison's sentence, hoping that she wouldn't remember Crystal's name or *Southern Style*. Although, if she did and called the magazine, Crystal would most likely tell her she was nuts and hang up—I hoped.

The call hadn't been a total bust, though. I'd learned a few important things. One, that someone named Sonny had been mentioned in the outline. I was willing to bet it was the same Sonny who'd been in the appointment book. So now the question became, was Sonny the person's real name or a code name? And if it were the latter, who might it be for? One of the current suspects, or someone else entirely?

Thinking about that possibility made my head hurt so I turned my thoughts to the other thing I'd learned, that Damaris Alexander had been responsible for hooking Jason up with the publisher. I tapped my phone against my chin. Perhaps my next move should be to talk to Damaris, see what, if anything, I could get out of her. I thought she was giving a talk this afternoon and I started to pull the schedule out of my tote when my phone beeped with an incoming text. It was from Jimmy: *Getting ready to announce the food truck winner. Get your buns over here.*

I slid my phone into my pocket, and as I turned to head back to the main area, I caught sight of none other than Damaris Alexander herself, standing beside a tree a few yards away from where the food trucks were gathering. But she wasn't alone.

She was deep in conversation with another woman—Fiona.

Thirteen

For a moment I stood uncertainly, torn between heading over to the judging area or boldly walking over to confront both Damaris and Fiona. The decision was made for me when Fiona suddenly threw her hands up, turned, and walked swiftly away. Damaris stood looking after her for a moment, then shrugged, whirled on her high heels, and headed in the opposite direction, into the crowd that was surging toward the judging area, all of them no doubt eager to hear who had won the trophy and the five-thousand-dollar prize. My thoughts were whirling—what on earth could that encounter have been about?

My phone pinged with another text from Jimmy: *Hurry up. It's starting!!!!!!!* Reluctantly I pushed further speculation about Fiona and Damaris's conversation to the back of my mind and picked my way through the throng of people to the makeshift stage that had been set up to the left of the food truck area. I saw Jimmy right in front, his camera trained on the stage. Sophie Brinkwater, dressed in navy slacks with a white turtleneck and gray-and-navy-checked vest, was smiling at the crowd, microphone in hand. Phoebe was there too, dressed more simply in black leggings and a green blouse, with a black cardigan knotted around her shoulders. She stood beside a small table a few feet away on which rested a large silver trophy with what I assumed was supposed to be a food truck on top of it. There were three white envelopes on the table as well. Phoebe plucked one from the pile, walked over and handed it to Sophie.

Sophie tapped on the microphone. "Attention, everyone," she said, and the murmuring in the crowd stopped almost immediately. "I want to thank all our entrants today, and all the foodies, home cooks and chefs who helped pick our winners. Let's give them a round of applause." Sophie clapped her hands and the crowd enthusiastically followed her lead. After a few moments she cleared her throat and spoke again. "It's time to announce the winners."

Sophie announced the second and third place winners, and I was pleased when the Thai food truck took second place. Once those prizes had been given out, Sophie said, "This was one close race, but our winner is . . . Everything But the Kitchen Sink!"

My lips curved in a smile as I joined in the clapping for the winner. After the Pappas brothers had accepted the trophy and envelope, Sophie addressed the crowd again. "Thank you so much, everyone! Please enjoy the rest of this afternoon's activities, and don't forget— the first round of Last Remaining Chef begins at six p.m. tonight in our upstairs arena! I understand there are a few seats left in the audience, and our volunteers will be upstairs outside the auditorium to sell tickets in about an hour. Enjoy."

Sophie put down the microphone and Phoebe came over, spoke softly to her. Sophie nodded and picked up the microphone again. "Members of the press," she said, "there will be a short period for photo ops and interviews with the winners commencing in ten minutes."

I saw Phoebe leave the stage and Sophie walked over to where the winners were standing. I saw her shake hands with all of them, and then reporters and photographers started to converge on the stage. I caught sight of Jimmy, camera in hand, right at the forefront of the crowd. I hesitated. I'd had the foresight to get interviews with each of the winners when we'd done the tastings, so now I felt comfortable leaving the photos and videos in Jimmy's capable hands. My time might be better spent tracking down Damaris and Fiona and maybe getting some answers. I turned away from the stage and in the direction of the main floor when a familiar voice stopped me cold.

"Tiffany Austin. Aren't you going the wrong way?"

I turned around and bared my teeth in a semblance of a smile at Francine. Today the newswoman was dressed in a tight lavender-colored dress that seemed to be little bigger than a washcloth. She teetered toward me in heels that matched the color of her dress and had to be at least four inches, adding to her already impressive height.

Gold bracelets jangled on one wrist, and the other hand clutched a microphone. I wondered if she slept with the thing, it always seemed as if it were attached to her body. She brushed a white-blonde curl out of her eyes and her perfectly arched brows rose. She waved the hand that clutched the microphone in the direction of the stage. "Shouldn't you be over there, interviewing the winners?"

I smiled sweetly. "I could say the same thing about you," I said.

"Those people are always ready and available for an interview." Francine moved closer to me. "So, any insights into the Barclay investigation you'd care to share? Like if Jason's murder is possibly related to this book he was writing?"

Twyla's warning came back to me, and I narrowed my gaze at her. "What makes you think I know anything about the investigation?"

"Oh, come on, Tiffany. I know that you're . . . close, shall we say, with the lead detective on the case? He practically browbeat me into not tagging you as the person who found Jason's body. And since you seem to have a penchant for getting involved in his murder investigations, well, it was just a natural assumption."

"You know what they say about assumptions, Francine."

She laughed. "Touché. So, how about it? Anything you'd care to share?"

"If—and that's a big if—I did know anything, I certainly wouldn't share it, not with you or anyone else," I snapped.

Francine clucked her tongue. "That's not a very charitable attitude toward a fellow member of the Fourth Estate," she said. "Why, I recall someone telling me, just yesterday as a matter of fact, that a reporter's job is to help keep the public informed. I believe you said that it's our civic duty."

"Thank you for throwing my own words back at me," I growled. "There's a difference between civic duty and grandstanding for the purposes of possibly horning in on a news story."

She frowned. "As usual, I have no idea what you're talking about."

Now I took a step closer to her. "I'm talking about you siccing

Bartell on Bob Gillette. I saw you watching Bob and Jason argue. You told Bartell about it, didn't you?"

Francine shot me a cat-ate-the-canary smile as she replied, "Someone had to. You obviously didn't. You witnessed it too and that was quite an argument."

I clenched my teeth. "It was over a trivial matter, Francine. Not something one would murder over."

"Sorry, but it didn't sound that way to me. Let me see, what did Gillette say again?" She made an exaggerated gesture of tapping at her chin. "Oh, yes. 'If you try something like that again, it'll be the last time you do.' That might not be an exact quote, but it's darn close. And you have to admit, it definitely sounded like a threat."

I swallowed. "I'll agree it doesn't sound too good when it's taken out of context, but once you know the whole story—"

"Look, if Gillette has nothing to hide, then he's got nothing to worry about," cut in Francine. She widened her eyes and added, "I was truly just trying to do my civic duty, as you yourself suggested. Gillette looked like he was going to burst a blood vessel. For all we know, he might have given Jason that shiner he was trying so ineffectively to hide. And, after I saw Gillette on tape sneaking around the banquet last night, a banquet he had no business being at—" She spread her hands. "What else could I do but advise Detective Bartell? I mean, once he saw Brent's video, I had no choice."

I gasped. "You mean the video shown on the news last night? Bob was on it?"

Francine shifted her microphone to her other hand. "Yes. I didn't show that part on TV though. I cut it off before Jason did his little hand gesture at me. But just as Jason waves his, ah, hand at me, Gillette can plainly be seen peering in the open door right in back of Jason. Granted, he was only there for a second or two, but he's quite visible once you freeze the tape." Her lips curved upward. "Detective Bartell seemed very grateful for the information. Very."

It was on the tip of my tongue to ask, "Just how grateful was he?"

but I restrained myself, figuring that was a question better posed to Phil himself. Her mention of Bob's appearance on the video also reminded me that I'd seen the gray-haired man on it too, something I needed to advise Phil about. I sniffed and said, "So, you have nothing to complain about. Seems like everyone got what they wanted."

"Not exactly," said Francine. "Of course, it felt good to do my 'civic duty,' but I can't help but think of the headlines there would be if I could be instrumental in handing the killer over to Bartell."

I stared at her. "Are you saying you'd confront the murderer?"

Her laugh tittered out. "Heavens, no. I'm not that brave. But if I could gather enough evidence that would lead Bartell right to him—or her, for that matter—I could see the headlines now. News at eleven! Francine Weston aids police in capturing killer of Jason Barclay!" Her face took on an almost dreamlike quality. "Why, I could write my own ticket!"

"And you wouldn't have to worry if you'll still have your job if the station is sold," I blurted out.

The smile faded from her face and her eyes narrowed down to slits. "What have you heard about that?" she asked, her tone sharp.

I shrugged. "Not much, really. Just that there's a rumor floating around town the station could be sold."

Francine seemed to relax a bit. "Joe's been talking about retiring for a while now," she said. "And he never does. The guy's a workhorse. He wouldn't know what to do with himself. No one at the station really puts any credence in that rumor," she added, but I noted her tone lacked conviction.

"I heard it seems to be circulating around a lot more this year. Maybe he's finally decided to bite the bullet. I know a beachfront home in Hawaii would surely tempt me to retire."

Francine tossed her head. "I'm not worried. My work will speak for itself. And you never answered my question. Is Jason's murder somehow connected to that book he was writing?"

"I have no idea," I said. I turned on my heel and started to walk away.

"Just a second, Tiffany." She was next to me in a nanosecond, making me wonder just how she did it in those heels. She held up her microphone, then dropped it to her side. "Off the record? You think helping Bartell is your exclusive territory. I've got news for you. You're not the only talented amateur sleuth in Branson, and it's time Bartell found that out. I'm sure he'd appreciate some competent help for a change."

"Like I said, keep dreaming," I said with a curl of my lip. "I happen to know Bartell prefers to work alone."

"Hah! Maybe he only thinks that because he hasn't hooked up with the right helpmate. I don't need to dream. I make things happen. And believe me, I'm very capable of making things happen with Bartell. With this investigation, and . . . who knows what else," Francine shot back. And with that parting shot, she whirled and flounced off back toward the staging area.

"Good riddance," I muttered. Now that Francine was gone, I slowed my pace to a crawl. I'd been right about her tipping off Phil, and apparently I'd also been right about seeing Bob at the banquet. No doubt he'd gone there to see Jason, but why? I found an unoccupied bench and sank into it. I pulled out my phone and hit the speed dial for Nita's number. Thankfully, she herself answered on the second ring.

"Hey, I got your message," she said. "I just haven't had a free minute to call you back."

"It's okay," I said. "I've had a pretty eventful day myself."

"So." Nita blew out a breath. "To answer your question, yes, that was Bob you saw down at the police station. Detective Bartell asked him to come down to clear up a few things."

"Let me guess. Was one of them why he happened to be at the banquet last night?"

"I should have figured you'd know about that," said Nita. "Yes, my ever-lovin' husband did go over to the banquet. We argued over it. He told me that he had unfinished business with Jason, and he had to confront him and get everything off his chest. I told him it was a bad idea."

"I understand Francine Weston got him on film. Bartell saw him when he viewed it."

"Yes, I know. Bob did go down there, but when he peeked in that room and saw Jason so drunk, he decided it wasn't the right time for a confrontation and he came straight back to the restaurant."

I felt a sense of relief surge through me. "He did?"

"Yep. He apologized to me, and we were together in Po'Boys the rest of the evening, from six thirty on, with plenty of witnesses, both staff and customers, to vouch for both of us, if necessary. He told all this to Bartell, and he said that Bartell told him he wasn't a potential suspect."

My ears perked up at that. "Bartell said that? Bob wasn't a suspect?"

"Yep. He didn't go into detail as to why, and Bob didn't ask." She paused and then, "I'm sorry, Tiff, but I have to go. We're really slammed right now. I'll catch you later."

Nita hung up and I leaned back against the bench, glad my friend wasn't on Phil's list and relieved that I could cross him off of mine, not that I'd ever seriously considered him a suspect. And I'd learned something else. I'd dealt with Phil long enough to know how that man's mind worked. For him to dismiss Bob from the suspect list so quickly, he had to have something concrete to go on. I hit Nita's number again, and once again she answered. "Okay, Tiff. What did you forget to ask?"

"Bob said that Bartell dismissed him as a suspect after hearing he was in the restaurant with you from six thirty on, right? He didn't ask Bob for proof of that?"

"Of course he did," Nita said with a laugh. "Fortunately, just before Bob arrived here, I'd just finished making a foot-long Po'Boy Loaf for a take-out order and it was a masterpiece, if I do say so myself. We had one of the waitresses take our photo with it. Bob thought we could put it on our website, good publicity, you know? Anyway, it had the time and date stamp in the corner."

"I see," I said. "I don't suppose you remember the exact time on the photo?"

"As a matter of fact, I do. It was exactly six forty."

I nodded thoughtfully, even though Nita couldn't see me. "Thanks, Nita. I promise not to bother you again—at least not tonight."

I hung up and took a moment to process what I'd just learned. Phil had dismissed Bob as a suspect after he'd seen that photo, which meant the photo was significant. I was betting the time stamp was the key. My fingers flew over my keypad as I sent my BFF yet another text. *Anything from Sample? Time of death very important.*

I hit send and leaned back on the bench. I waited ten minutes, then fifteen, then sent another text saying essentially the same thing. Another ten minutes passed. Nothing.

I slid my phone back into my pocket. It was almost time for me to meet Jimmy and head over to Guy Goodwin's tent for our early supper and interview. I only hoped that Hilary's radio silence meant that she was right now, maybe at this very minute, getting info from Howard Sample.

Fourteen

"Welcome, welcome. Jimmy, it's a pleasure to see you again. And this lovely lady is the friend you mentioned? The food blogger?"

I smiled and extended my hand. In person, Guy Goodwin looked pretty much the same as he did on his weekly cable show: a very tan man with a scraggly goatee and white-blonde hair that he wore tied back in an equally scraggly ponytail. He was dressed in his usual attire of khakis and a short-sleeved shirt, the better to show off the myriad tattoos that graced his muscular arms. "It's an honor to meet you, Chef Goodwin," I said.

Guy Goodwin threw his head back and let out a booming laugh. "Please, call me Guy. Jimmy doesn't bother with the *Chef* nonsense, and any friend of Jimmy's is a friend of mine." He gave me a long, searching look. "He tells me that you are a former chef yourself."

I felt my cheeks start to color. "Yes. I was the assistant head chef at the Madison in New York, under Leonardo Puccini."

"Ah, the Madison Hotel. I know it well." Guy's nose wrinkled. "I can understand your decision to leave. Puccini always was a bear to work with. Not an angel like myself." He closed one eye in a deliberate wink before he added, "I see they are represented in the competition by Chef Jeffrey Marki. Do you know him?"

"Yes. Jeff was one of my sous chefs when I was there. He's very good—or shouldn't I express an opinion?"

Guy laughed. "Express away. I'm not one of the judges. I'm only the referee."

We joined in the laughter and then Jimmy asked, "So, Guy. Who are the judges? Anyone I know?"

Guy reached out and clapped Jimmy on the back. "You might know them. After all, you know most of the culinary world after doing all those cookbook covers." Guy turned to me and said with a wide grin, "He does everyone's covers except mine. I'm getting a complex."

"I'd do yours in a nanosecond. Talk to your agent," groused Jimmy good-naturedly.

"Don't think I won't. Anyway, about the judges. You might know them as well, Tiffany. Chef Ariana Bell, Harold Trent and Deena Davidson."

"That's a nice mix of judges," I remarked. "A chef, a food editor and a food critic. I'm familiar with Chef Bell's seafood, particularly her lobster Newburg, but I'm afraid I only know the others by reputation."

"Well, I've told them about you and your blog, and they've all agreed to be interviewed," said Guy. "I suppose I should be flattered. Several of the critics and chefs approached me, offering their services as judges. Even that man who was found in the fountain." He shook his head. "Terrible thing."

I exchanged a quick look with Jimmy, and then Jimmy said, "Do you mean Jason Barclay?"

Guy nodded. "Yes. I caught him up here, wandering around backstage. He said he'd been looking for me to offer his services. Although he didn't seem too disappointed when I told him all the slots had been filled," Guy mused.

"When was that?" I asked.

"Late yesterday afternoon. The day he was killed." Guy shoved his hands into the pockets of his khakis. "Enough talking about unpleasant things. So, Tiffany, before we eat, let's get down to business. What would your readers like to know about *me*?"

• • •

Jimmy and I spent the next half hour interviewing Guy Goodwin on video and snapping photos, not only of the chef but of the delicious dinner dish he'd prepared. The ten-alarm Chicken he'd prepared was fantastic, and I felt like I was in heaven with each bite I took. The chicken, while spicy, was not overly so and was seasoned to perfection. The sauce that accompanied it was tangy without being overbearing.

Yup, I was definitely in heaven, all right.

Once we'd cleaned our dinner plates and were seated with steaming cups of coffee and some whiskey and cola bread pudding, Guy started to talk about the competition. "The twenty finalists all prepared their top dishes this afternoon while the food truck competition was being held," he explained. "The judges have selected the top four, which will be announced at the beginning of tonight's competition. They'll sample the top dishes and narrow the field to three. Four cooking challenges will follow, two tonight, one Saturday, and one Sunday afternoon between the final two. Then, at the end of the conference, the winner of Last Remaining Chef will be announced."

"Do you have any idea who the four finalists are?" I asked.

"Not a clue. I'll find out same as you in about an hour when the show starts." He grinned at me. "You're hoping that Marki is one of the finalists, I bet. You'd like to see your former protégé in the competition?"

I was spared answering as a freckle-faced lad of about eighteen thrust his head into the room. "Hey, Dad, the sound engineer needs you onstage to check something."

Guy waved his hand at the boy. "My son, Tyler. I'm teaching him the ropes. This will no doubt take a while, so I'll see you two at the competition. I've reserved seats for you right up front."

Guy and his son exited and Jimmy leaned into me. "Boy, won't the other reporters be jealous? I doubt any of them will have seats in the front row."

"I wouldn't put it past Francine Weston to sneak into the front row," I said. "Especially if she sees me there."

"Excuse me."

We looked up as Tyler came back into the room. "Sorry to interrupt, but my dad forgot his notebook." He walked over to a small table and picked up a spiral-bound notebook that lay there. He glanced over at the serving table and grinned. "Let me guess. ten-alarm chicken?"

"Yes, and it was delicious," I said.

"My dad's teaching me to cook," Tyler said proudly. "I guess you could say he's prepping me to take over the family empire, since my other two brothers haven't displayed any interest in cooking. Thor wants to be a dentist, can you imagine? I can't think of anything more yucky than poking around in people's mouths. And Sonny wants to be a scientist."

I stared at Tyler. Thor? Sonny? I slid my gaze over to Jimmy, but his expression was bland. I wondered if he were thinking the same thing I was. Allison Dugan had mentioned those two names as being in Jason's outline, and we'd both seen *Sonny* written in the appointment book. Could they possibly refer to Guy Goodwin's sons?

"How old are your brothers?" Jimmy asked. "Maybe they'll change their minds."

Tyler waved his hand. "I doubt it. They're both in college. Thor's twenty-one and graduates this year, and Sonny's twenty and he graduates next year. Me, I graduate high school in June and I'm hoping to get into the CIA."

I smiled. "I imagine you mean the Culinary Institute of America. That's where I graduated from."

Tyler goggled at me. "So you're a chef and a food blogger? Cool. What restaurant do you work at?"

"Actually I'm a former chef. I guess you could say I'm retired."

Tyler gave me a once-over and shook his head. "You look waaay too young to retire, if you don't mind my saying so."

I laughed. "I don't mind. So, Tyler, are your brothers here at the competition too?"

"Nah, they couldn't take the time away from classes. They go to school in England. Thor goes to Oxford, and Sonny attends the University of London. Just between you and me, I think my father is looking forward to having one of his kids go to school in the States."

"I bet he is," chimed in Jimmy. "Your brothers have interesting names."

"Oh, they're nicknames," said Tyler with a wave of his hand. "Sonny's real name is Salvatore, and Thor's is Theodore."

"Interesting," remarked Jimmy. "I can see how you'd get Sonny from Salvatore, and Thor is just a shortened version of Theodore, rather than Ted?"

"Right. But we call him that because his favorite comic book character is Thor," said Tyler. "Like they call me Spidey."

"For Spider-Man," said Jimmy with a grin. "I get it."

"You should see people's faces when we call each other by our nicknames," Tyler said with a grin. He tucked the notebook under his arm. "I've gotta get this down to Dad. You guys take your time."

Tyler exited the room and Jimmy looked at me. "Well, if both Tyler's brothers are in England, there's no way either one of them could be Barclay's killer—not that I really thought they were."

"Neither did I, but you have to admit it was an amazing coincidence. We did learn something valuable, though."

"Yeah," said Jimmy. "That Jason Barclay was up here snooping around. I'm not buying that story about him wanting to offer his services as a judge, are you?"

"No. I think it's more likely that he might have been meeting another person who's mentioned in his book. A backstage area would certainly be private. Tyler's comment about his brother's nicknames got me to thinking. Maybe the Thor mentioned in Jason's outline could be a nickname, maybe for another Thor comic fan, or maybe someone else named Theodore. Ditto Sonny."

"A nickname," said Jimmy thoughtfully. "Or a code name. A possibility, I suppose. But for who?"

"That's the million-dollar question," I said. "There's no one on my suspect list named Theodore, and I greatly doubt any of them are Thor comic book fans. The only one who's in the clear right now is Bob

Gillette. Bartell hauled him in for questioning but then told him he wasn't a suspect. I think it's got something to do with the time of death."

"Then maybe we should see how much success your pal Hilary had finding that little detail out before we make any more plans." Jimmy held out his hand. "Right now, my dear, we've got a competition to cover."

I nodded. I didn't tell Jimmy the other thought that had entered my mind. That perhaps the Thor and Sonny in Jason's appointment book did refer to Guy's sons, and the person Barclay had the real meeting with was the boys' father, Guy Goodwin.

• • •

I had to admit, Guy's people had done a fabulous job transforming the upstairs portion of the Civic Center into a replica of his show set. The area behind the double glass doors had been transformed into a mini supermarket. The only thing that marred it were all the cameras, lights and wires scattered about. There were four workstations set up at the front of the supermarket, complete with every modern kitchen appliance known to man. Off to the left of that was a long table, where I presumed the judges would be sitting. Guy was in the center of the stage, talking with a woman who was wearing a baseball cap and a long-sleeved tee that had *Director* emblazoned on the back. Workers wearing earbuds and microphones buzzed around them, adjusting plates and bowls and lights. Phoebe and Sophie Brinkwater were backstage as well, watching the proceedings with great interest. One of the convention volunteers showed us to our seats, which were, as promised, right in the front row. I noted that the press area was over to the left a few rows back, and I recognized a few of the reporters who were already seated there. There was no sign so far of Francine or Brent.

Jimmy nudged me with his elbow. "We getting lots of jealous

looks from the reporters over there," he said. "Bet they're wondering how we rate."

"I bet they are," I said, and then sucked in a breath as I saw Francine and Brent arrive. As they took seats in the press area, I slumped down a little bit in my seat. The last thing I needed was Francine coming over and making a scene!

The auditorium was beginning to fill up now, and the noise level definitely increased. A pretty dark-haired woman accompanied by two other women took the seats on either side of Jimmy and me. Jimmy leaned over and whispered, "That's Guy's wife and her sisters." His grin widened. "Looks like Guy put us in the family and friends row."

Three other men and women arrived and took seats. The judges, Ariana Bell, Harold Trent and Deena Davidson, emerged from the back and took their places at the table. I saw Chef Bell and Harold Trent wave at the other occupants of the row and assumed that they were their guests. A few minutes later a tall, sandy-haired man came and took the last seat. Deena Davidson waved at him enthusiastically.

"That's Paul Mongo," whispered Jimmy. "He's Deena's fiancé. We met when I was doing a shoot for *L.A. Magazine*. He's a pretty good photographer too." He snapped his fingers. "Say, he's got even more contacts than I have. He could know something about your gray-haired photographer friend. I'll have to corner him during intermission and pick his brain."

Before I could reply, Guy stepped onto the center of the stage and pointed to a cameraman who stood by the double doors. "Are we ready?" he called out. The cameraman nodded, and Guy clapped his hands loudly.

"Good evening, everyone," his voice boomed out. "Welcome to our special Foodie National Convention edition of *Last Remaining Chef*!"

The crowd responded with loud clapping and cheering. Guy introduced Sophie, who made a short speech on how honored the convention was to have Guy and his crew there. When the applause for

that died down, Guy said, "Thank you, Ms. Brinkwater. And now it's time to introduce the deciding factor in this competition—namely, our judges!"

Guy introduced each one by name. Ariana Bell received the loudest applause. Once that was done Guy continued, "Four dishes were selected in a preliminary round. Now our judges will sample them all and narrow the competitors down to three. The three finalists will compete in two rounds of games and cooking tonight, and each will be assessed a point value. After tomorrow evening's competition, the chef with the lowest score will be eliminated, and the last two will compete Sunday afternoon for the title of Last Remaining Chef!"

Thunderous applause greeted that announcement. Then Guy snapped his fingers and a white-coated man appeared, wheeling out a cart on which rested four silver-covered platters. "Each dish is only labeled with a number that corresponds to one of our contestants. One dish will be selected as the judges' favorite. So—let the competition begin!"

The white-coated assistant pulled the cover off of the first dish, revealing a mound of tasty-looking seafood atop a mound of white rice. He spooned a portion of the dish onto three plates and put them in front of the judges, along with a set of silverware. The audience went into a hushed silence, watching as the judges forked the food into their mouths and chewed, their expressions giving away nothing. This was repeated with the other three dishes. When the last bite had been taken, Guy asked each judge for their input. For the most part, they were complimentary. I noticed that all three judges agreed on the beef Wellington as the best dish, and I found myself hoping that was the one Jeff had prepared. I'd taught him how to make that dish. When the judges finished giving their critiques, Guy introduced the finalists. Jeff was indeed number three, and even though he smiled and waved at the audience, I could tell he was nervous. Once all the finalists had been introduced, Guy asked the judges for their decision.

"The judges' favorite was unanimous. Chef number three's beef

Wellington," said Ariana Bell. I couldn't hide my wide smile at that announcement!

"Congratulations, Chef Jeffrey Marki of the Madison Hotel Restaurant in New York," Guy said. "Jeff, for having the best dish you get an advantage in the first round."

Jeff looked relieved and stepped back. Harold Trent announced the other two finalists, numbers one and four. One was a man, a chef from a restaurant in Oregon, and four was a woman, a sous chef from an upscale hotel restaurant in Washington State. The disqualified finalist, number two, a junior chef from Cincinnati, looked disappointed but made his exit with good grace.

"So, here we have our finalists," Guy's voice boomed out. "Chef Jeffrey Marki, from the Starlight Restaurant at the Madison Hotel in New York. Chef Adelaide Spinnel from the Downtowner Restaurant at the Cambridge Hotel in Tacoma, Washington. And our last finalist, Chef Sullivan "Sonny" Brinker from the Palisade Restaurant in Eugene, Oregon . . ."

My mouth went dry and I stared at the man onstage. I glanced over at Jimmy and saw his lips were clamped tightly together, and I wondered if he was thinking the same thing I was.

Could Chef "Sonny" Brinker be the mysterious Sonny mentioned in Jason Barclay's appointment book?

Fifteen

I put my suspicions aside and concentrated on the competition. The first event was to be what Guy lovingly referred to as a budget battle. The chefs were to create a spicy lunch dish and each were given twenty dollars with which to buy their ingredients. The next hour passed quickly as the chefs shopped in the makeshift supermarket, then went to their workstations to prepare their dishes. Guy himself even participated, and I figured it was more to show off for the audience than anything else. He settled in at the fourth station and in less than the half hour allotted to the contestants created a chili dish that the judges raved over. I couldn't help but feel a bit proud when, at the end of the first round, Jeff's spicy Mexicano Burger received the highest score.

There was a brief intermission as the techs set up the stage for the second round, and Jimmy leaned into me. "I see Paul's all alone over there. Seems like a good time to have a little chat with him."

Jimmy moved off in Paul's direction, and I took the opportunity to head backstage. Guy had given Jimmy and me passes that gave us free rein backstage to interview the contestants, and I immediately homed in on Chef Sonny. He'd come in second behind Jeff and was only too willing to talk about his Chicken Supreme sandwich. "I knew I should have added more paprika," he said, twisting his lips into a rueful grin. "More ghost pepper wouldn't have hurt either."

"It's a tight race," I said. "There are only three points separating the finalists. Do you have a strategy?"

Chef Sonny grinned. "Just to cook to the best of my ability. That's what got me here."

"Thanks for your time," I said. "If you're interested, you can read your interview on my blog post tomorrow."

He chuckled. "Of course I'm interested. I need all the publicity I can get."

I shut off my recording app and slid my phone back into my pocket. "So, Chef Sonny, how do you like Branson so far? I take it you're staying here at the Branson Towers?"

He pulled a face. "I was supposed to, but I ended up at the Cardinal Inn. There was a bad storm and my flight from Eugene was canceled. I had to scramble to get another to get here in time, and even at that I barely made it." He ran a hand through his hair, messing up the sides. "I hate connecting flights, but I had to take two, and I didn't arrive here till eight a.m. this morning. And, of course, when I arrived, they informed me that since I had forgotten to notify them I'd be late, they'd given my room away. They did call the Cardinal Inn, though, and arrange for accommodations. By the time I got settled, I had just enough time to get over here, set up and make my dish for the preliminary round. Thank goodness they liked it."

"That was fortunate," I murmured. I'd check on the flights, but I had the feeling Chef Sonny was telling the truth. And even if he were the Sonny in the appointment book, he couldn't have murdered Jason if he'd arrived this morning.

I said goodbye to Chef Sonny and paused to take a quick look around backstage. I didn't see Jeff or Fiona anywhere and I wondered if they might be avoiding me. If so, it was probably Fiona who wanted to do the avoiding. Chef Adelaide waved me over and I spent the next fifteen minutes chatting with her. We'd just finished when the lights started blinking, signaling everyone that the second game was about to begin. I hurried back to my seat and found Jimmy there. He looked at me as I sat down. "Any luck?"

I shook my head. "I have to confirm with the airlines, but it looks as if Chef Sonny is in the clear. He had plane trouble and didn't arrive until eight this morning. He couldn't have killed Jason." I shifted slightly in my seat and leaned closer to Jimmy as Guy came back onstage. "How did you make out?" I whispered. "Did you show Paul the photo?"

"Yep. He didn't recognize him, but he said he'd check with some of his cronies who do a lot of freelancing and get back to me." Jimmy held up his hand with his fingers crossed. "He's got a lot of good contacts, so hopefully he can turn up something."

I slumped back in my seat as Guy announced the next game. The contestants could only use items found in the odd-numbered aisles. As they started to wheel their carts down the aisles I felt my phone ping with an incoming text. I pulled it out and my heart started to beat a little faster when I saw it was from Phil. It was simple, just four words: *We need to talk.* I frowned. That phrase never boded well, and I found myself feeling a bit apprehensive as I texted back: *I agree. Competition should be over in an hour. Meet me at my place around ten?*

A few seconds later, a response: *Can't wait that long. Can you get away? I'm in the parking lot.*

Uh-oh. I texted back: *On my way.*

That apprehensive feeling I mentioned? It just increased a hundredfold.

• • •

I whispered to Jimmy where I was going and he offered to come with me for moral support. I was tempted, but in the end I assured him it wasn't necessary. I made my way downstairs and out of the Civic Center into the parking lot, where I saw a dark sedan parked off to the side, a few feet away from the KPTX van. I started toward it, and the driver's door opened and Phil emerged. His jaw was set, and there was a steely glint in his eyes I hadn't seen since—well, since I was a prime murder suspect and he'd had me in his interrogation room. I plastered a wide smile across my face and walked over to him. "You know, we've really got to stop meeting like this," I said lightly.

Phil didn't answer, just stood, staring at me. Okay, this was going to be fun. I stared back, smile gone, my lips clamped tightly together. Finally he leaned forward and jabbed his finger under my nose.

"Tiffany, didn't I ask you to stay out of this investigation?"

I swallowed but didn't flinch. "Hello to you too," I said. "I believe you mentioned something about not wanting me to play detective."

His brows drew together in a deep frown. "I said more than that," he said gruffly.

"True. You did say something about me being a possible target."

"That I did. Obviously you haven't taken it seriously."

I squared my shoulders. "Don't tell me what I do or don't take seriously," I snapped. "And while we're on this subject, I think you owe me a thank-you for texting you about Francine and that tape."

For a second he looked taken aback, and then he nodded. "Okay, I'll admit I do. That tip turned out to be very helpful."

"It sure was. It cleared Bob Gillette." At his sharp look I added, "I saw Bob with you when I was at the station giving Brandon my statement. And then Nita told me that you eliminated him as a suspect."

"Yes, your friend is off the hook," he said. "You, however, are a different story."

I widened my eyes and tried to look innocent. "I don't know what you mean. I didn't kill Jason." I raised my hand and made a crossing motion over my heart.

"Oh, come on, Tiffany," he said. "You know darn well what I meant. You just can't resist playing detective, can you? I know you and that photographer were in Barclay's room over at the Cardinal Inn."

Uh-oh. "I was going to tell you all about that when I gave my statement," I said, "but you didn't take it, Brandon did, and I didn't want to tell him. I wanted to tell you in person." I paused. "How did you find out, or can't you tell me?"

"Oh, I can tell you. Once I showed her my badge, the chambermaid on that floor was extremely forthcoming to us about letting in a man she assumed was Mr. Barclay and his female companion. I showed her your photograph and she identified you."

Hm, so much for Jimmy's ten-dollar bribe. Apparently the chambermaid suffered from a bad case of loose lips. I leaned forward, my hand over my heart, and batted my eyelashes at Phil. "I'm touched. You carry around my photograph?"

"Don't change the subject," Phil growled. "What I want to know is, how did the two of you know Barclay had another hotel room?"

"We found that out purely by accident. And before you ask, I didn't touch anything directly." I related the whole story about finding the key card and our subsequent investigation. He listened impassively, not saying a word, and the silence continued after I finished. It stretched out for so long that I was tempted to pinch his arm to make sure he was still alive, but then he cleared his throat and barked out, "It didn't occur to you that key card could be evidence, that you should have reported it to me at once?"

"Of course it occurred to me," I said. "But I had no idea who that key card belonged to. It could have been lying in that grass for hours, days. It might not have had anything to do with Jason's murder, in which case I would have been wasting your time." I paused. "It turned out to be a good call on my part, too. The card belonged to a seventy-five-year-old woman here for Foodie Fest. Of course, anything's possible, but I'm guessing the odds that she's the killer are pretty slim to none."

Phil let out a breath. "I'll admit you lucked out, but one of these days I'm going to have to give you a little lesson on what I do and don't consider a waste of my time," he ground out. "What else have you put in that category?"

"You remember I did tell you I heard footsteps, and I thought I saw a flash of red? Well, Fiona Puccini was wearing a red dress."

He shot me a sharp look. "Fiona Puccini?"

"Yes. She's the daughter of my former employer. She was a chef in training when I was there." I paused and then added, "She's engaged to Jeff Marki, my former sous chef. Jeff is here competing, and she's here with him." Phil made a hurry-up motion with his hand and it was all I could do to resist sticking my tongue out at him. "Anyway, earlier that evening I overheard a snatch of a conversation between Fiona and Jason. They appeared to be . . . arguing about something."

Phil's head snapped up, and he reached into his jacket pocket, whipped out his notebook and pen. "You heard them arguing? When was this?"

"Shortly before the banquet started. I'd gone to the ladies' room, and I happened to see the two of them together in an alcove."

He let out a moan. "Why didn't you tell me about this last night?" he demanded.

"To be honest, it slipped my mind. I'm telling you now," I said. "I caught the tail end of their conversation. A few minutes after I got there Fiona left, and Jason left a few minutes after her."

"Approximately what time did this happen?"

"I can't say exactly, but I think it was around six thirty, give or take a few minutes. I went to the ladies' room and I know I got back to the banquet after seven. I thought I was late, but Rain—that's Rainbow McGill—said they'd made an announcement that it would begin a bit late."

Phil tapped the edge of the pen against the notebook. "I don't suppose you happened to hear what Jason and Fiona were arguing about?"

I hesitated, then nodded. "Yes. Jason told Fiona that he'd decided to put some incident in his book, and she seemed to be upset over that." I paused and then added, "There was someone else nearby who I'm certain overheard that conversation, a gray-haired man that I think was following Jason. Rain and I ran into him earlier in the bar, and he was most unpleasant. Anyway, when Jason left, I saw that man follow him. I figured he was after a photograph." I paused. "Unless he had something more sinister in mind."

Phil's eyes lit up with interest. "Can you describe this man?"

"He had shaggy gray hair, a lantern jaw, he was built like a linebacker and he had a sour disposition. He's in one of Jimmy's cocktail hour photographs. You can only see the guy's profile, but that mop of gray hair and lantern jaw is pretty distinctive." I paused. "He's also in Francine's video. You have to freeze the frame or you'll miss him, but . . . he's at the tail end of the video. You can see him at the bar when the camera makes its sweep."

"I can check them out, but it doesn't sound as if they'd be of much help." He raised his pen, pointed the tip at me. "Would you be willing to confer with the station sketch artist? You got a good look at him, and I think a sketch would provide a clearer likeness."

Now I leaned against the sedan hood, folded my arms across my chest. "Let me get this straight. Now you want my help?"

Phil let out a long sigh. "I always want your help when it's feasible. What I don't want is you inserting yourself into the actual investigation and possibly getting hurt."

I bristled. "I wasn't doing investigating per se. I was just trying to find out if what I found at the crime scene was actual evidence germane to the case."

"I think you also need a lesson on what police consider actual investigating," said Phil. "For example, looking into that key card on your own is investigating. When you found it, you should have called me immediately."

I made a face at him. "I told you why I didn't."

"So you did." Phil put his hand up to his temples, massaged gently. "Now, is there anything else you need to tell me?"

"Yes." I looked down at my hands. "It's about the notations in Jason's appointment book."

Phil's hand dropped to his side. "Wait, what? You looked through that book? You said you didn't tamper with any evidence."

"No, I said I didn't touch anything directly. Don't worry, I didn't compromise your evidence. I wrapped a Kleenex around my fingers."

He groaned. "Am I going to like this?"

I sighed. "Probably not. But in the spirit of full disclosure, I'm going to tell you anyway."

Phil leaned back and listened as I told him everything I'd learned so far: the rumor Twyla had shared about Damaris, the conversation I'd overheard between Damaris and Jason, and my thoughts on who might be the other initials scribbled in the book. When I'd finished, he was silent for a few moments, and then he cleared his throat.

"I'll check out this Hugh Hudson," he said. "And Damaris Alexander too. I agree, I don't think Goodwin's son could be this Sonny, but it is possible he might have used the son's name as a placeholder for a meeting with the father." He paused before adding, "Now, is that everything? There's nothing else you're keeping from me?"

Hilary's admonition to "fess all" rumbled through my brain, but I ignored it. "Nothing concerning Jason's murder," I said finally. Then I added in a light tone, "You know, I'm only doing all this to help clear things up so we can have our dinner date Sunday. That is, if you still want to."

His lips twitched upward just a fraction. "You are incorrigible, Tiffany Austin. And of course I want to keep our Sunday dinner date." He looked deeply into my eyes. "So, do I have your word? No more investigating?"

"You know, I'm not the only amateur sleuth in town you should be concerned about," I said. "Francine Weston has told me that she thinks she can be of immense help to you. She informed me that not only am I not the only amateur sleuth in town, but she has visions of somehow securing evidence that will lead you straight to Jason's killer."

Phil's hand shot up, massaged at his temples again. "She said that, did she? And did she happen to mention how she was going to go about securing this evidence?"

"Nope, and I didn't ask. But she intimated she was hoping to get a huge story out of it—and also get in your good graces." I believe she referred to you as 'quite a hunk,' and she also mentioned you were extremely grateful to her for providing that videotape."

"I'm not that grateful," growled Phil. "That tape just enabled me to cross one suspect off the list. And who knows, perhaps it will add another to the group." He reached out, put his thumb under my chin and turned my face up to his. "Believe me when I say hell will freeze over before that woman gets in my good graces."

I leaned into him. "What about me? Am I in your good graces?"

"For now. Just make sure you stay that way." He glanced at his watch. "I'd better get going. I want to go back to the station, look over those photos again. So, what do you say? Can you drop by the station around nine tomorrow and see the sketch artist?"

"I was going to check in at the office first, then go to the Civic Center for the Market Games competition, then wander around and get some random interviews before the next round of the Last Remaining Chef competition begins at six. Market Games starts tomorrow morning at eleven thirty, so I should be able to squeeze you in."

"Great. I'll see you around nine, then." He started around to the driver's side of his car, stopped. "Oh, heck," he said. Then he walked back over to me, took me in his arms and gave me a long, satisfying kiss on the lips. "I think that should hold us both till Sunday," he said as he released me.

I took a moment to steady myself. "Speak for yourself," I said. "If you don't solve this case . . ."

"Please don't say you or Francine Weston will do it for me," he said. Then he jumped into his sedan and roared off. I stood there, rooted to the spot, feeling more than a little euphoric.

Not only had I scored a good night kiss, but I'd managed to distract Phil away from the fact that I'd never answered him when he asked for my word that I wouldn't continue investigating. Because if anyone was going to play Nancy Drew and help Phil close this investigation, it sure wasn't going to be Francine.

I glanced at my watch. The final Last Remaining Chef event for the day was almost over, so it really didn't pay for me to return to the auditorium. I had more than enough content for my blog post, and Jimmy had promised to forward me any additional photographs of the event, so I decided I might as well head for home and get an early start on writing everything up. I'd just slipped behind the wheel of my car and was about to press the ignition button when my phone beeped with an incoming text. I whipped it out, thinking it might be Phil, but it was from Hilary. My heart beat faster as I read the short message:

Barclay TOD estimated between 6:55 and 7:15. You owe me!!!!!!!!!

I texted Hilary back immediately, thanking her for coming through. She responded with: *I'm at Trends. U can meet me here if U want. Got some more info.*

I texted back: *On my way.*

A few seconds later I got her response: *Then dinner's on you.*

Sixteen

Fifteen minutes later I slid into a parking spot right across the street from Trends. The bar was modeled after an English pub and was a favorite of the magazine staff, probably because it was only two blocks away from the office. As I came through the front door, I saw Hilary seated in a booth near the back entrance. I pushed my way through the throng of people who were clustered around the bar watching a sporting event and slid into the unoccupied side. Hilary grabbed a fistful of peanuts from the complimentary bowl, tossed them in her mouth, chewed, and then cocked her head at me. "Geez, I thought you'd never get here," she grumbled.

I grabbed a fistful of peanuts for myself. "Grumpy, are we?"

"Yeah, well." My BFF slumped down in her seat, folded her arms across her chest and glowered at me. "I've decided I hate detective work."

I bit back a sigh. Regular Hilary could sometimes be a handful, but I really hated dealing with petulant Hilary. "No, you don't. You like it. You only hate it when it involves Howard Sample," I remarked.

"That's because every time I contact him, I can tell he's hopeful that it will lead somewhere. I hate leading him on."

I leaned across the table and said, "Might I remind you that cozying up to Howard the first time was entirely your idea?"

"Yeah, and it was a bad one. I didn't realize the fatal effect I had on him." She sighed and straightened up a bit. "He made me feel so bad that if I weren't so nuts about Mac, I'd actually consider giving him another chance."

I raised an eyebrow. "So, what? His job doesn't creep you out anymore? I believe that was the main reason you dumped him."

"Oh, it still creeps me out. That's another reason I hate doing this. I have to pretend to be interested in it, which I am not."

"Well, hopefully this will be the last time you'll be pressed into service. So tell me, how did you manage to get the time of death out of him?"

Hilary's lips twisted into a crooked smile. "I have a confession to make. I didn't exactly get the info out of Howie."

I frowned. "Pardon?"

Hilary plucked a napkin from the dispenser on the table and started to fiddle with its edges. "I managed to get out of work a little early, and I decided to bite the bullet and went right over to the County Coroner's Office. I suppose I should have called ahead, but I thought maybe the element of surprise might tip the scales in my favor."

"That's good thinking," I said. "Surprise never hurts."

"Yeah, well, in this instance it did, because when I got to the office, Howie wasn't there. He'd gotten a call from someone in Baker County asking him to consult on a case." She pushed the napkin off to the side and tapped at a plastic menu lying on the table. "I imagine you're not hungry, seeing as you've been tasting samples all day long."

I pointed an accusing finger at her. "You're changing the subject," I said sternly.

Hilary's eyes widened. "No, I'm not. I believe my text message said specifically that you were buying dinner."

She started to pick up the menu but my hand shot out and slapped it back down. "I'm perfectly willing to buy you something to eat, but first things first. You said Sample wasn't in the office?"

"Nope. He was gonzo. Not expected back until late." She picked up the napkin again. "Do you mind if we order first? Crystal kept me hopping today. She was all upset about some chick who called her, wanting to continue their earlier discussion, and Crystal had no clue what she was talking about."

I gulped and looked down at my hands. "Really? That's . . . odd."

"Yeah. Anyway, Crystal told her she was crazy and hung up, then paced around the office ranting that she never called the woman. It put her in a worse mood than usual though. She had me running around all afternoon. I only had time to grab half of a ham sandwich for lunch, and I'm starving."

I'd been friends with Hilary long enough to know that she would withhold information until her hunger was sated, plus, I felt a bit guilty because I was ninety-nine-point-nine percent certain the woman who had upset Crystal was Allison Dugan, so I signaled the waitress. Hilary ordered a spicy chili burger and double cheese fries, and despite all the food I'd consumed today, I found myself a tad hungry myself, so I ordered a mini-platter of my favorite appetizer, potato skins. We both ordered cups of Mexican coffee. I enjoyed the way Trends prepared it: just the right mix of brewed coffee, brown sugar, Kahlua and tequila.

When the waitress brought our food and coffees, we spent the next fifteen minutes eating and sipping our drinks. Once Hilary had cleaned her plate, she pushed it off to the side, then took another sip of coffee before she spoke.

"The cause of death was blunt force trauma," she said. "They think the killer might have used one of those stone statues that are scattered around the fountain. According to the handyman, one is missing. They've searched the grounds twice and it hasn't turned up."

I tipped my mug and a little coffee sloshed onto the table. I set the mug down quickly before I could spill more. "How did you find that out?"

Hilary smiled smugly and took another sip of coffee. "That's not all I found out. They found traces of meta-something in his blood. Don't ask me to pronounce the medical name, but it's some sort of muscle relaxer. They checked with Jason's doctor. He never prescribed that meta-whatever it is for him."

I leaned forward. "Metaxalone? Could that be the drug?"

Hilary thought for a moment, then nodded. "That sounds familiar. How did you know that?"

I let out a sigh. "Jeff occasionally has muscle spasms from a childhood injury he sustained. I remembered that he takes that particular drug. I also know that some of the side effects can be drowsiness and dizziness." I tapped at my chin. "Maybe Jason wasn't as drunk as we thought. He could have been suffering side effects from the drug."

Hilary frowned. "You think someone slipped it into his drink?"

"They might have. And the alcohol could have sped things up. He was sloshing down those Scotches pretty fast."

"Well, we know Jeff didn't do it," said Hilary. "But Fiona could be another story. She and Jeff share a room, so she'd have access to the drug."

"Maybe, but Jeff can't be the only one in the universe who uses that drug. Maybe someone else does, like one of our other suspects."

Hilary cut me an eye roll. "When are you going to stop making excuses for that woman?"

"I'm not," I protested. "I'm just exploring possibilities."

"Yeah, every possibility except the one that Fiona might be guilty. Think about it, Tif," Hilary said. She lifted her hand and started to tick off on her fingers. "She had motive, according to that argument you overheard. She had opportunity, and she had means—Jeff's drug. So . . ."

"We're not certain she had means," I said stubbornly. "The drug isn't what killed him. And there are others who had just as much motive and opportunity, maybe more. Like Damaris Alexander, for instance." I paused, rubbed my fingers across my forehead. "She and Fiona were together earlier today. I saw them. They were deep in a pretty intense conversation."

"Oh my gosh!" Hilary clapped her hand across her mouth. "Do you think maybe the two of them were in cahoots? That they did this together? Fiona could have slipped Jason the drug to make him woozy, and Damaris could have finished him off!"

"I'll agree that their connection needs some investigating," I said. "Damaris is pretty high on my list. She was responsible for leading Jason's agent to her publishing house, which could be the deal Damaris referred to in their argument. Then there's the rumor Twyla told me about, that Damaris and Jason were lovers, and she confessed some sort of crime that happened in her youth to him. He might have threatened to put it in his book." I drummed my fingers on the table. "The time of death is somewhere between six fifty and seven fifteen. I know Damaris didn't show up to the dinner till close to seven thirty. She got the text from Jason asking her to accept Dana's award at six forty-five, so what was she doing in between then and the time she arrived at the banquet?"

Hilary pushed her mug off to the side. "You think she was late because she killed Jason?"

"It's a possibility," I said. "Then there's Hugh Hudson. He came in late too. He said a waiter spilled wine on his tie and he went to change."

"As alibis go, that one's pretty flimsy," observed Hilary. "And what would Hudson's motive be for offing Jason?"

"Same as Damaris's and Fiona's. He might be in Jason's book. I noticed Jason giving Hugh some pretty dirty looks at that kickoff luncheon. They'd argued earlier. Hugh said it was because Jason wanted to pick Hugh's brain about his crime reporting days, but maybe he was threatening him with exposure in his book." I paused. "And then there's Sophie Brinkwater. No one saw her until the banquet started."

"Sophie Brinkwater? The convention organizer?"

"Yep. I overheard her and her assistant talking, and I'm positive it was about Jason. I think Sophie knows him better than she let on. He could have something on her too."

Hilary dabbed at her lips with her napkin. "Maybe she's the Sonny in the appointment book," she suggested. "Sonny could be a nickname for Sophie."

I shot my friend an admiring glance. "Hey, that's good. I didn't think of that." I picked up my mug, saw it was empty, and pushed it off to the side. "I think my priority tomorrow, after I see the station sketch artist, will be to find all three of them and grill them a bit."

"Well, just be careful. You're my best friend, and I don't want anything to happen to you. Who else would bring me samples of gourmet food?"

The waitress came with the leather folder containing the check, and I slid enough cash inside to cover our tab and leave a generous tip. As we rose to leave, I looked at Hilary. "You never told me, since Howard wasn't there, how did you find all this out? Did you break into his office? Please tell me you didn't."

Hilary's grin widened. "I didn't have to. Do you remember Margaret Katz?"

"Margie? Sure I do." Margie Katz had been the head cheerleader when we'd been in high school. She'd been a Farrah Fawcett look-alike, right down to the hair. She'd also been one of the ditziest girls in school. Last I'd heard she'd gone to community college to study business administration—or maybe it was home ec. I never could remember. But she'd always been good at sewing. In senior year she'd made all of the costumes for our production of *Our Town*.

"Well, she's working as an admin at the coroner's office," Hilary said. Okay, business administration. "And, you'll be pleased to know, she's just as ditzy now as she was in high school . . . maybe ditzier. She happened to be updating the Barclay file when I dropped in to see Howie, and we got to chatting."

My eyes widened. "She told you what was in the file?"

Hilary gave me a look of mock horror. "Oh, no, she'd never do that. Margie is very ethical. Her words. But what she did do was leave the file on her desk for a few minutes while she went into the next room to get something for one of the techs." Hilary gave me a look of mock innocence. "I mean, she left it right out there on the desk, open, no less. It was practically an open invitation for me to take a quick look."

I shot my pal an admiring glance. "Good work."

"Thanks." Then with a wicked grin she added, "After all, I learned from the best."

Seventeen

I spent a fitful night tossing and turning. I dreamt that I was being chased by Damaris down a long corridor. At the end of the corridor was Hugh Hudson, holding a large rock. He threw the rock at me, and it missed me and hit Phil on the side of the head. Phil went down, and Francine was suddenly there, bending over him, holding her microphone close to his lips. I started toward them, but a hand on my arm stopped me. I whirled around and it was Fiona, her eyes large. "Please don't tell Jeff," she whispered.

"Don't tell Jeff what?" I whispered back. "Did you kill Jason?"

"She didn't. I did." I looked up and saw Damaris, an evil grin plastered across her face.

"No, I did." Now Hugh Hudson bent over me. "I killed the cad."

"You're all wrong." Sophie Brinkwater appeared out of nowhere and stood, hands on hips. "I did."

Francine stood up and pointed dramatically. "None of them did. There's your killer."

I turned and saw a figure standing off in the distance. His or her face was shrouded in shadow, and they wore a long robe, making it impossible for me to discern if it were male or female.

"I solved it! I solved the murder, Philip," Francine crowed. She cradled Phil in her arms. "I did it!" she shrieked.

Phil's eyes shot open and he looked at Francine. "You certainly did," he said softly and pulled her face down to his. I woke up, bathed in sweat, just before their lips met.

Needless to say I didn't sleep the rest of the night.

● ● ●

I arrived at the police station promptly at nine Saturday morning and was shown to a small office in the back, where I met Sandy Hemsher, the station sketch artist. Sandy was a petite blonde who was very talented with a pencil, in spite of sporting nails that I estimated to be at least four inches long. In less than a half hour she'd drawn an excellent likeness of the gray-haired man that was so lifelike I thought he'd speak to me right off the page. "Thank you so much for coming in, Ms. Austin," she said as she set down the pencil. "I'll make sure Detective Bartell gets this right away."

"Thanks," I said. I wanted to ask if I could get a copy of the sketch, but I figured she'd most likely have to ask Phil's permission, and the chance of him agreeing to that were about as good as me winning the lottery. "I hope it helps."

Sandy smiled. "If there's nothing else you think I should add to this, you're free to go. Thank you for your cooperation." She scraped back her chair. "I'll walk you out."

We'd just entered the corridor when an officer hurried over to Sandy. "Ms. Hemsher, Detective Gobin would like a word with you about the sketch you did in the Ballentine case."

As Sandy hesitated, I touched her arm. "You go on," I said. "I've been here enough times that I can find my own way out."

"Great," Sandy said, looking relieved. "Well, thanks again for your help."

Sandy and the officer moved off and I turned in the opposite direction toward the main entrance. A door at the far end of the hall opened, and I saw Brandon Hoffman emerge, a file folder in his hand. He crossed over to another door, knocked, then opened the door and walked in. I quickened my steps down the hall and paused before the door I'd seen Brandon open, which was labeled *Conference Room 1*. In his haste to enter, Brandon had left the door open a crack and I paused before the tiny open space and peeped in. Seated at a long table was Phil. The table was littered with papers scattered helter-skelter, and a mug was pushed off to the side. The folder that had been in Brandon's hand was now lying open in front of Phil.

"We might have caught a break," I heard Brandon say. "The hotel pharmacist confirmed that he issued a prescription for metaxalone for one Jeffrey Marki, and it was picked up late Thursday afternoon by his fiancée, Fiona Puccini."

"Fiona Puccini, huh? Well, that is interesting." There was a brief moment of silence during which I was certain I could hear the gears turning in Phil's head, and then he said, "Keep checking the other pharmacies in and around town. See if anyone else might have also picked up a prescription. In the meantime, I think I'll head out to the Branson Towers and have a little chat with Ms. Puccini."

I heard the sound of a chair being scraped back and I immediately beat feet out of there before I might come face-to-face with Phil, which definitely would not be a good idea right now. I kept walking and didn't stop until I was outside in the parking lot. Then I paused to take stock of the situation.

I felt partly responsible for Phil circling in on Fiona. The fact that she'd picked up the metaxalone for Jeff, coupled with what I'd told Phil about seeing her with Jason and her wearing a red dress and the flash of red I'd seen, had no doubt elevated her to "person of interest" status. My thoughts flew back to the theory Hilary had broached last night, about Fiona and Damaris being in it together. I'd pooh-poohed it then, but . . . could there be some truth to it?

I hurried to my car, slid inside and hit the ignition button. Hopefully I'd be able to connect with Damaris and maybe Hugh Hudson and Sophie Brinkwater as well, and start getting some more answers before Fiona ended up in a jail cell.

• • •

I made a short detour to the office before heading out to the convention center. Even though it was Saturday, I knew Dale would be in the office, and if I were lucky, maybe Twyla too. Lady Luck, however, wasn't so inclined to smile on me today. I stopped by Twyla Fay's office first, but she wasn't there. Gladys Galvin, who also worked on the Household Tips and Tricks feature, was in the office, and she informed me that Twyla had attended a fashion show in Cushing last night and wasn't expected in today. Next I went to Dale's office. He wasn't in either, but Callie, his admin, was. She assured me that yes, he'd gotten my blog post, he'd thought it was great, and he'd be in later today. "He left something for you," she said, and handed me a box tied with a white ribbon. I tucked it under my arm, and as I turned to leave, a sudden thought struck me and I looked at Callie. "Say, how did that board meeting go the other day?" I asked. "I heard it was something about an acquisition?"

Callie glanced up from her monitor and looked at me over the rims of her glasses. "Wow, then you heard more than me. No one has a clue what that board meeting was about." She leaned forward. "What did you hear? What sort of acquisition?"

I glanced quickly at my watch and let out a little moan. "Oh, gee, look at the time. I've got to get going if I'm going to cover the Market Games. See ya." I beat a hasty retreat before Callie could quiz me further. I hurried back to my car, and once inside, I opened the box. Inside was a good-sized computer tablet, and a white envelope. I slit open the envelope and pulled out a sheet of paper on which was written: *I put in a request for a camcorder for you. Until I get approval, I hope the enclosed will help. It has a high-def camera! Dale. PS: It's fully charged so you can use it right away.*

I tossed the box in the backseat and slid the tablet into my tote, then pulled out my phone and sent Dale a quick text. *Thanx for the tablet. Any news about that board meeting?*

I started to put my phone away when it pinged with an incoming text. I read the short message from Dale.

You're welcome. No news yet, but sometimes that's a good thing, right?

I sighed as I hit the ignition button. Was no news good news? In this case, I certainly hoped so.

• • •

I'd told Jimmy I'd meet him at the convention center's main entrance around ten, and sure enough he was there waiting for me. I showed him the tablet Dale had given me. "Not bad," he said, after giving it a thorough going-over. "It's the latest model with all the bells and whistles. Big screen, heavy-duty battery, keyboard, camera—two, in fact. It's more like a mini-computer. Personally, I prefer the camcorder for pictures and videos, but I can see why your boss thought this would be a good alternative. It's a big improvement over your phone." He handed me back the tablet. "And now let's get down to business. It's time for a progress report." Jimmy grabbed my elbow and steered me over into a far corner. After taking a quick glance around he said in a low tone, "I heard back from several of my contacts, and no one knows anything about the gray-haired man. I'm still waiting to hear from Paul. If I don't hear by noon, I'll ping him again." He made a little bow. "Your turn."

I told him about my conversation with Hilary the night before, ending with my trip to the police station and overhearing what Phil had said about Fiona. Jimmy let out a low whistle. "It does sound as if Bartell has zoomed in on your friend," he remarked. "Do you think it's possible Hilary's theory could be on the money? That they were in on it together?"

"My first inclination would be to say no, but then again maybe they met and bonded over whatever it was Jason had on each of them. I thought I'd try and track down Damaris before the Market Games start, see if I can get anything out of her."

"She's here. I saw her come in about fifteen minutes ago, while I was waiting for you," offered Jimmy. He pulled a program out of the pocket of his pressed jeans, ran his finger down it. "Ah, she's scheduled to give a talk on her specialty, Southern cooking, at ten thirty in Section 16-C. If you hurry you might be able to catch her before it begins. Need me to come with you?"

I shook my head. "No, I think it's best if I go it alone. I'll meet you upstairs at eleven thirty for the Market Games."

I took off like a shot and made it to Section 16-C by ten after ten. There was quite a crowd clustered around the entrance to the seating area, and I noticed many of them held copies of Damaris's cookbooks, no doubt hoping for a chance to get them autographed. I made my way through the throng and over to the volunteer table. Two girls were seated there, and thankfully I recognized one of them. I walked over to the table and smiled at the brunette. "Hello, Gillian. Remember me?"

Gillian returned my smile. "Of course." She gave the other girl a nudge with her elbow. "This is Tiffany Austin," she said. "She writes the Bon-Appetempting blog?"

The other girl looked at me, all smiles. "Gee, I never miss your blog, Ms. Austin. I just love it! What can we do for you today? Are you here for Ms. Alexander's talk? It's SRO, but I'm sure we could squeeze you in."

"Actually I was hoping to have a word with Ms. Alexander before her appearance, if that's possible," I said.

"She's very popular with the press today," said Gillian. She inclined her head toward the tent situated in back of the designated event area. "Francine Weston is in with her now, but if she leaves before the talk begins, I'm sure she'd be glad to see you."

"Thanks," I said. "I'll just hang here for a bit." A small group of women bustled over, and I moved away from the table. Francine was with Damaris? I frowned. Somehow I doubted that she was there to get an interview for the news show. The two volunteers were occupied and not paying attention to me, so I circled around to the back of the tent and Damaris's private area. I could hear a rumble of voices emanating from said tent, so I walked over and leaned closer.

"You have some nerve," I heard Damaris say. "I don't think I like your accusation, Ms. Weston."

"I'm not accusing you of anything," I heard Francine say. Her tone practically dripped honey. "I'm just asking a simple question. You were late getting to the awards banquet the other night. What delayed you?"

Damaris blew out a sharp breath. "Just what business is that of yours?"

"My business is getting at the truth," replied Francine. "I have a civic duty to report the truth to the American public."

"Since when?" Damaris sneered. "I spoke with that detective the night of Jason's murder. I don't have to say anything to you."

"No, you don't have to, but it's only a matter of time before the police find out the depth of your relationship with Barclay. They'll have more questions for you, ones you can't avoid, including your late banquet arrival. You know how easily things can get twisted in an investigation. Wouldn't it be better to get your side of the story out, reveal what happened to the public, rather than get caught up in a messy investigation?"

There were a few moments of silence, during which I figured Damaris was digesting what Francine had said. Then Damaris said, in a tone none too pleasant, "I was late getting to the banquet because I kept changing my mind on what to wear."

"Really?" Francine's tone held just a tiny hint of incredulity. "You were late because you were making wardrobe changes, and not because you were having a conversation with Jason Barclay?"

"It's the truth," huffed Damaris. "I didn't see Jason at all that evening."

"But you did get a text from him, asking you to accept Dana Carlyle's award," persisted Francine. "Why did he choose you?"

"I have no idea," shot back Damaris. "And unfortunately we can't ask Jason now, can we?"

A pause and then: "You and Jason were lovers at one point, during which you told him something you'd done in your youth, something you didn't want made public. He threatened to put it in his book."

I stood there, my mouth open. Francine must be a better reporter than I'd given her credit for. How on earth had she found that out?

Damaris also seemed a bit taken aback by Francine's attack. "I don't have to tell you anything," she mumbled.

"No, but as I said, the police will haul you in for questioning about your connection to Jason. You know how things can get twisted. Play ball with me and I'll make sure the public learns the true version—your version."

There was another slight hesitation and then Damaris said, "That was a long time ago. Yes, I was foolish enough to actually believe he loved me, foolish enough to confide in him. He promised me that he'd never reveal that little piece of my past to anyone." She let out a breath. "Then he told me he'd changed his mind. He'd decided that little incident would make good reading, that it would help him get on all the bestseller lists. It didn't matter to him what it might do to me, to the image I've so carefully cultivated over the years."

Francine's voice rose an octave. "So you were mad at him. Furious with him."

"Of course. Wouldn't you be? But I wasn't mad enough to kill him, if that's what you're getting at. I was late to the banquet just as I said. I'd taken a nap, and I overslept. Then I changed my dress a number of times. And when that . . . that cad texted me to accept Dana's award, well . . . I was nearly even later. I should have really changed my dress again." Damaris's tone brightened as she added, "I've got a witness. One of the chambermaids was in my suite, changing the towels. I paid her to be a sort of fashion commenter—helping me select an outfit. Her name is Suzette, I believe. Ask her, she'll verify what I've told you. And now, I think you've wasted enough of my valuable time. I must leave or I'll be late for my scheduled talk."

I moved away from the tent flap and behind a nearby pillar seconds before Francine emerged, a pensive expression on her perfectly made-up face. I wondered if she'd actually expected Damaris to confess to murdering Jason. Francine paused, whipped out her phone, looked at the screen and made a face. Then she shoved the phone back into her pocket and walked swiftly away. Damaris emerged a few minutes later, a book tucked under one arm and her head held high. She made her way to the area where the talk was to be held and I heard lots of applause and whistling as she entered. I waited a few moments before emerging from my hiding place, but my head was swimming.

If Damaris's alibi checked out, then she could be crossed off the list, but how on earth had Francine learned all that info about her? It was the same information that I'd shared with Phil last night in the parking lot . . . and then it hit me. I raised my hand and gave myself a good, hard smack right across my forehead.

The KPTX van had been parked a few yards away from where Phil and I had had our little conversation. Had Francine followed me and hidden inside the van? She could have easily overheard us talking. It was the only thing that made sense. I smiled as I thought that if that were the case, she'd also have heard Phil's less-than-flattering comments about her, maybe even have seen Phil and me lock lips. But my smile faded as another, even more troubling thought struck me.

If that were the case, then she'd also heard what Phil and I had discussed about Hugh Hudson and Fiona, and that probably meant she was on the hunt for them too.

"You really are determined to show me up, aren't you, Francine?" I muttered. "Well, we'll just see about that. I've got to find Fiona and Hugh Hudson and talk to them before you sink your claws into them."

But where did I begin? I had no idea where either one of them might be right now, and I could only hope Francine had the same problem. I started to move forward, but I was so engrossed in trying to figure out my next move I didn't watch where I was going, and the next thing I knew I'd collided with another warm body. "Oh, I'm so sorry," I began, and then I stopped speaking as I recognized who it was I'd bumped into.

None other than Fiona Puccini.

Eighteen

For a second the two of us just stood and stared at each other. Then I found my voice. "Hello, Fiona," I said softly. "It's been awhile."

Fiona, for her part, looked like a deer caught in the headlights. She averted her gaze from me and stared down at the floor. "Yes, it has," she finally said.

"Sorry about bumping into you like that. I wasn't paying attention to where I was going," I said. When I received no response, I added, "I read about your engagement in the paper. I'm very happy for you both."

Her stance seemed to relax a bit, and she raised her gaze from the floor to meet mine. "Thank you for that, Tiffany," she said, albeit a trifle stiffly.

Another silence stretched between us, and then I cleared my throat. "So, I'm assuming that you're here to support Jeff in the Last Remaining Chef competition?"

She nodded. "Yes. It's a big deal for him to be in this. He nearly fainted when Father told him he'd chosen him to represent the Madison."

I nodded. "I can just imagine. Winning this would be quite a feather in his cap, not to mention what it would do for the Starlight Room."

"Father would love it if he won the grand prize," Fiona mused. "All that free publicity! Not to mention the ten grand they award the winning chef. It would really help, you know, with planning the wedding." She paused and then added, "Jeff's pretty nervous, but I told him he has nothing to worry about. His talent will speak for itself."

"Yes, Jeff is an extremely talented chef," I responded. "Your father always liked to put him down, but I always knew he had what it takes to be an excellent chef."

Fiona wrinkled her nose. "Father is quite adept at putting most people down. Except you. He tried hard, but he could never find fault with your cooking." She glanced at her watch and then added, "It's been nice bumping into you. Literally, but I really have to get going."

"Wait." I reached out and touched her arm. "I need to talk to you, Fiona. It's important."

Once again, that deer in the headlights look crossed her face. "Talk to me? About what?"

I decided not to waste time beating around the bush, not with Francine on the prowl. "I know about you and Jason Barclay."

Her gaze skittered away from mine. "I'm sorry. I don't know what you mean."

"I overheard you talking to Jason the night he was killed," I said. "I know he was holding something over your head, something he threatened to put in his book."

Fiona's eyes narrowed. "You overheard us? Were you spying on me?"

"Not intentionally," I said. "Look, Fiona, I had to tell Bartell what I overheard. If I hadn't told him and he found out I knew about it, I'd have been guilty of withholding information in a murder investigation."

Fiona pushed her hand through her hair. "Well, I wasn't the only person who argued with Jason that night. I saw him talking with a silver-haired man in a black jacket. And neither of them seemed particularly happy." She raised her gaze to meet mine. "They had a very brief conversation, and then Jason tossed his drink at the guy and stalked off."

"I see," I said. "And this happened right before your meeting?"

She nodded. "Yes. I imagine the conversation was short because Jason was drunk. He kept slurring his words, and his gaze seemed unfocused."

"That could have been a result of the metaxalone," I murmured.

Fiona sucked in a breath. "Metaxalone! You're kidding! Jeff takes that for his shoulder. I picked up his prescription at the hotel pharmacy earlier that day. Jason took that too?"

"Jason didn't take metaxalone." I leaned in closer to her and said, "The police are going to question you about picking up that prescription. They might think that since you had access to the drug, you could have slipped it in his drink, then got him out to the fountain and killed him."

"What? That's ridiculous." She tugged at a strand of hair. "I hated Jason, that's true, but I would never kill him or anyone else. Even if I really, really wanted to."

"I believe you," I said. "The Fiona I knew could never kill anyone. You always used to feel sorry for the lambs and cows, remember?"

To my surprise she laughed. "I still do," she confessed. "I specialize in pasta and vegetarian dishes, much to my father's dismay. But people like to have those choices on the menu." Then she sobered as she added, "You remember when Jason came to review our restaurant? Well, he contacted me a few weeks later and asked me out. You were going with Jeff at the time, so . . . I said yes. Biggest mistake of my life," she added bitterly. "We got to talking and I confided in him about something I'd done when I graduated high school. Something I'm really not proud of." Her face twisted into a grimace as she added, "Something my father definitely would not approve of."

"Does this secret of yours have anything to do with photographs?"

Her head jerked up. "Yes, but how—"

I held up my hand. "You don't have to go into detail if you don't want to. I just heard a rumor that he had revealing photographs on some girl in New York."

"I was very young," Fiona murmured. "I thought I might want to be a model, and a 'friend' hooked me up with a guy who took some photos that, well, let's just say they displayed my assets to advantage. I thought the negatives had been destroyed, but somehow Jason got his hands on them. He contacted me, said that he had them and was considering putting them in this book of his. I begged him not to. He said he'd think about it. He . . . he wanted me to . . . to . . ."

I held up my hand. "You don't have to go any further. I get the drift. He really was a cad, wasn't he?"

"That's putting it kindly." Fiona put up her hand and twined her fingers in the chain around her neck. "He got my phone number and texted me. He told me he'd be at this convention, that he hadn't made a final decision on whether or not to put some of those photos in the book, but he was willing to listen if I had anything to say. He warned me against having my father contact him. He said he knew stuff about him that he could use too. When I got here I texted him, and he told me to meet him in that alcove that night. He said there was no need for a discussion, he'd decided to put the story and some of the less, ah, revealing photos in the book. He said he'd use an alias for my chapter, and said I looked so different from those photos now no one would recognize me. I said my father would, and that was bad enough. He said not to get him involved, nothing he might say would change his mind. That's when I told him he liked to ruin lives." She paused. "I also said I wished he were dead. I did. But I didn't kill him."

I looked at her. "But you were in the vicinity where he was killed, right around the time of the murder, weren't you?"

She looked down at her feet. "Yes," she said softly. "I went outside after our . . . meeting. I needed a breath of fresh air, and I needed to think about what I was going to do." She sighed. "I knew Jason wasn't going to relent, so I had to decide how to break the news to my father . . . and to Jeff. Jeff knows I've been keeping something from him. I just haven't had the courage to tell him."

"One thing I know about Jeff is that he's very understanding, especially with people he loves," I said softly. "And he loves you, Fiona. Believe me, he will understand."

Her lips twitched upward slightly. "Probably more than my father will. That's who I'm really afraid of," she admitted.

Having had my own experiences with Leonardo, I was inclined to agree with her. "Finish telling me what happened," I said. "You could have seen or heard something that might help catch the real killer."

She clasped her hands in front of her. "Like I said, I went for a walk, and I ended up near the fountain. I could hear voices, but they were very low. I couldn't tell who was talking, and I didn't want to see anyone, so I just stopped and stood for a few minutes. I was just about to turn around and go back the way I'd come when I heard a cry and then a splashing sound. I was undecided about what to do, so I just didn't do anything for a few minutes. Then I went over to the fountain and I saw the shoe sticking out of the bowl. I went and looked and I saw Jason and . . . I panicked. I hurried away and I cut through the shrubbery and back to the hotel."

"That's when I must have seen you," I said. "Or rather, I heard your footsteps and saw a blur of red when you cut through the shrubbery. At first I thought I might have imagined it."

"I wish I'd imagined that entire evening," Fiona said bitterly. "If only I could go back and do everything over again." She nibbled at her lower lip. "When I got back to the hotel I realized I didn't have my room key. I panicked a bit because I thought I might have dropped it near the fountain, but I didn't want to go back and look for it. Jeff found me and I went to the desk and got another. Then later on, I found the key card. It had fallen out of my purse and was under the dresser in our room." She looked at me. "I felt relieved. I was so afraid I'd dropped the key card near the fountain, and if the police found it . . . but I guess I'm a suspect anyway." She gave me a fearful look. "Do you think that detective is going to arrest me?"

I shook my head. "So far the evidence against you is circumstantial. He can't prove you were anywhere near the murder scene, and he can't prove that you slipped that drug to Barclay. He needs something more concrete, like finding the murder weapon in your possession or an eyewitness." I shot her a crooked smile. "Me seeing a flash of red and you wearing a red dress doesn't cut it as incriminating evidence."

"I don't even know how Jason was killed," said Fiona. She closed her eyes. "I only know when I looked into the fountain, there was a blob of red under his head."

"Did you happen to see a phone lying around? They haven't found Jason's."

"No, but then again, I wasn't looking for one." Suddenly her eyes flew open. "I did see a black button though. It was lying on the ground in front of the fountain."

I frowned. I was positive I hadn't seen a black button anywhere near the fountain. "Are you sure?" I asked Fiona.

"Yes, yes," she said, her tone excited. "I almost stepped on it. I'm positive. It was right there in plain sight."

I put both my hands on her shoulders. "Look, when Detective Bartell questions you, be sure you tell him that. And be honest with him. Trust me, he'll know if you're holding something back." I paused and then added, "If I were you I'd tell Jeff all about your dealings with Jason and I'd do it sooner than later. Oh, and if a reporter named Francine Weston should approach you, I'd be careful what I said to her. My advice would be stick to 'no comment.'"

"I have no intention of speaking to any reporters," Fiona said. "And I'll think about telling Jeff, but I really hate to do it before the end of the competition. He'd worry and I don't want to throw him off his game. And speaking of Jeff, I've got to be going. I didn't plan on being away this long, and he's probably wondering what happened to me."

"One last question," I said. "I saw you yesterday talking with Damaris Alexander. I noticed you seemed upset."

"Oh, her." Fiona puckered her lips as if she'd just bitten into a lemon. "I'd seen one of her cookbooks in Jason's apartment, and from the inscription I figured they must have had a relationship at one point. It was one of those gushy phrases, you know, that you say when you first fall for someone. Anyway, I thought maybe she knew something about his book, but she got very testy when I asked her. She said that it was most likely a dead issue now, like him, and she didn't want to be bothered about it. So then I said what would happen if they decided to publish the book anyway, and she just smiled like a Cheshire cat and said, 'Well, they'd have to find the book first.' She was very dismissive, said I should concentrate on living my life and forget about it. I got fed up with her condescending attitude and I just walked away."

"Thanks, Fiona. You've been a big help." I squeezed her hand. "I hope Jeff wins the competition. I'll be rooting for him."

"Thanks." She suddenly smiled at me, a big, genuine smile. "I'm glad I ran into you, Tiffany. You—you've made me feel a whole lot better. And I promise, as soon as I get a chance, I'll tell Jeff everything. I don't want to start our life together with any secrets between us."

She hurried off and I watched her go. I doubted that she'd confess anything to Jeff until after the competition, and I only hoped that wouldn't be too late. Then I turned my thoughts to Damaris. Why was she so positive the book wouldn't turn up? Or was it wishful thinking on her part? That black button Fiona insisted she saw disturbed me too. I was positive I hadn't seen one by the fountain. Had the killer returned in between the time Fiona left and I arrived and removed the button, possibly also confiscated Jason's phone? That could mean the footsteps I'd heard hadn't been Fiona's, but maybe the killer's?

If that were the case, I'd only missed running into him or her by scant minutes.

I closed my eyes and tried to visualize what people had been wearing that night. Damaris had been in a royal blue gown, but if memory served correctly, Hugh Hudson had worn a black jacket. He might be the silver-haired man in the black jacket Fiona had seen talking to Jason. I thought Sophie Brinkwater had also been wearing a black jacket. I'd have to double-check Jimmy's photos, but I was pretty sure I was right. It would be interesting to find out if either Sophie or Hugh had a button missing from their jackets.

I pulled out my phone and pressed the speed dial number for Phil.

The call went to voicemail, and I wondered if he'd gone to interrogate Fiona. I decided my news about the button could keep for now, so I disconnected without leaving a message, then glanced at my watch. It was almost time for Market Games to begin. I made a mental note that the minute it was over, I was going to track down Hugh Hudson and Sophie Brinkwater and try to get some answers.

Nineteen

It was a full house for Market Games, which didn't surprise me at all. The cable show, hosted by Chef Rocco Martone, was second in popularity to Guy Goodwin's show. It featured professional, amateur and home cooks alike, all competing in different games that took place in a supermarket (of course). Today the contestants were a sous chef from a restaurant in Madison, Wisconsin, a line chef from Illinois and a home cook from Trenton, New Jersey. There were three challenges in all, and after the first round the line chef and the home cook remained. It didn't surprise me. The two were fierce competitors and avid watchers of the show, although to be honest my money was on Betty Baldwin, the home cook. She seemed particularly fierce to me. Then again, she was from New Jersey.

There was a brief intermission before the last round and Jimmy and I wandered outside. Jimmy looked at his phone, then motioned to me. "It's Paul," he mouthed, then turned away to take the call. I glanced around the crowded area. I caught sight of Francine, trusty microphone in hand, talking to Chef Rocco over in one corner, Brent and his trusty camera at the ready. Well, at least she was here and not off searching for Hugh Hudson, Sophie Brinkwater or Fiona.

Jimmy finished his call and came over to me, a perplexed look on his face. "What's wrong?" I asked. "No luck with Paul?"

"I wouldn't say that," said Jimmy. "It's just . . . odd. One of Paul's contacts thought the guy did look familiar. He suggested that we try and contact a crime reporter named Hugh Hudson. He seemed pretty sure Hugh would know who the guy is."

"Hugh Hudson, huh?" I tapped at my chin. "That is interesting. Hugh did mention Jason wanted to pick his brain about his crime reporting days."

"Think it might have had something to do with our mystery man?"

"It might," I said. I stole a glance over at where Francine was chatting with Chef Rocco. The two of them had big smiles and seemed to be getting along famously. Obviously Chef Rocco was a sucker for bottle blondes with big blue eyes and low-cut blouses. I swung my gaze back to Jimmy. "There are several talks starting shortly that Hugh might be interested in. One called 'The Food Critic: The Unsung Hero' starts in ten minutes. I let out a long sigh. "Unfortunately, Market Games will be starting back up at about the same time."

"You go on and see if you can track down Hudson. I'll hold down the fort here," said Jimmy.

"Great. And would you mind forwarding me that photo of the bar? It's not as good as the police sketch, but it'll have to do."

He grinned at me. "I did that once I was done with my call."

I touched his arm. "You've really been a big help with all this, Jimmy. I'm going to miss you when you go."

"Know what? I'll miss you too. I can't remember when I've had so much fun."

• • •

I went downstairs and made my way over to Booth 18-F, where the food critic talk was to be held. Sure enough, I spotted Hugh Hudson on line. Rain was with him. I hurried over and touched his arm. "Hello, Hugh," I said. "Rain."

Both of them smiled at me and then Rain said, "Well, hello, Tiffany. I'm surprised to see you here. I would have thought you'd have been upstairs covering Market Games."

"I was," I admitted. I looked straight at Hugh. "I came down here hoping to run into you. There's something very important I need to discuss with you before the police do."

"The police!" Rain let out a gasp. She grabbed Hugh's arm. "Oh, my goodness, what is it? Does it have anything to do with Jason's murder?"

Hugh sounded puzzled as he said, "I've already spoken with that

Detective Bartell. I told him all I knew about that evening, which wasn't a lot."

I gave a quick glance around. "I'd really rather continue this conversation in private," I said.

Hugh glanced at Rain then back at me. Then he shrugged. "Okay, fine. But let's make this fast."

We walked over to a bench a few yards away and sat down. I looked at Hugh. "You said you spoke with Bartell. Did you tell him you had words with Jason Barclay shortly before he was killed?"

Hugh's cheeks paled a bit. "What?" The word came out a croak.

"There's a witness who can put you speaking with Jason not long before I discovered his body," I went on. "Still want to stick to that story about being late because a waiter spilled wine on you?"

Hugh was silent for a few moments and then he said, "Okay. A waiter didn't spill wine on me. Jason tossed his Scotch at me. I reeked of it so I hurried back to my room and changed. And that's the truth. I didn't see Jason again that night."

"What were the two of you arguing about?"

"He wanted some information on a story I'd done some time ago," Hugh said. "One that I was working on around the time I decided to forsake true crime for food." His tongue came out, licked at his lips. "It had to do with the mob. Not pretty stuff."

"The mob?" I remembered what Twyla had said about Jason having a fling with a 'Mafia princess' that hadn't ended well. "Did it have anything to do with a Mafia kingpin's daughter, by any chance?"

"Not a daughter. A girlfriend," said Hugh. "Sonja Blackman. She was the main squeeze of a mobster named Donny 'the Wiz' D'Amico in Chicago. Long story short, five years ago Sonja got fed up with being a mobster's main squeeze and decided to strike out on her own. To help finance her new life, she stole a notebook from Donny that contained the names of some of his most valuable contacts, along with twenty grand from his safe. She also stole one of Donny's Cadillacs. I'd gotten a tip that she was in New York, and I was trying to track her down when I decided I'd had enough of writing about crime. I turned all my notes over to another reporter, Dave Caruso, but he wasn't really invested in working on anything connected to the mob, so eventually the trail and the story went dead."

"So that's what he wanted to pick your brain about the day of the kickoff luncheon?"

Hugh nodded. "Jason cornered me the night of the banquet. He wanted access to any notes I might have kept about Sonja. I told him to talk to Caruso, and he said he'd done that and Caruso had destroyed the notes. I told him as far as I was concerned, that story had died when I switched careers, and it was something he was better off staying out of. After all, this is the Chicago mob. You don't mess with them. That was when he said that he couldn't stay out of it, that it was personal. I told him I wouldn't help him even if I could, and that's when he threw his drink at me and stormed off."

"He said it was personal? Do you think he had an affair with her?"

Hugh shrugged. "I have no idea. But knowing Jason, it wouldn't surprise me."

A mental image of Jason's appointment book reared itself in my mind's eye. "Did D'Amico have a nickname, or a pet name, for this Sonja?" I asked.

Hugh nodded. "Yes. He used to call her Sonny. Why?"

"I think it could be possible Jason made contact with her."

I told Hugh about seeing the name Sonny on Jason's appointment calendar. Hugh was silent for a few moments and then he said, "Jason had a lot of resources at his fingertips. He could have tracked her down. If that's the case then she must be somewhere close by."

"She could be closer than we think," I murmured. I pulled out my phone and opened Jimmy's photo, then thrust my phone in front of Hugh. "Take a look at this. Does the man in the far corner of this photo look familiar to you? One of Jimmy's contacts said you might know who he is."

Hugh looked at the photo, and his jaw dropped. He gave me a

sharp look. "How—where was this taken?"

"Jimmy took it Thursday night. This guy was at the bar at the banquet, and Rain and I sat next to him. Later on I saw him following Jason." I looked at Hugh. "You do know who he is," I said, "don't you?"

Hugh set his lips. "I sure do," he replied. "If I'm not mistaken, that's Trent Saville. Or as he's better known in certain circles, 'True Shot.'"

"True Shot?"

"Yeah. He got that nickname because he never misses his target. He's a hit man for D'Amico's mob."

Twenty

"**A** hit man?" I let out a gasp. That was a revelation I hadn't expected. "Are you sure?"

"Oh, yes. That's him all right. He's a bit older and a lot thinner, but I'd know that jaw anywhere," said Hugh. "You said he was following Jason?"

"I can't be absolutely certain, but it seemed that way to me," I said. "But hit men don't usually conk people over the head when they kill them, do they?"

"That's definitely not Trent's style," said Hugh. "He'd have put a bullet right between Jason's eyes."

"I don't think Jason was his intended target," I said. "It's possible D'Amico somehow found out about Jason's interest in his former girlfriend, and he sent the hit man here hoping Jason would lead him to her."

Hugh considered this for a few moments, and then nodded. "That would make more sense. He'd want revenge. No one crosses D'Amico and lives to tell about it. It seems logical that Sonny could have killed Jason to protect herself."

"What did Sonny look like?" I asked.

"She was a very pretty girl. Long, strawberry blonde hair, big blue eyes—her best feature if you ask me—and legs that went on for days. But I doubt very much she looks anything like that now. In order to have stayed under D'Amico's radar all this time, she'd have had to alter her appearance dramatically."

"Plastic surgery?"

"Most likely. She'd have had the money to do it." He gave me a sharp look. "You aren't thinking of trying to track down Sonny yourself, are you? Because that would be a huge mistake."

"I have no intention of confronting anyone. Besides, Detective Bartell has a pretty strong opinion about me helping in his investigations." I looked at Hugh. "You should give Bartell a call, tell him what you just told me about Saville."

Hugh frowned. "To be honest, I'd rather stay out of the whole thing. I'm sure Bartell will find out about Saville on his own."

"I'm sure he would too, but things might move along faster if you help."

Hugh sighed. "You're right. Okay, I'll give him a call."

"Good. You're doing the right thing. I'm sure if you tell Bartell how you feel he'll keep your name out of it." I paused and then added, "Francine Weston is hot on the trail of this story, and she wants to be the one to lead Bartell in the right direction. To that end, she just might track you down and question you."

Hugh made a face. "Francine Weston, eh? Well, she won't get any information out of me. And now, if that's all, I'll give Bartell a call before the talk begins."

I stole a glance over at the line, saw Rain looking over at us. "If I were you, I'd call him now, before you get back on that line," I said.

Hugh chuckled. "Good idea. It wouldn't do for Rain to know what we were talking about. The less she knows, the better."

"Agreed. If Rain asks you what we discussed, tell her I asked about the button."

"The button?"

"Someone thought they saw a black button near the fountain, but when I found the body I didn't notice one. You had a black jacket on that night. You aren't missing a button, are you?"

"Nope," he said with a lopsided grin. "I can definitely assure you that all my buttons are accounted for."

I left Hugh to make his call and went back upstairs to Market Games. Out of the corner of my eye I noticed Francine giving me a sharp look as I slid into my seat. Jimmy leaned over and whispered, "Any luck?"

"More or less. I'll fill you in later."

The final round was just ending, and as I'd predicted, Betty

Baldwin, the home cook from the Garden State, won with her caprese pasta. Once Rocco had congratulated her, given her the prize money and trophy, and said goodbye to the audience, Jimmy and I immediately hurried backstage. We separated so Jimmy could get some photos of the dishes and the other contestants and I told him I'd meet him in the tasting area in an hour. I saw Francine approaching out of the corner of my eye and I made sure that I got over to Betty first. She was flushed and nervous but more than willing to share not only her joy at winning, but the recipe for her winning dish. I wrapped up my interview and headed for the seating area just off the entrance to the set. I pulled out the tablet and called up my favorite search engine. I typed in "Sonja Blackman—images" and was rewarded with over five hundred hits. I typed in "Sonja Blackman" and this time added D'Amico's name. I was rewarded with a color photograph of D'Amico leaving a courthouse. A blonde woman in a black fur coat stood slightly off to his left. I agreed with Hugh—she certainly was pretty, and her wide blue eyes were certainly her dominant feature. She didn't resemble anyone I knew, making me think Hugh was right about the plastic surgery. Suddenly I was assailed by the feeling that I wasn't alone. I looked up and found Francine standing over me. "What are you doing here?" I snapped as I shut the tablet off.

"Looking for you, of course," Francine said sweetly. "I noticed you were conspicuously absent for practically the entire second half of the event," she said sweetly. "Where were you? Out following a hot lead on Jason's murder?" She gestured toward the tablet. "What were you looking at?"

I blew a stray hair out of my eyes before I replied, "Gee, Francine, don't take this the wrong way, but it's really none of your business. And if you were so concerned about where I was, I'm surprised you didn't follow me. I know you're good at that."

Her eyebrows went up dramatically. "My, my, someone's pretty full of themselves," she said. "What makes you think you're important enough to follow?"

"I don't think I am—but you do. You followed me last night, didn't you?" I said.

She had the grace to flush. "Why would I follow you?"

"Because even though you said your goal was to help Bartell, you've become fixated on solving Jason's murder all by yourself, and you have it in your head that by following me you'll get some sort of lead that will help you do just that. I know you hid in the KPTX truck last night when I was talking to Bartell in the parking lot, and I know you got an earful. How else would you have known to ask Damaris all those questions?"

Too late, I realized my mistake. Francine's eyes narrowed. "And just how do you know I was with Damaris? You were following me," she rasped.

"I was not! I went to talk to Damaris myself and you were already there."

"So you hung around outside and listened to my private conversation with her?"

"You two weren't exactly whispering," I said. "I suppose you've already questioned the maid, and Damaris's alibi checks out."

"I guess you'll just have to wait for my story to break to find that little detail out," Francine hissed.

"Fine. No problem." I shoved the tablet back in my bag, then looked over my shoulder at Francine. "Just remember this, Francine. Eavesdroppers rarely hear anything good about themselves."

"If you're referring to Detective Bartell's comment about me, it won't be long before he changes his mind," she shot back. "Hell won't freeze over before he'll admit being grateful for my help."

I turned my back and walked away. No sense trying to deal with a woman who was delusional. I had bigger fish to fry. I only hoped that if she tracked Hugh down, and I was pretty certain she would, that he'd keep his promise not to say a word. I also hoped that Hugh had managed to get in touch with Phil, which reminded me—he'd mentioned heading over to the Branson Towers to talk to Fiona. If he'd missed finding her there, he might be somewhere around here.

"Ms. Austin!"

I looked up and saw Phoebe striding purposefully toward me, brows drawn together, lips drooping down. She paused in front of me and said dramatically, "I noticed you bothering Hugh Hudson earlier, and arguing with that other reporter just now. Have you made it your mission in life to disrupt this convention?"

I stared at her. "Disrupt the convention? How am I doing that?"

Her lips thinned and her brown eyes flashed. "It's my understanding that you've been bothering some of our volunteers with questions—you and that photographer. I'd like it to stop. There are police investigating Mr Barclay's murder. We don't need the waters muddied by someone looking for a big story butting in."

"I think you have me confused with Francine Weston," I said. "I'm not looking for a big story. I-I'm just trying to help."

"I doubt the police appreciate your help," Phoebe said coldly. "As for Francine Weston, she's been nosing around as well. I'll have a word with her myself. We don't need any more trouble around here. If you're here to report on the convention, report on the convention. Don't involve yourself in matters that don't concern you."

And with that, she turned on her heel and stalked off. I looked after her and shook my head. "Wow, what got into her?" I grumbled. I wondered if Sophie Brinkwater might have put her up to it. Well, she wasn't going to discourage me. If anything, she'd whetted my appetite to find out the truth. As I debated taking a detour over to the hotel, my cell rang. I fished my phone out of my pocket and looked at the screen. Unknown Caller. I hesitated, then hit the accept icon. "Tiffany Austin."

"Tiffany Austin." The voice on the other end of the line was deep, gravelly. "You're the blogger chick, right? The one who found Barclay in the fountain?"

I felt a chill run down my spine. "Who is this?"

Harsh laughter, then, "I think you know. You've been trying to find me, haven't you? You even went to the police station this morning, had a sketch drawn up.”

I almost dropped the phone. I paused, looked swiftly around the area. There were lots of people around, but I didn't see a trace of the man on the phone. “You—you're Trent Saville,” I whispered.

“I prefer to be called True Shot,” he replied. “I hear you're somewhat of an amateur sleuth, a good one. I also hear you want to make sure your friend didn't kill Jason.”

“Did you kill him?”

“No. I was never supposed to kill him. But I've got a good idea who did.”

My throat was so dry I could barely get the words out. “Sonja—Sonny?”

He barked out a harsh laugh. “We might be able to help each other, you and I. Interested?”

I swallowed. “How might we help each other?”

“You want to clear your friend of Jason's murder. The best way to do that is to find Jason's book.”

“And just how would finding Jason's book help you?”

He laughed. “It would help me find the person I've been looking for. In return, I'll make sure the cops know your friend had nothing to do with Jason's death. Now, meet me in the back parking lot in ten minutes and I'll explain the whole plan to you.”

“Hold on a sec—” I stopped speaking. The line had gone dead. I shoved my phone back in my pocket and stood uncertainly for a moment. On the one hand, I had to admit I was curious as to just what Saville—True Shot—would have to say. On the other, I knew Phil would blow a blood vessel if he knew I was planning on meeting a known hit man in a deserted parking lot.

To be honest, I didn't think it was such a great idea either, but . . . could I pass this opportunity up?

No, I couldn't, but I wasn't about to be stupid, either.

I pulled my phone out again and hit the speed dial number for Phil. I got voicemail. “Listen,” I said, “This is Tiffany. I just got a call from the gray-haired guy. Hugh Hudson knows him. He's Trent Saville, a hit man for the Chicago mob. He wants to meet me in the back parking lot, he said he had information that could prove Fiona didn't kill Jason. I'm on my way there now. Meet me if you get this."

I disconnected and hurried toward the side exit. Halfway there I was stopped by two women who were avid readers of my blog. I didn't want to just diss them, so I paused to pose for a selfie with them, I signed their programs, and I answered a few polite questions about restaurants and recipes before I was finally able to get away. I hurried outside and took a quick look around, then headed in the direction of the back parking lot, where the food truck competition had been held. The lot was deserted now, except for a few cars and SUVs that I figured probably belonged to the Civic Center employees or maybe a few of the convention volunteers. When I reached the edge of the lot, I paused. There was no sign of Saville anywhere.

"Maybe he changed his mind," I murmured. I'd had no intention of going through with the meeting anyway unless Phil showed up. I took a quick look around again and this time I paused. At the very edge of the parking area was a white van. A large shape was sprawled off to the side of the bumper.

I moved forward cautiously, approached the van and looked down. Trent Saville stared at me with sightless eyes, one perfect bullet hole in the middle of his forehead and, judging from the red stain on his shirt, another bullet in his chest.

And as I stared at the body I heard a groan behind me and then Phil's voice. "God, no. Not another one."

Twenty-one

Phil whipped out his phone and called for backup and then turned to me. "I got your message," he said. "I came straight out here. Did you see anyone?"

I shook my head. "No. I thought the lot was deserted. I was just about to leave, actually, when I noticed something sprawled off to the side of the van. When I got closer, I realized it was a body . . . Saville's."

Phil leaned over for a closer look at the body. "It looks like the work of a professional." He reached up and pinched the bridge of his nose, a sure sign he was getting a headache. "We'd gotten a positive ID on him before I got your message. Our FBI contact identified him immediately."

"So did Hugh Hudson," I said. "I told him to call you."

"I got his message too," said Phil. "I'll contact him later." He reached out, touched my arm. "Are you sure you're okay?"

I nodded. "Sure. You'd think I'd be used to this by now," I added with a wan smile.

Phil's lips puckered. "You said in your message that Saville had information that would clear Fiona of murdering Jason Barclay?"

I shifted my weight to my other foot. "He didn't say that exactly," I admitted.

Phil shot me a sharp gaze. "No? Then what did he say?"

I let out a deep breath. "He said he was never supposed to kill Jason, but he had a good idea who did. Then he said the best way to clear Fiona of Jason's murder was to find his book—his manuscript. He said it would help him find the person he was looking for, and in return he'd make sure you knew Fiona had nothing to do with Jason's death."

Phil's eyebrows drew together. "And just how was he going to do that?"

"I have no idea. He wanted me to meet him here and he was going to explain his plan to me." I paused. "Want to know what I think?"

Phil sighed. "No, but you're going to tell me anyway so go ahead."

I resisted the impulse to stick my tongue out at him and instead said, "I think that Saville was sent here by a mobster named D'Amico to track down a former girlfriend of his—Sonja Blackman—who's been missing for years. I think that Jason somehow managed to track her down and he was going to publish that information in his book. It's possible that she might have killed Jason to protect her identity."

Phil's eyes narrowed. "Just how did you find out about Sonja Blackman?"

I averted my gaze, stared down at the ground. "Hugh Hudson told me."

Phil was silent for a few moments after that, and finally said, "So you think Sonja—Sonny—killed Jason."

"Yes. And I think she killed Saville too. I mean, think about it. She lived with a gangster for years, she'd most likely be familiar with the gangland style of killing. I bet she was a great shot too. It seems to me that Sonja is the obvious choice."

"It would appear so, but I've learned through the years that sometimes the obvious choice isn't always the right one," answered Phil. "If you'll recall, early on in our association you were on the top of my suspect list for a murder."

"Okay, okay," I grumbled. "Point taken."

"No, I don't think it is," said Phil. He put his thumb under my chin and turned my face up to his. "I don't know what it will take to get it through that thick skull of yours that there's real danger involved here. Up to now I know you haven't taken my warnings seriously."

I tapped my foot. "What do you mean, I haven't taken you seriously? Of course I have."

"No, Tiffany, you haven't," Phil said. "Not only did you continue investigating on your own by interrogating Hugh Hudson, you were willing to put your life in danger by meeting a professional hit man."

"Hold on a minute," I said, waving my hands. "I had no intention of meeting him unless you showed up. I was walking away when I saw the body."

"Still . . . what if he'd surprised you before you could leave? What then? I greatly doubt you'd have walked away. Saville wouldn't have let you, no matter what he promised. It would be your body lying there with a bullet between the eyes." He moved closer to me and said in a softer tone, "It does no good to argue with you. You seem to think you're impervious to danger. I can't be everywhere at once. If you should get yourself into a situation, I might not get there in time to rescue you."

"Who says I'll need rescuing?" I said. "I told you I have no intention of confronting the killer, or killers, directly. I meant it when I said I was leaving. The thought that he might have surprised me honestly didn't occur to me."

"And that's my point. Sometimes you don't think things through, especially when you're in your investigative mode. In your zeal to get to the bottom of things, you just act."

I knew he was right but I wasn't about to give him the satisfaction. "Hey, I'm not the only headstrong person you should be worried about," I said. "Francine Weston is pretty determined to solve this thing."

"Yeah, well, I don't care about Francine. I care about you. And I'd really like for you to stay in one piece."

I forced a smile. "I'd like that too."

We stared at each other for a long moment, and then Phil started to lean into me. His lips were only scant inches from mine when we both heard Brandon Hoffman's voice. "Detective Bartell?"

We reluctantly broke apart. "Over here," shouted Phil. A few minutes later Brandon appeared, followed by two EMTs wheeling a gurney. "Get some men over here to cordon off this area. And we'd better give Jacobsen at the FBI a call."

Brandon whipped out a notebook, made a notation. "I'm on it."

Phil turned to me. "You can give your formal statement tomorrow. Do you want me to have someone escort you home?"

"Home? Gosh, no. I still have to go over my Market Games post with Jimmy, select photos and video for the blog, and I've got Last Remaining Chef Part Two starting at six."

"Are you sure you're up to all that?" Phil began, but was interrupted by a strident, "Detective!"

We both turned to see Sophie Brinkwater striding toward us. She stopped before Phil and placed her hands on her hips. "One of your men just told me that someone else was killed back here," she huffed.

Phil nodded. "Yes, Ms. Brinkwater, that's true. We'll have to cordon off this parking lot. It's now a crime scene."

"Swell." Sophie rolled her eyes. "This convention is turning into a real murder-fest. First Barclay and now . . . whoever. This isn't the sort of publicity I wanted for this event."

"Be thankful the man wasn't killed inside the Civic Center," snapped Phil. "Then I might have had to shut the rest of your convention down."

Sophie ignored him and put a hand to her head. "I'll have to get with Phoebe, see what way is best to spin all this. And we'd best do it before that nosy reporter gets wind of what happened back here. Talk about a buttinsky!"

She turned on her heel and whipped out her cell phone. "Phoebe?" I heard her say as she started to hurry away. "We have a situation."

Phil turned away to speak to one of the officers, and I took that opportunity to hurry after Sophie. "Ms. Brinkwater," I called. "Could I have a word?"

Sophie, having finished her conversation with Phoebe, slid her phone back into her jacket pocket and faced me, arms across her chest. "Yes? What is it?"

"I couldn't help noticing that you didn't ask Detective Bartell any questions about the body that was found," I said.

Sophie's eyebrows went up. "I don't need to know the gory

details," she said. "All I need to know is that there was another death at this conference."

"Be that as it may," I said, "The dead man's name was Trent Saville. Is that familiar to you?"

She looked at me. "I don't know anyone by that name."

"Are you sure? Maybe you're more familiar with his nickname, True Shot?"

She shook her head. "Sorry. Now, if you'll excuse me . . ."

I wasn't about to be put off that easily. "Could I ask where you were just now? When you heard about the, ah, incident in the parking lot?"

"I was in my office going over the schedule for Last Remaining Chef tonight. I stepped outside for a breath of fresh air and I saw the officers heading toward the parking lot, so I inquired what was going on."

"I see. And you were alone in your office? No one was with you?"

"I was alone. Normally my assistant, Phoebe, would have been with me, but she had to go out on an errand." Her eyes narrowed. "What's with all these questions? Are you with the police? Wait . . . no, I recognize you now. You're a reporter, aren't you? Tiffany something?"

"Tiffany Austin. I'm a food blogger. I write a weekly column for *Southern Style* magazine."

"Yes, I remember you now. You wanted chef interviews. It seems to me that you should be at Market Games instead of in the parking lot finding dead bodies," Sophie said with a curl of her lip. "You're just as bad—or maybe worse—than that other reporter, the one with the dyed blonde hair and skimpy dresses. Phoebe said that you were trouble. I didn't take her seriously, but now I'm changing my mind."

"I've already gotten a lecture from your assistant about interfering," I said.

"Good. Then I take it you will listen and stick to food reporting."

She started to walk away, but I hurried and fell into step beside her.

"The night of Jason's murder you were wearing a black jacket," I said.

She stopped so abruptly I nearly bumped into her arm. "What?"

"The night of the banquet you had on a black jacket," I said. "Did you happen to lose a button from it?"

She shook her head. "That jacket has snaps, not buttons. But I think you might have lost a few of your buttons." She made a whirling motion against her temple. "Loco," she said.

And with that, she turned on her heel and walked swiftly away.

• • •

After my conversation with Sophie turned out to be a bust, I texted Jimmy and told him to meet me in a small seating area that was near the parking lot. He found me fifteen minutes later, bearing a take-out tray with two Cokes on it. As we sipped our drinks, I filled him in on what had happened. When I got to the part about finding Saville, he nearly dropped his camera.

"Oh my gosh," he cried. "You certainly do have a habit of finding dead bodies, don't you?"

"It's a talent. One I'd rather not possess." I tapped at his camera. "Think you've got a photo of Sophie in there from Thursday night? I'd like to verify that jacket of hers did have snaps."

Jimmy scrolled through his photos, finally handed the camera to me. "There's a good one of her at the podium," he said.

I looked at the photo. Sophie stood on the podium, Phoebe standing slightly off to her left. Her jacket was open at the top, and I could see there were indeed snaps, not buttons, on it. I frowned at the photo. Something about it struck me as not being right, but I couldn't put my finger on just what it was. "Yep. The jacket has snaps." I handed the camera back to Jimmy. "Sophie said she was alone in her office around the time Saville would have been shot. Phoebe was out, so there's no way to verify Sophie's alibi."

"Her alibi? You think she needs one?" asked Jimmy.

"She might. When I first got this assignment, I did a little research. Sophie Brinkwater has worked for the events planning company for the past five years, but I couldn't find anything on her prior to that."

"That's not so unusual," remarked Jimmy. "Not everyone puts every detail of their life on social media."

"True, but you'd think there would have been something, some mention of prior positions. I didn't think too much of it before, but now . . . it's almost as if Sophie Brinkwater didn't exist before five years ago."

Jimmy's eyes widened. "Wait, don't tell me you think Sophie Brinkwater is really Sonja Blackman?"

"Think about it. Most people who switch identities keep the same initials. In this case, SB—Sonja Blackman, Sophie Brinkwater. And it's not only the lack of information, there's more. The first day of the convention I overheard her talking to her assistant about Jason. It sounded to me as if she'd known him before this event. Then Twyla Fay mentioned Jason having an affair with a Mafia princess—only I think Twyla had the terminology wrong. It was a girlfriend, not a daughter." I tapped at my chin. "Jason wanted to ask Hugh about Sonja Blackman's disappearance. I think Jason must have met her after she got a new identity and he had an affair with her. She must have gotten a hint the mob was on her tail and she up and left New York—and Jason."

"You think that upset him? Jason was a master at loving and leaving."

"I think it was different with Sophie, or whatever she called herself then. He told Hugh it was personal. And when he was talking to me about love, he referred to it as an emotion for fools. He must have really fallen for her, and he was bitter when she left him."

"Yeah," agreed Jimmy. "That would play into his conceit. No one leaves him, he does the leaving."

"Right. Anyway, I bet he used every resource at his command to track her down, and when he did, he threatened to expose her identity in his book. And, knowing Jason, I bet he couldn't resist the opportunity to hint to D'Amico that he had a lead on his missing girlfriend. What Jason didn't expect was that D'Amico would send his hit man here to keep an eye on him, figuring he'd lead him to Sonny and he could settle the score once and for all."

"Wow," said Jimmy. "This sounds like the script of a bad B movie."

"Doesn't it though?" I tapped at my chin. "The two of them were after the same thing for the same reason—Jason's book."

Jimmy rested his chin in his palm. "So . . . any ideas on where the book could be?"

"I've been thinking about that." I pointed my finger at Jimmy. "You said Jason was a control freak, right? And he was a paranoid control freak to boot. He kept that book shrouded in secrecy, and now I can understand why. So, if you were a paranoid control freak who didn't want anyone getting your hands on your book, what would you do?"

Jimmy thought for a few moments before he answered. "I can tell you what I wouldn't do. I wouldn't keep it on my hard drive. I'd want it to be portable, where I could keep tabs on it."

"Exactly," I said. "And what would be the best way of toting around a document?

"A flash drive," Jimmy said without hesitation. "That way he could carry it around with him. It makes perfect sense." Then he frowned and added, "Except there was no flash drive on the body, right? So then whoever killed him must have taken it."

"Maybe not. I don't think Jason kept it on his person. Yes, he was paranoid, and yes, he liked to be in control, but he wasn't stupid either. He wouldn't have kept it on him because he wouldn't have wanted to take a chance on possibly losing it. He'd have wanted it under lock and key, but someplace where only he knew where it was."

Jimmy's eyes lit up. "Like a safe deposit box?"

"I thought of that, but I remember Bartell told me that they checked both hotels in case Jason might have rented a safe deposit box, and they turned up zip. It has to be somewhere else, but where?"

Jimmy snapped his fingers. "Remember Guy Goodwin telling us that he caught Jason wandering around backstage? Maybe he hid it somewhere on the set?"

I gave my head an emphatic shake. "I doubt Jason would have hidden it on the set. He might have considered it, maybe even been backstage scouting out the area, but in the end he probably felt there were too many people hanging around. Think of it—the chefs, the crew, the cameramen are constantly wandering around back here, and the risk of it being found would have been too great. He was probably on the set to meet one of his victims, maybe even Sonja herself. No, the flash drive is somewhere else, but where?" My eyes slitted as I thought, and then I looked at Jimmy and asked, "What about a locker?"

"A locker?" Jimmy frowned. "You mean like a gym locker?"

"Exactly," I said. "He could have rented one at either hotel's pool or gym, but once again, the hotel would have a record of it and the police would have found out."

"What about the airport or train station?" suggested Jimmy.

"Trust me, Bartell would have checked there too," I said. "No, it would have to be a locker off the beaten path, a locker no one would know about—wait!" I reached out and dug my nails into Jimmy's forearm, causing him to yelp. "There's a section of lockers here in the convention center. They're in back of the main stage, right across from Phoebe Fitzgerald's office."

Jimmy disengaged my hand from his arm. "I bet they're probably strictly for employees of the Civic Center. I doubt just anyone could use one."

"I'm sure that's true, but Jason wasn't just anyone. I'm betting he managed to get his hands on one of those lockers somehow. But how can we find that out?"

Jimmy inclined his head toward the side entrance, where two

female volunteers had emerged, sipping drinks. "Perhaps I could make a discreet inquiry."

We ambled over to where the girls stood, and they looked up as we approached. "Hey, Jimmy, Ms. Austin," one of the girls said. "How's things? Did you enjoy Market Games?"

"We sure did," said Jimmy.

The blonde, Audrey, leaned over and said in a half whisper, "Is it true they found another dead body? That's so creepy."

"Unfortunately, it's true," I said. "A body was discovered in the back parking lot."

Both girls shivered. Then the redhead, Cecily, murmured, "This convention is turning into more of a horror gathering than a foodie one. Do you think the police will shut the convention down?"

I shook my head. "I don't think so. But they have to investigate any sudden death, even if the guy just died of a heart attack."

"Oh, do you think that's what happened?" Cecily asked. "I hope so. Two murders is a bit much."

"Oh, I agree," said Jimmy. He leaned in a bit closer. "Let's switch to a more pleasant topic. I wonder if either of you two ladies could answer a question for me."

"Why, sure, if we can," said Audrey. "What's the question?"

"I heard there are lockers here in the Civic Center," he said. "And I was wondering if they were limited to employees of the center, or if they were open to the general public." He touched the camera hanging around his neck. "It would be helpful to have a place close by where I could store my equipment, instead of having to wear it around my neck all the time. There are times when it's nice to be unencumbered—like when I'm talking to pretty girls."

Both girls giggled and then Cecily said, "I know the area you're talking about. It's back by the offices. I'm not sure anyone uses them though."

"Aaron would know for sure," Audrey put in.

"Great. Who's Aaron?" Jimmy asked.

"He's in charge of the volunteers. As a matter of fact, he's right over there." Audrey pointed to a tall, thin man a few yards away, smoking a cigarette. She lifted her arm and called out, "Aaron. Yoo-hoo. Can you come here a sec?"

Aaron frowned, but he crushed out his cigarette and came over to us. He gave both Jimmy and me a cursory glance before turning to the girls and saying, "My break's almost over. What do you need?"

Cecily inclined her head toward Jimmy. "This is Jimmy Devane, the famous photographer. He was asking about those lockers in the office area, if maybe he could use one." She glanced at her watch and gave Audrey a nudge. "Speaking of breaks, ours is over too. We've got to get back. Aaron, you be nice now," she added, wagging her finger.

I had an idea the word *nice* wasn't in Aaron's vocabulary. That was confirmed a few moments after the girls had departed. He turned to us and said in a rough tone, "Those lockers are strictly for employees of the Civic Center."

I looked Aaron straight in the eye. "We have reason to believe an exception was made," I said coolly. "A locker was used by a non-employee, wasn't it?"

Aaron set his lips. "I don't know what you're talking about."

"Fine." I pulled out my phone and held my finger poised above the keypad. "You can either tell us or tell the police. Your choice."

He looked startled. "The police? Why would they be interested?"

"Because you may have given a locker to a murder victim," I said calmly.

"A . . . a murder victim." His face turned pale, and the belligerent look vanished. "Don't—there's no need to involve the police," he said quickly. He gave a quick look around and then continued, "A man did approach me Wednesday inquiring about using one of the lockers. He said that he had some valuables and he didn't trust them to the hotel lockbox, and these lockers were pretty secluded and no one would ever think of looking there. I told him the same thing I told you, but he was most persuasive."

"Persuasive as in he offered you money?" Jimmy asked bluntly.

Aaron shifted his weight from one foot to the other and averted his gaze. "I'd rather not say," he mumbled.

"Okay, fine," I said. "What did he look like?"

"Tall, good build, dark hair, well-dressed. He only gave me his first name. I think it was Justin, or something like that. He wanted the most inconspicuous locker, so I gave him the one at the very end, bottom of the row, 638. The lockers have built-in combination locks. I told him he had to set his own, so only he could open the locker. That seemed to please him." He shot us a distressed look. "Are you going to tell the police? If any of this gets back to my boss, I could lose my job."

"We'll be discreet," I said. "Since you cooperated, your name won't be mentioned."

Aaron looked as if he might kiss me, or Jimmy, or both of us. He reached up and swiped at the sheen of sweat on his forehead. "Thank you," he murmured.

"In the future, though, I'd think twice before doing anything you don't have the proper authorization for," I said in as stern a tone as I could muster.

"Oh, don't worry. I'll never do that again," Aaron said. He gave us both a brief nod and then scurried off.

Jimmy looked at me. "Nice work. So, I guess the next order of business would be to see if Jason's manuscript's in that locker. How do we do that? Break in? It would take us hours, maybe even days, to try and figure out the combination, so short of blasting it open with dynamite . . ." He reached up to scratch at his head. "I guess the prudent thing would be to tell Detective Bartell and let him handle it."

"I would do that, but it's only a theory. I need hard proof before I involve Bartell. He's got enough on his plate right now," I said. "And since he hasn't yet given me his lecture on what he does and does not consider pertinent information, I'm making an executive decision not to tell him until I'm positive of Sonja's identity." I thought for a moment, then snapped my fingers. "Say, we might already have the information we need." I whipped out my phone again and this time called up the photos I'd taken of Jason's appointment book. I pointed to one of them. "See that string of numbers? 638-12-4-19-82?"

"Yeah. You thought they might be a phone number."

"Now I'm changing my mind. Aaron said he rented Jason number 638, right?"

"Right." Jimmy's tone turned from guarded to excited as he stared at the other numbers. "These other four numbers are probably the combination. So what are we waiting for? Let's go have a look at that locker."

He started forward but I grabbed his arm. "Hold on, hold on," I said. "Now isn't the right time. Sophie and Phoebe are probably down there in their offices, and I'm sure there are other people around too. It's too dangerous. We might be seen. I think it's best that we postpone our investigation until later."

"Later, as in during the Last Remaining Chef taping?"

"Exactly. Sophie and Phoebe will be in attendance, and it'll be pretty deserted down here. I looked at the program. Last Remaining Chef is the only event scheduled for tonight. This area will most likely be deserted. And if I do find that manuscript in the locker, I'll hit the speed dial for Bartell immediately. Knowing him he'll probably be in the area, investigating the latest homicide."

"Okay, but don't you think it would look too obvious if neither one of us were at the taping? I'm sure your good pal Francine will have her eagle eye on you, and if she doesn't see you around . . ."

"You're right, Francine could be one big complication. She's followed me once already. Plus, she saw me looking up Sonja's photograph. I don't know how much she actually saw, though." I pushed the heel of my hand through my hair. "We need to create some sort of diversion to get Francine out of the way."

We both sat silently for a few minutes, and then Jimmy said, "I've got an idea. I know a guy who happens to work at KPTX, and he owes me a favor. I'll get him to call Francine and pretend to be calling for her boss. He can send her out on some emergency to cover."

"It might work," I said. "If the emergency is big enough."

Jimmy grinned. "Don't worry, it will be."

"Okay then, once she leaves we'll leave separately. I'll go to the lockers, and you can stand guard at the stairway. If Francine—or anyone, for that matter—pops up, give me some sort of signal so I can hide. Can you whistle like a whippoorwill or something?"

"My dad and I used to go fishing a lot. I can do a mean duck call. Want to hear?"

I held up my hand. "Save it for later. With any luck, you won't have to make like Donald Duck, and I'll get Bartell the proof he needs to catch a killer."

Twenty-two

It was another SRO crowd at the second installment of Last Remaining Chef. Jimmy and I went backstage shortly before the competition was to start, and while he took some random photos, I did a brief interview with each of the three finalists, Jeff, Sonny Brinker and Adelaide Spinnel. I did Jeff's interview last. He appeared to be quite calm, but I knew Jeff well enough to tell when he was nervous, and he definitely was. When I finished my interview, I reached out and touched his arm. "Good luck, Jeff. I know you'll make the finals."

He smiled. "Thanks. I hope you're right."

As I turned to go I saw Fiona standing in the shadows. She raised her hand and gave me a thumbs-up. I wasn't sure if that was a comment on my interview or if she was trying to tell me she'd confessed all to Jeff and everything was fine. I hoped it was the latter. I saw Sophie and Phoebe backstage too. Phoebe glanced in my direction and nudged Sophie with her elbow. The two of them shot me dagger looks as I hurried by.

Francine had been backstage too, and the minute she saw me start to leave she cut short her interview with Chef Adelaide and hurried over to me. "Any news on the latest dead body?" she asked.

"Boy, you just get right to it, don't you," I said. "No hi, how are you, just any news on the dead body?"

Her lips thinned. "My sources tell me the guy was a hit man," she said. "Any thoughts on how a hit man ended up shot, execution-style, in the back parking lot?"

"I have no idea, Francine. Maybe he expressed an opinion someone didn't care for."

"Or maybe the same person who killed Jason killed him. That book he was writing must really be something."

"So I've heard. But since Jason is dead, and the manuscript is missing, it's irrelevant."

"I wouldn't say that." Francine placed a hand on her hip. "After I saw you looking up photos, I did some digging myself. That woman was Sonja Blackman, and she was involved with a Chicago mob king named D'Amico. She took off and vanished five years ago." She tapped her foot. "I had to ask myself, why would Tiffany be looking at that photograph? And then it hit me. Maybe Jason managed to find her, and he was going to reveal that fact in his book."

It took every ounce of my willpower to make my tone remain neutral. "That's quite a theory."

"Isn't it though. The Mafia has been known to hold grudges," said Francine. "And they don't like their dirty laundry aired in public. It wouldn't surprise me if that hit man had been sent here to kill Jason, to prevent his telling that story in his book."

"Lots of things wrong with that," I couldn't resist pointing out. "For one thing, Jason wasn't killed by a hit man, he was conked over the head with a hard object. The hit man is the one who was killed execution-style."

To my surprise, Francine wrinkled her nose and said, "Yeah, I admit I haven't quite got all the loose ends tied up. But I'm close, I feel it." She shot me a sharp look. "You must have some sort of theory about all this. Why else would you have been looking up that woman's photo—oh, nuts!" She fished her phone out of her pocket, looked at the screen. "Wow—sorry to cut our chat short, but there's an emergency I've got to cover. A five-alarm fire just broke out at City Hall and there's a big meeting going on there tonight." Her head whipped around. "Brent!" she shouted.

Brent was already hurrying toward Francine. "Yeah, yeah, I got a text too. We'd better move it."

"Right." She raised an eyebrow at me and added, "The sooner we get over there and cover the story, the sooner I can get back here and finish my chat with Tiffany."

The two of them hurried off and Jimmy sauntered over to me. "I take it she got the text," he whispered.

I looked at him. "That was a pretty good distraction—a five-alarm fire. But once she finds out there isn't one, she'll rush right back here."

"Oh, I think they might be delayed a bit," said Jimmy. "It's all part of that favor I called in."

I held up my hand. "I don't need to know any details, but thanks."

"No problemo. Hopefully by the time she gets back, we'll have the manuscript in Bartell's hands."

The intro theme for Last Remaining Chef started up just then, and the audience began clapping enthusiastically. Jimmy and I had taken seats near the back of the press area tonight, and we'd made sure to select aisle end seats. I saw both Sophie and Phoebe standing in the wings, their eyes riveted on the stage. Guy Goodwin came out and gave his intro, then introduced the chefs. Tonight was an elegant dinner challenge, made for under twenty-five dollars. As the contestants manned their shopping carts, I gave Jimmy's arm a squeeze and then I slid my tote over my shoulder and slipped away. I took the stairs two at a time and made my way over to the entryway that led downstairs. I hurried down the short flight of steps and made my way swiftly down the corridor.

The locker area started right in front of Phoebe's office and stretched halfway down the hall. I remembered Aaron saying 638 was all the way at the end so I went down to the last row of lockers. Sure enough, there it was, second from the bottom. I called up the photo on my phone of the string of numbers and put them in. Then I held my breath and turned the handle. The door creaked open, revealing a flat metal box. I pulled the box out partway and slid back the latch. Then I lifted the lid and looked inside.

A flash drive lay on top of a manila envelope marked *Photos*. I reached in picked up the flash drive and set it over to the side, then I reached for the envelope. I raised the flap and looked inside. There were at least a dozen photos crammed inside, along with several strips of negatives. I looked at the first one. Yes, she was younger and thinner, but it was definitely Fiona. Anyone who knew her would recognize her. I thought about Leonardo's reaction to these photos and I shoved the photo back into the envelope, then dropped the envelope into my tote. That done, I turned my attention to the flash drive. Before I notified Phil, I wanted to be certain the flash drive did indeed contain Jason's manuscript. I reached into my tote bag, whipped out the tablet, and inserted the flash drive into the port on the side. After a few moments a document icon appeared on the screen. I clicked on it, and the document opened. The title page read, *Tender to the Bone—A chronicle of my life*

"Interesting title," I murmured. I had a feeling the contents of the book would be far from tender. The next page was a chapter breakdown. There were twenty chapters, each on a separate tab and categorized by a different name. I saw one marked "Hugh," another marked "Damaris," and one labeled "Fiona." I clicked on the Fiona tab and read what was there. Apparently Jason had only just started to write this chapter. There were a few paragraphs about meeting Fiona, but nothing about the photographs. I closed the tab and continued going down the list. The next-to-last tab was entitled "Sonny." My heart pounding, I clicked on it and the chapter opened. I skimmed what was written there quickly.

Sonja Blackman, aka Sonny, had been the girlfriend of mobster Donny "the Wiz" D'Amico for ten years. Five years ago she'd gotten tired of the life and took a valuable book of his contacts and twenty grand from his safe and hit the road in a stolen Cadillac. Along the way she'd picked up a female hitchhiker. Long story short, there had been an accident. The hitchhiker was killed but Sonny got away with only a few injuries. She switched backpacks with the hitchhiker and assumed her identity. She spent a short time in New York, where she became involved with Jason. And then . . .

> One day she just up and vanished without a word. I
> was frantic—an odd situation for me. I used all the
> resources at my command to try and find her and then,

lo and behold, I got a lead. She was working for an event planning agency and was at this moment in Branson, Georgia. She'd been assigned to the National Foodie Convention. It seemed a godsend when, a few days later, I heard about Dana Carlyle's auto accident. I immediately had my agent call and offer my services as a replacement. I told her that it was because I wanted to drum up some favorable publicity for the book, but the real reason was because I planned to confront Sonny. After all, this was my chance to find her, to even the score. I was certain that D'Amico would pay dearly to learn the whereabouts of the woman who'd made a fool out of him—and me. But before I notified D'Amico, I had to be sure. I arranged for her to meet me at another hotel, away from the convention. Her appearance had changed drastically—no doubt due to good plastic surgery—but I knew it was her. Without contact lenses, there was no mistaking those cornflower blue eyes. So now I can reveal the truth, dear readers, that Sonja Blackman is alive and well and is going under the name of . . .

My eyes widened as I read the name there. "My gosh, I didn't see that coming," I murmured. "Sonja Blackman isn't Sophie Brinkwater after all. Sonny is . . ."

"Me," said a voice behind me. I whirled and looked straight into Phoebe Fitzgerald's eyes, which were now a brilliant shade of blue, not brown. The gun she held in her hand was pointed directly at my heart. She held out her other hand, wiggled her fingers. "I knew you'd eventually find it for me. I read all about those other cases you were involved with. You're such a little snoop."

My fingers closed protectively over the tablet. "Where . . . Wait, did you do something to Jimmy?" I asked. My throat was so dry I could hardly get the words out.

She threw her head back and let out a sinister laugh. "Oh, he's just taking a little nap for now. I knocked him out and dragged him underneath the stairway. Unfortunately, I'll have to dispose of him as well. Can't leave a trail." She waved the gun at me. "Now, take your cell phone out and put it on the floor where I can see it, then step away from the locker."

I hesitated, then pulled my phone out and set it on the floor. I took a step away from the lockers, my hands in the air. "You'll never get away with this," I said. "Bartell already suspects you."

"That detective suspects Sonja Blackman, but he has no idea who she might be. I've laid some groundwork that will put another person under his microscope."

"Sophie," I murmured. "You're going to try and make Bartell believe that Sophie is you?"

"Why not? You did, didn't you?" Phoebe's lips twisted upward in an evil leer. "I've been keeping an eye on you ever since I found out you were going around asking questions. I looked you up online and found out you've helped the police in two murder cases." She paused. "I tried to talk to you, to get you to mind your own business, but apparently what I said didn't sink in. I overheard you and your photographer friend make your plans for tonight, and I decided right then and there that the time was right to make my move."

"You'll never get away with it," I said again. "Bartell will have tests run. Fingerprints, DNA. He'll find out that Sophie isn't you."

"Tests can be faked, especially if you know the right people and you have enough money," Phoebe said calmly. "By the time Bartell figures it out—*if* he figures it out—I'll be long gone, with another new identity. Hopefully for the last time." She let out a chuckle. "Bartell will probably be off his game, you know, what with grieving for you and all. But I'm sure that other nosy reporter, Francine What's-her-name, will be up to consoling him. Unless she gets in my way too, and then . . . oh well. At this point, what's one more body?"

My tongue darted out and I licked at my lips. Maybe if I could keep her talking I'd think of some way out of this mess—or maybe someone else might wander down here. As if she'd read my thoughts, Phoebe said, "Don't think anyone will come to your rescue. Everyone is upstairs at the taping, and for the few stragglers I put one of those yellow *Wet Floor, Do Not Enter* signs at the entryway."

Swell. I figured my best bet right now was to keep her talking. Maybe Jimmy would come to and go for help. "You murdered Jason," I said. "Because he exposed your identity in his book."

"Of course I killed Jason. He was a fool. He went on and on about how I'd broken his heart and had to pay. Who was he kidding! The guy had no heart. I offered to buy him off, but he called it chickenfeed. Said his book would net him twenty times that amount. I tried to reason with him but he wasn't having any of it. He said I had to pay. He told me he'd decided to leave for New York immediately and give the manuscript to his editor. He still had some pages to flesh out but he could do that on the plane. Then he couldn't resist adding that he'd sent an anonymous message to D'Amico, saying that he should be on the lookout for not only a book but a forthcoming movie that could deliver me to him. That's when I lost it. I knew there was no reasoning with him. He turned away to fiddle with his phone, and I grabbed that rock from beside the fountain and swung. He went down like a sack, right into the fountain. His body made such a splash my blouse was soaked. I had to hurry back to my office and grab a black cardigan to cover it up. That red blouse had black buttons on the cuff, and in my haste to get away I snagged a button on Jason's cufflink. I had to hurry back and get it. Later on I sewed it back on the sleeve of my blouse."

"So it must have been you I heard, and not Fiona. That flash of red I saw was your blouse—before you covered it up with the cardigan. But what I'm really interested in is just how you managed to take down a pro hit man. You killed Trent Saville too, right?"

"Yeah, I knew Trent. The minute I saw him in that bar—just before I spiked Jason's drink with that drug to make him drowsy—I figured he was there for me. It was Lady Luck that I happened to overhear your conversation with him. I went right out to the back lot. He never saw it coming." She paused. "I'm an excellent shot, as you're about to find out. But it won't do to have another body found here." She fished in her pocket, held up a set of keys. "You and I, we're going to take a little ride. In Sophie Brinkwater's car, of course. And that's where your boyfriend Bartell find your body."

Suddenly we both stiffened at the sound of clicking heels, and a second later Francine appeared. "Oh, here you are! Nice try, Tiffany, but that phony dispatch didn't fool me for a minute—say, what's going on here?" she said, as her gaze focused on the gun in Phoebe's hand.

"What the hell?" Phoebe spun around and her fist shot out, connecting with Francine's jaw. Francine let out a moan and slumped to the floor.

The next few moments passed in a blur. I took advantage of Francine's momentary distraction to hurl the tablet at Phoebe. It struck the hand holding the gun, causing her to yelp in pain. The gun went off and flew out of her hand, skittering across the floor. She lunged for the gun and I jumped on top of her. I grabbed a hunk of her hair and pulled, eliciting more yelps. I tried to reach for the gun, but she reached out, grabbed my arm and twisted it, making me cry out.

"You interfering witch," she hissed. "It will give me great pleasure to rid the world of you."

"I could say the same," I gasped. I wriggled out from underneath her and brought up my knee. It hit her square in the stomach. She fell back with a grunt. I struggled to my feet, but she reached out again and gave me a push that sent me reeling against the wall. She scrambled to her feet while I lay dazed and snatched up the gun. "Say goodbye, Tif—oh!"

A shadow had loomed up behind Phoebe, a shadow that moved quickly. Phil grabbed the wrist that held the gun with one hand and clamped the other around its barrel, snapping it out of her grasp before she could react. "Well, well, what have we here? A lucky thing I happened to be heading over to the Last Remaining Chef set. As I passed this way, that woman Rain stopped me. She said she thought she heard a gunshot from down here."

I managed to get into a sitting position. I pointed at Phoebe. "Her name isn't Phoebe Fitzgerald. It's really Sonja Blackman," I gasped. "She killed both Jason and Saville." I pointed to the tablet that lay a few feet away. The screen was cracked, but the flash drive was still in the port. "Jason's book is on that flash drive. Everything's there. And if that's not enough . . ." I pointed to my cell phone, still where I'd placed it. "I hit the record button before I put it down. You can hear her recorded confession."

Phil removed a set of handcuffs from his pocket and snapped them on Phoebe's—Sonja's—wrists. He went over, picked up the phone, and a second later we heard Phoebe/Sonja saying, "Of course I killed Jason."

"She knocked Jimmy out," I said.

"I saw him under the stairs. I texted Hoffman to call for an ambulance." He glanced over at Francine's inert form. "She's out cold."

"Phoebe—or rather Sonja—clocked her pretty good. I imagine she'll be pretty pissed she missed all the excitement." I managed a small grin. "I never thought I'd say these words, but this is one time I was really, really glad to see Francine."

Twenty-three

"And now I'm pleased to congratulate the winner of the Foodie Fest special edition of Last Remaining Chef—Chef Jeffrey Marki!"

I clapped loudly as Jeff made his way to the center of the stage, his face wreathed in smiles, to accept the trophy and ten-thousand-dollar check from Sophie Brinkwater. I'd missed seeing Jeff make the finals last night with his chicken Alfredo lasagna, but both Jimmy and I were on hand to see his beef Wellington win out over Chef Adelaide's hearty beef stew.

After Phil's men had led Phoebe/Sophie away, he insisted one of the EMTs look both me and Francine over. Jimmy too. He'd regained consciousness shortly after Phoebe was taken into custody. He got a once-over from the EMTs as well, but aside from a splitting headache, he seemed just fine.

Guy Goodwin came to the center of the stage and shook Jeff's hand. "Here you have him, everyone. The first winner of the Last Remaining Chef National Foodie Association competition, Chef Jeffrey Marki of the Starlight Restaurant, Madison Hotel, New York! Jeff, we hope you'll come back to defend your title next year!"

Jeff clutched the envelope containing the check to his chest. "Count on it, Chef Guy," he said.

"There you have it, everyone! We'll see Chef Jeff next year, and in the meantime, don't forget to join us for another episode of *Last Remaining Chef* every Wednesday at nine on cable channel 54!"

The lights went up, and everyone started to slowly file out. Jimmy looked at me with a grin. "Bet you're happy. Not only did your protégé win the title, but you aided the police in solving a double murder." He reached up to touch the back of his head gingerly. "I can't believe I let you down. I never even heard her coming. She was like a jungle cat. By the time I realized she was behind me, the butt of her gun connected with my head. Thank goodness I inherited the Devane famous hard head."

I squeezed his arm. "Don't feel bad. Saville was a pro, and he never saw it coming either."

Jimmy nodded toward the stage. "I guess we should get backstage for your final interviews." He glanced around. "I don't see your pal Francine anywhere around."

"She's probably back at KPTX, getting her feature story together," I said. "Neither Bartell nor I could deny her an exclusive interview, considering it was thanks to her I was able to get that gun away from Phoebe—I guess I should say Sonny. It was the least I could do."

"Ditto," said a voice behind me. I whirled around and bumped straight into Phil's chest. He reached out a hand to steady me. "I figured I'd best track you down," he said, "before you blew up my phone with all those messages."

"I think you two could use some privacy," said Jimmy. "I'll be backstage."

Jimmy left and I turned to Phil. "You surely can't blame me for being curious about the outcome," I said.

Phil crossed his arms over his chest. "No, but I can blame you for taking it upon yourself to investigate that locker without informing me. Your little run-in with Sonja Blackman could have been avoided, and then neither one of us would have been beholden to Francine."

"Be honest," I said, jabbing my finger at his chest. "That's what really bothers you, isn't it? Being grateful to Francine, and not me investigating."

"Maybe. But you and I are definitely going to have to have a chat on when I should be informed of your investigations, since it's apparent to me it's a habit you are loath to break," Phil said. "In the meantime, though, you'll be happy to know that right now Sonja alias Phoebe is safely locked up. We had to notify the FBI, of course. It's possible they might offer her immunity if she rolls on D'Amico and his illegal activities. She said that she still has his book of contacts."

I frowned. "I can appreciate the FBI's wanting to nab D'Amico, but I don't like the idea of her getting off scot-free," I said.

"Well, it's all still up in the air. I think it depends on how much she trusts the FBI to keep her safe. As she put it, even if they throw D'Amico in jail, he still has his network. She said if they gave her solitary in jail at least she'd be alive."

"I'd like to say I feel sorry for her, but I can't," I admitted. "While I can appreciate her wanting to make a new life for herself, I can't condone the way she went about it. She planned to kill me and frame Sophie Brinkwater, then take off and assume a new identity." I looked at Phil. "What happened with the flash drive? Jason's book?"

"Right now it's evidence, but I've notified Jason's agent and that editor. They're hopeful that everything will be cleared up soon and they'll be able to publish the book. Of course, a lot of it is going to have to be rewritten. I've got a feeling the FBI is going to want to delete that chapter about Sonja, especially if a deal is made."

I had a feeling the chapter about Fiona would be deleted as well, since Jason wasn't around to write it and I'd taken the packet of photos. "So I guess everything is cleared up except one mystery. Who gave Jason that black eye? He said he ran into a door."

Phil chuckled. "Oddly enough, he was telling the truth. He'd had a little too much wine at that luncheon and he did slam the side of his face into the hotel room door. We got a statement from the hotel doctor who he called to treat it."

"Well, what do you know. That's probably one of the few times in his life Jason ever told the truth." My phone buzzed just then and I pulled it out, looked at the text. It was from Dale.

Mystery solved. Manchetti apparently thinking of buying KPTX. More to come.

"Well, well," I said. "Here's an additional mystery solved." I showed Phil Dale's text. "Looks like Francine and I might be coworkers soon. There's been talk of the station being sold for a while now, and she said that Manchetti had been thinking of expanding before Roberto went to jail. I guess he decided to go ahead with it."

"So that would explain Francine's zeal in tracking down stories," said Phil. "She's trying to prove her worth. It's sad, but in deals of that sort, people almost always get laid off."

"I know," I said. "I just hope one of those people isn't me."

"I doubt that. After all, you helped clear Manchetti's son of murder. The guy's got to be grateful."

"Maybe so," I said, wrinkling my nose. "But I have to wonder what my role would be if that happened. If I didn't get laid off, would they keep the blog, or would they put me somewhere else—maybe working with someone?"

"You mean with Francine?" Phil said bluntly. "I can see where that would worry you, but nothing's cast in stone, right? I've always found it's best not to worry about anything until it becomes a reality. And speaking about reality, is our dinner tonight still on?"

I beamed at him. "So, then. Eight o'clock at my place? I thought I'd make chicken Alfredo lasagna, the dish that put Jeff in the finals. After all, I did teach him how to make it."

"I'll definitely look forward to that," said Phil. "So, after you wrap this up, what's next for you? And please don't say another murder."

I made a face at him. "It's not like I deliberately go out looking for it," I said. "Besides, I've decided this was the last time. I'm done with solving crimes."

Phil cocked his head at me. "You say that now," he said. "But it's like a magnet to you. You can't resist."

I laughed. "Never say never, right? Anyway, I got a text a few days before the conference from a girl I went to culinary school with. She and her aunt are moving here from Atlanta and opening up a Spanish-Portuguese restaurant."

"Spanish-Portuguese cuisine? That's different. We don't have any upscale restaurants that feature that cuisine as far as I know."

"She's asked if I would review their restaurant on opening night and feature it on the blog. I said of course—assuming I'll still have a blog by then."

Phil laughed. "They wouldn't can it that quickly," he said, "but I still don't think you have anything to worry about. One day at a time."

"I know, I know," I mumbled.

"As for tonight, I myself am looking forward to some delicious lasagna." He leaned forward, gave me a light kiss on the lips. "Just a little preview of what you can expect later," he murmured.

He gave me a casual wave and moved off. I picked up my tote bag, and as I turned to head toward the backstage area, Fiona came hurrying up to me. "Fiona," I said. "I was just on my way to interview Jeff."

"Yes, Jimmy said you were coming. But I wanted to talk to you first. Alone." She reached out and grabbed my hand. "Jeff and I had a long talk last night after he made the finals. You were right. He understood completely. He even offered to come with me when I tell Father."

"You might not have to tell Leonardo anything." I reached into my tote bag and pulled out the packet of photos I'd taken from the locker. I pressed them into her hand. "There are negatives in there too," I said. "So you don't have to worry about them popping up anywhere. If I were you, I'd destroy them."

Fiona stood for a moment, staring at the envelope. Then she flung her arms around my neck in a massive bear hug. "How can I ever thank you," she murmured.

"Just you and Jeff be happy," I said. I didn't even bother to hide the catch in my throat. "That's all the thanks I need."

Recipes from the Bon-Appetempting Blog

Chef Jeffrey Marki's Chicken Alfredo Lasagna

6 chicken tenders (or 2 medium chicken breasts)
salt to taste
½ teaspoon black pepper
1 teaspoon cayenne
1 teaspoon garlic powder
2 tablespoons olive oil

For Alfredo Sauce:

5 tablespoons butter
½ chopped onion
1 tablespoon minced garlic
salt to taste
2 tablespoons Italian Seasoning
5 tablespoons flour
3 tablespoons olive oil
2 cups whole milk
1 cup cream
1 cup grated Parmesan cheese
You will also need about 14 lasagna sheets and 3 cups of shredded mozzarella cheese

Combine salt, black pepper, cayenne, and garlic powder in a bowl. Coat the chicken tenders in the mixture.

Pour olive oil into skillet, then cook tenders on high until they are thoroughly cooked and seared on both sides—about 5 minutes each side.

Next, make the Alfredo sauce. Melt butter in a nonstick pan over high heat, add the onion and sauté for 3–4 minutes. Add garlic and cook for another 2 minutes. Add spices and flour, cook another 2 minutes. Lower the heat and add the milk and cream. Stir until thick, then turn off heat and remove from stove. Add Parmesan cheese. Taste and adjust spices as needed.

Preheat oven to 375. Spread 2–3 tablespoons of sauce on bottom of pan, then start layering: lasagna sheet, sauce, chicken. Should make about 3 layers. When done, sprinkle mozzarella cheese on top. Cover with foil and bake in oven for 45 minutes. Remove from oven, let rest for 10 minutes at room temperature, then serve!

Chef Adelaide's Hearty Beef Stew

2 pounds beef stew meat
½ teaspoon each of black pepper and garlic salt
¼ cup flour
4 tablespoons olive oil
3 tablespoons cold butter
1 small onion, minced
3 garlic cloves minced
1 cup red wine
4 cups beef broth
2 beef bouillon cubes
2 tablespoons Worcestershire sauce
2 tablespoons tomato paste
4 medium carrots cut into cubes
1 pound baby Yukon Gold potatoes, halved
1 cup frozen peas
¼ cup cold water
3 tablespoons cornstarch

Cut meat into one-inch cubes. Sprinkle with black pepper and garlic salt. Sprinkle flour over the meat.

Heat the olive oil in a large skillet and cook meat until brown on both side. Transfer to slow cooker.

Reduce heat under the skillet and add butter, onions and garlic. Cook for 5 minutes. Add a splash of wine and transfer to slow cooker. Add all remaining ingredients to the slow cooker except for the peas, cold water and cornstarch. Cook for either 7 hours on high or 4 on low, until the vegetables and potatoes are tender. Add peas during last 15 minutes of cooking. To thicken, add the cold water along with 3 tablespoons of cornstarch. When gravy is thick turn off and serve.

About the Author

While Toni LoTempio does not commit—or solve—murders in real life, she has no trouble doing it on paper. Her lifelong love of mysteries began early on when she was introduced to her first Nancy Drew mystery at age ten—*The Secret in the Old Attic*. She and her cat pen the Urban Tails Pet Shop Mysteries, the Nick and Nora mystery series, the Tiffany Austin Food Blogger Mysteries, and the Cat Rescue series. Catch up with them at Rocco's blog, catsbooksmorecats.blogspot.com, or her website, tclotempio.net.